9/9

baring

arms

Other Me and Mr. Jones Mysteries

Missing Member

Also by Jo-Ann Power

Allure
Never Say Never
Never Again
Never Before
The Nightingale's Song
Gifts
Treasures
Remembrance
Angel of Midnight
You and No Other
The Last Duchess of Wolff's Lair
The Mark of the Chadwicks

baring

arms

Jo-Ann Power

THOMAS DUNNE BOOKS   ST. MARTIN'S MINOTAUR   NEW YORK

This is a work of fiction. All of the characters, organizations, and events portrayed in this novel are either products of the author's imagination or are used fictitiously.

THOMAS DUNNE BOOKS.
An imprint of St. Martin's Press.

BARING ARMS. Copyright © 2008 by Jo-Ann Power. All rights reserved. Printed in the United States of America. For information, address St. Martin's Press, 175 Fifth Avenue, New York, N.Y. 10010.

www.thomasdunnebooks.com
www.minotaurbooks.com

Library of Congress Cataloging-in-Publication Data

Power, Jo-Ann.
    Baring arms / Jo-Ann Power.—1st ed.
        p.   cm.—(A Me and Mr. Jones mystery)
    ISBN-13: 978-0-312-36541-7
    ISBN-10: 0-312-36541-1
    1. Women legislators—United States—Fiction. 2. Washington (D.C.)—Fiction. 3. Texas—Fiction. I. Title.
    PS3616.O883B37 2008
    813'.6—dc22

                                                              2008026427

First Edition: November 2008

10   9   8   7   6   5   4   3   2   1

For my three sweethearts—Ann,
Jason, and Stephen

Acknowledgments

An author never creates in a vacuum. And for those who have given me their time and shared so generously their knowledge and insights, I am immensely grateful:

David Ransom, Majority Leader and Congressman Steny Hoyer's communications director, who very graciously gave me a private tour of the Capitol and shared his invaluable insights, time, and laughter.

Kevin Morison, communications director of the Metropolitan Police of the District of Columbia, for providing the precise details I needed to lend credence to the plot.

Friends, old and new, many anonymously contributing to my attempt to create the verisimilitude of working in the nation's capital today.

Once more to my friends and colleagues in the Saturday Morning Critique Group, a cluster of talented authors dedicated to creating strong fiction—and to one another's success at it: Linda Carroll-Bradd, Mary Fechter, Deloris Lynders, and Megan Galloway-Winkler.

Nancy Brooks, my assistant and friend, who performs the role of Right Arm so very well that I am truly blessed.

To Steve, who continues to be my anchor, my adviser, my plot doctor, and my proofreader.

And finally to those who really take Carly Wagner and her world most seriously: my agent, Jay Poynor, and my editor, Marcia Markland—my fondest wishes and gratitude for allowing her life, love, and the pursuit of happiness . . . and criminals.

Cast of Characters

Characters in alphabetical order by first name:

Aaron Blumfeld—Carly's chief of staff in her Washington office.

Abe Lincoln—Carly and Jordan's pet chimp.

Alistair Dunhill—minority whip, deceased; father of Zachary Dunhill.

Antonio (Tony) Salazar—Carly's legislative aide, recently hired after discharge from Army and service in Iraq; weapons and technology expert with friends in Pentagon.

BEN—acronym for Zach Dunhill's robot.

Brad Wilson—friend or acquaintance of Mr. Jones.

Butch (no last name)—Rocking O Ranch foreman, hails from Colorado; hired by Sadie O'Neill.

Carly Wagner (née O'Neill)—fifth-term congresswoman from the Twenty-third Congressional District of Texas.

Chad Elliott—director of "Rawlings for President" Campaign for Senator Louise Rawlings, senior senator from Texas; known as "The Wizard."

Dana (no last name)—Carly's newest press aide.

Donald Graves, Dr.—director and president of Metro Hospital and Health Care Group.

Dustin Hyde (Dusty)—Carly's perennial opponent for her seat in the House for the Twenty-third District.

Edward (Ed) Aguirre—undersecretary of defense for acquisition, technology, and logistics; retired one-star Army general; friend of Carly's.

Esme Navarro—Carly's office manager in Uvalde, flies Piper Cub; descendant of fighter at the Alamo.

Frank Wagner—Carly's first husband, deceased.

Goodwin Deeds, Judge—father of Nicholas and Nicole, husband of Marie.

Graham McGinty—detective of the Metropolitan Police Department of the District of Columbia.

Gunther Halstead—currently governor of Nevada and second in delegate count in presidential primaries of Carly's political party.

Henry Bunting—senator from Kentucky, husband of Norreen, father of Sherry.

Jim Wyatt—gaming organizer.

"Big" John Casey, Judge—Carly's granddaddy and mentor, father of Sadie, deceased.

John Sullivan—FBI agent.

Mr. Jones—a security expert employed by a firm specializing in investigation, protection, and guarding high-profile people.

Jordan Underwood—Carly's daughter and only child, age twelve; daughter of Leonard Underwood.

Kirk Crandall—minority whip, replacing deceased Alistair Dunhill; representative from a California district.

Leonard (Len) Underwood—Carly's ex-husband, father of Jordan, lobbyist in the defense industry, married to fourth wife, Leslie.

Leslie Underwood—wife of Len Underwood; cable TV news commentator.

Louise (Lou) Rawlings—senior senator from Texas; aka "Grandma" Lou from Dallas, Texas; current front-running candidate for party's nomination to president.

Marie Deeds—wife of Judge Goodwin Deeds, stepmother to Nicole and Nicholas Deeds.

Mickey ("Mickey G.") Gonzales—reporter for *San Antonio Express-News*.

Ming Yu-Bao—Carly's Chinese housekeeper, law student at Georgetown University.

Paul Turner—convicted corporate CEO who was sentenced by Judge Deeds to prison, husband of Barbara.

Raymond Barr—vice president of the United States and from Carly's opposing party, husband of Thea.

Reiko Ishimura—student at Georgetown University, friend of Ming's.

Robert Trainor, Dr.—psychiatrist, deceased.

Sadie O'Neill—Carly's mother, widow, part owner with Carly of Rocking O Ranch in southwest Texas.

Samuel Lyman—junior senator from Mississippi, friend of Carly's.

Sarge Brown—detective with Capitol Police, Homicide Division.

Sebastian Marconi—congressman from Carly's opposing party, head of Defense Appropriations Subcommittee.

Sherry Bunting—daughter of Henry and Norreen Bunting, friend of Jordan's.

Susan (no last name)—receptionist for William Preston Scott.

Ted O'Neill—Carly's father, who disappeared when she was sixteen; presumed dead.

Victoria (Vickie) Enrici—gaming organizer.

William Preston Scott—minority leader of the House, congressman from Georgia.

Zachary (Zack) Dunhill—Alistair Dunhill's son, Jordan Underwood's childhood friend.

one

Locking lips with a man who trips my heat index off the charts is a treat I rarely savor. Well, let's get honest here and reveal all. I haven't kissed a man in almost five years. Haven't wanted to. Haven't felt motivated.

Now, I'm no nun. Celibacy is not my chosen condition, nor my profession, and no, my hormones are not in the Dumpster. Okay, so I am forty-two, but judging by tonight's events, I can still get wildly interested in getting busy.

Truth is, I think a lot about hooking up. And with this man whom I'm about to smooch, too. So my main reason for the dry spell is more a lack of time than interest. My work fills my days, almost 24/7. And my name recognition combines with my high-profile job to make trading saliva with a man a potential front-page affair.

And affairs are what a lady in my hot seat can never have. Why? Because I'm Carly Wagner, five-time elected congresswoman from the Twenty-third District of Texas, a divorcée with one child, a Washington staff of seven and a district staff of six, a political party that hates to love my politics, my humor, my sass, and—yes, my face and figure. So you see, who I'm kissing is always a story someone wants to tell.

And this is also true for the man whose lips I currently contemplate sampling. Because he's the junior senator from

Mississippi with the charisma of Jack Kennedy, the brains of Einstein, and the rhetorical skills of a Bible-bangin' preacher.

The fact that it's taken Sam Lyman over two years to get up the gumption to ask me out reflects his careful way of doing things. Including the way he set up tonight's scrumptious little dinner at a teeny table for two in a dimly lit Georgetown restaurant.

I like his attention to detail. Scrupulous.

I like his style. Meticulous.

I like his hair. Blond with golden highlights that no beautician streaks.

His jaw. Square as a board.

His eyes. Kind of oh–baby, baby, baby blue.

And his freckles. Very Redford.

Plus his chuckle.

And yes, I love his rich, full, un–Botoxed lips.

We're up against the inside of my front door. Me, with my back against the frame. He, with his front against me. His fingers wrap around my wrists, my hands drop to his waist. His breath mingles with mine. He smells of the port he had with his crème brûlée. Mine must reek from the garlic that spiked my bouillabaisse. Neither one of us is breaking for a mint.

"Alone at last," he's crooning in a molasses baritone that melts most women's socks every time he opens his mouth.

"We could have been here sooner," I chide him in a voice I note is husky with come-and-get-me-big-boy umph. "But you had to have dessert."

He rubs his nose against mine. "Just a pinch of sugar before the main event."

I chuckle. "Why, Senator," I whisper to the man whose southern drawl crawls right up my libido, "how you do compliment a lady."

He grins, lopsided like a kid. "I've been waiting a long time to do this."

Really? Who'd have known? "Took you forever to rustle up

the nerve to ask me for a date." Because I'm a real Texas lady who waits for the gentleman to do the courtin'.

"Well, shucks, ma'am." He's doing his Ole Miss shy-boy routine while using my official title, courtesy of Miss Manners's Washington rules of address. "I had to be sure you wanted to dine with me."

I arch a brow. "You've either been working too much, Senator—or you just decided you had to test-drive the party's keynote speaker." Ever since he called last week to ask me out, I've been pondering whether or not his sudden motivation is sparked by our leaders' recent announcement that they've chosen little ol' me to kick off this summer's presidential convention. I don't know Sam well enough to vouch that he's above stealing my limelight.

"Maybe," he says with a laugh as he nuzzles my ear, "they've sent me to seduce you into being more of a knee-jerk politico—and less of a maverick."

Ha! "That'll take more than one kiss."

Chuckling, he trails his warm lips down my throat to the hollow of my collarbone. "So, maybe you could shut up, then, and let me see how far I can get."

Unh-hunh. I am trying not to moan as he blows on my skin in a sultry invitation to racier acts. "Dunno how far that is, but I do like where you're headed."

He's now trailing back up to my cheek, and I'm squeezing my legs together at the playful path he's making to my mouth. And then, at the hovering, panting moment before impact, he sighs, "We could go, well"—he gives me a peck—"in a lot of places"—he gives me another one—"together." And he lets go of my wrists and I lift my arms around his broad shoulders to plunge my fingertips into his thick, soft, curly hair. . . .

And Abe, my daughter's and my pet chimpanzee, starts to howl like the monkey he is. The shrill vibes make my date raise his face, gaze into space, and ask, "What the hell . . . ?"

I wince. "Abe Lincoln," I say, putting a name to our family

watchman. "Remember? I told you about him. Quiet, Abe!" I instruct firmly from where I stand. "He's in his cage in the kitchen. I guess he heard you and wants out so that he can meet you." Abe has this unexplainable antipathy, though, to men with blond hair—so I have locked him up to ensure I have no problems here tonight.

Sam grins wryly. "His timing is awful."

I stand on my toes to get nearer and whisper, "Abe can wait."

"A few long minutes, I hope." Sam pulls me closer, and I'm back to where I'm almost purring with interest as he says, "Then we can . . ." Sam cocks an ear.

Outside, a car with a horsy muffler groans into park. Doors slam, and two women shriek in delight as they clatter up the sidewalk in high heels and onto my front porch. From the racket, you'd swear they were two construction workers firing nail guns.

Sam and I are staring at each other. "Oh, no," I groan, knowing these two are my soon-to-be-full-time Chinese housekeeper, Ming, and her best friend.

"Who is—" Sam begins to ask when I am shoved flush against him with the force of someone barreling through the door.

"Ugh! Wait just a minute!" I object loudly, and turn to see my young, laughing housekeeper halted in her tracks with her girlfriend crashing into her from behind.

"Oh, Taitai Wagna!" Ming exclaims, bug-eyed, her Oriental deference for me freezing her into porcelain. "I so sorry! Reiko and I did not think you are home!"

"Clearly." I try to be congenial in my adversity. But Ming, at five-foot-four and ninety pounds soaking wet, possesses the exquisite face and form of an ancient goddess. Getting angry at her is nigh on impossible because she is always so perfect at everything she tries, but yelling at her tonight for bad timing would be really unjust. Besides, she is a very smart cookie of twenty-two who studies law at Georgetown University. Two years ago she started to clean house for me occasionally, and this week she'll finish moving in with me and my daughter to help me with cooking and car pools to Jordan's summer camp. She and her friend Reiko Ishimura, who is a Japanese exchange student also at Georgetown, are as inseparable as . . . yes, I will draw the bad analogy, Siamese twins. "You must be more quiet outside," I say, declaring the guidelines for living in patrician Georgetown. "The neighbors are not tolerant of excessive noise."

Reiko shows her Japanese heritage and bows to me in apology, an act that Ming, as a good communist, would never offer a Westerner. "So very sorry, Wagna-san." Reiko repeats, "So sorry."

"Please remember in the future," I instruct.

The two young women examine Sam and me, then check each other's eyes. What they conclude makes them giggle. They join hands, and Ming tugs at Reiko. "We go to my room. Okay, Taitai?" She inclines her head toward the stairs. "I want to show Reiko. Then we go back to old apartment, yes?"

"Yes," I smile, eager to have them disappear.

We watch them climb the staircase, and when we hear a door shut, Sam circles his arm around my waist again. "So let me try this one more time before they come down."

I bat my lashes at him like a silent film star. "The sooner we get started . . ."

He licks his lips. "The sooner we get somewhere." He kisses me so softly that I am starving for the full monty. "How's that?" he asks, and I answer by pulling his head down so that our lips melt into each other's.

And the phone rings.

I freeze.

So does he.

It rings again.

He groans.

I wait while it rings a third time.

"Let it go," he instructs me, and lowers his mouth.

But I open mine to object and he stops short, knowing I am eager to listen. Will he dub me unromantic at heart . . . or just plain curious about my caller?

Then the voice mail feature kicks in with the digital android-voiced mechanized message that declares in broken English, "Please. Leave. A message."

"Congresswoman Wagner," begins a man's bass so Darth Vader–deep that it sounds as though it rises up from the tunnels of hell. "I need to talk with you, ma'am. Pick up."

"Carly, who is—" Sam asks, but I'm shushing him to listen.

"Ma'am," the voice repeats while I hear someone chatting in the background. A child? A young girl? "Just a minute," says the man to the other in a tone of command so absolute and so unforgettable that I'm mesmerized. And fuming.

"Carly?" Sam asks again.

Oh, brother. I'm trying to stop the steam from coming out of my ears because if I get torqued in front of Sam, he'll demand details I shouldn't ever give him. Or anyone. Yes, I know this voice, all right. I recognize it from my recent wish-I-could-forget-it-all past.

"Ma'am," demands my caller, "I know you're in there. I know your Tahoe is in the garage." In the background, I hear a car engine passing.

Outside, I hear one simultaneously going down the street.

Sam pulls away to peer down at me with those incomparable blue eyes that are going from balmy to polar-cap icy. "Who *is* that?"

Oh, I know, I know . . . and I definitely do not want to. I bite my lip.

"Ma'am!" insists the voice on the line. "I must talk to you. Pick up."

Sam now no longer resembles the hot tamale who was seducing me two minutes ago. Frowning, he's more of a cool, pissed-off cucumber.

I know his problem. Few people talk to him or me with

anything other than abject respect—and few order us to do anything—and if they do, it is with a deference that would make an etiquette teacher grin like a fool.

"Carly," Sam persists, "who is that?"

I wince. I want to curse. I search for an explanation that sounds plausible. "An old acquaintance." *Right, Carly, that's sure to cure Sam Lyman's curiosity.*

"From where?"

I examine Sam, his ardor gone like the wind at the persistence of this other man. He's jealous, which is flattering, but if I reveal how I know my caller, Sam will think I am certifiable or perhaps a woman he should never acknowledge ever again, let alone date. But I have to give him something or he's going to walk out thinking I'm also rude.

I offer, "He's someone I got to know a few months ago." A man who helped me solve a crime. A murder. A man who saved my curvaceous ass from death. A man who was a cipher, a nameless entity that no one wanted to claim they knew—and no one wanted to claim they hired to save me.

"Carly," Sam perseveres, "I'd say from the sound of him you know him really well."

"Ms. Wagner, ma'am, I must talk with you personally. Now." The voice on the phone proves Sam right. "And I will not leave any message."

Sam steps backward. "Whoa, what a guy. Surly as well as demanding."

"Sad but true," I affirm. "Forgive me, Sam, I have to answer this."

I know I won't like what my caller has to say. I never did. Never would. He is a smooth-talking sonovagun who invaded my life two months ago after I discovered a dead man in my office chair. He'd been hired by someone, a friend, a foe, who knew what, to protect and preserve my reputation. He'd dubbed himself a bodyguard, a detective, a security expert with orders to defend me from anyone who might harm me. He is younger than I, yummy to look at, and maddening to have to work with. But he certainly helped me get the job done when it came to rounding up bad guys and gals. In the end, because I never quite knew who had hired him—and had no idea who to thank for the gift of his time and effort—I never knew if he was truly friend or foe. To this day, I still do not know how he came to me and at what cost to my honor and reputation.

And I guard both like a sober virgin coed at her first frat party. I have to.

Because keeping my job depends on it.

And the man on the other end of that line is a professional private investigator with spooky Special Operations training who takes jobs for the mission and the money—and maybe not in that order. He's a hi-tech dude who never shares who he works for. Or why they hired him.

And the very fact that he is calling me means one of a few grim possibilities. One is he's here to present me with his invoice for the favor. But chances that the operative would deliver the kind of bill a congresswoman gets for saving her life and rep are slim and none. The second possibility makes me want to cough up my gourmet dinner. Mr. Jones has got himself a new load of trouble—and he's trying to dump some of it on me.

With most of my pistons still firing on the much-anticipated prospect of a hot and heavy hookup with the hunky junior senator from Mississippi, I'm wondering how do I get Jones off the phone and out of my life.

Wouldn't I be able to go on with my life if I just drop everything right now, do what good Texas girls do when varmints invade, and go get my gun and shoot the bugger?

Also known as fat chance.

Leaving Sam Lyman standing by my front door, I walk to my hall table, snatch up the receiver, and make a beeline to my kitchen. "What are you doing calling me?" I light into the man on the other end. "I have no business with you. Shouldn't. Correction, won't. Hear me? Will. Not. Ever. Again."

"Right. I hear you, ma'am," says my caller—and I grind my teeth because I catch a hint of humor in his voice. "But listen—"

"No. I won't. Whatever you're calling for, forget it. We're done. I have no patience for cold callers. Don't do surveys. Won't buy anything. Do not want to donate. And I certainly do not want to change my phone company. Although, on second thought, I might change my phone number."

"Now, ma'am," he drawls, sweet-talkin' like a cowboy who's been shunted off to ride the dumbest horse in the barn, "you know I could learn whatever number you take, so don't—"

"Listen to me, Jones." I forgo addressing him with the courtesy of *Mr.* Seething into my receiver, I lock eyes with Abe Lincoln, who does indeed resemble the Great Emancipator when he's scowling at me like he is now, concerned for my distress. "Whatever you are selling, I don't want any."

"Ma'am, you—"

"So long, Jones. It was great fun . . . but it was just one of those things. Go away."

"Can't," he spits back.

"Must." I do him one better.

"If I go—" he counterattacks.

"I'd be much obliged."

"How 'bout your daughter?"

Jordan. My daughter. I halt in front of my kitchen island. My only child is my prize, my joy, my personal talisman of all that is good in the world. "What about her?"

"I have her. Here with me. You definitely want to let us in."

Now I am not only frustrated but scared for the one person whom I love most. "Just how do you have Jordan with you?" I realize I must be screeching. I lower my voice so Sam can't hear me and Abe won't go ape-shit at the thought of his favorite little girl in trouble. "She went to a gaming party with her friends in Rockville. They are all good children and she—"

"Ma'am, I have her with me by special permission from the

Montgomery County Police. I asked them to let me bring her home."

I startle, alarmed that Jordan would be in any situation that the local Maryland police would release her to Jones. Yes, he does have a license he shows to law enforcement. I have never seen it, but I've seen him brandish it. And whatever it is—a private detective's license or a security firm's identification—they do accept it. Though beats me why they honor a guy who looks, sounds, and moves like a ghost through the night, a flesh-and-blood paramilitary X-Man whose favorite color is black. Black in balaclavas and hi-tech cat suits, black in tees and jeans, Volvos and Hummers, matched with a funny-money, nothing name like Mr. Jones.

"Give me three minutes," I instruct him, acceding to his demand. Why he has Jordan with him—and how he got her—are stories I have to hear. "I have a guest."

"Check. For certain you don't want Senator Lyman to know any of this."

I inhale. Jones knows who I have in here? Maybe Jordan told him. But if she didn't, why should I be surprised Jones knows who I let into my home? The last time he walked into my life— and into this house—he knew I made a mean marinara and that I favor green silk panties. I shouldn't be surprised at anything he knows . . . or can learn.

He intrudes in my reverie to say, "I brought your daughter home on condition that no one knows the police allowed me to."

I feel myself nodding, accepting what he's saying.

And that has me asking myself what could have gone wrong at Jordan's computer game party that the Montgomery County police would be called in. And why would my daughter need to be extracted? What could go awry that a dude like Mr. Jones would be involved? Admitted? Trusted? Entrusted with my daughter?

Jones croons through the line, "Ma'am, I can hear your wheels grinding. I'll tell you everything I can. First, get rid of Lyman. Ming and her friend, too. Then let us in."

Someone's chattering again in the background at Jones and the voice is one I now recognize. Jordan. And she's grousing at Jones, finishing her monologue with, "Yeah, and hurry up, too." I note she doesn't sound scared, just irritated.

"I hear you," I tell Jones, wondering how the hell I get Sam out of here with some catfish story he's sure to smell for the stinker it is. "I need to tell Sam——"

"Tell him anything, but do not say I have Jordan. We don't want my favor from the police spread around town. And neither do you."

Jordan mutters something that ends with, ". . . like I care."

Shocked and dismayed at her growing cynicism the past two months, I am now bent on getting her fanny in here so I can chew her up one side and down the other. Sure, she seems to be ungrateful to Jones for a good deed for which I am now suddenly beholden to him. But in addition, I am now dying of curiosity.

"Okay." I start to say adios, when I realize I need to ask him, "Where are you?" I had a house alarm system installed two weeks ago—and though we're still working out the kinks, I have to plug in a code to open any entrance to my home.

"Tsk-tsk," he scolds. "Guess."

Right. *Where else?* "My garden gate."

"Check."

I grind my teeth. "I'll come open it. Wait."

"What I do best, ma'am. What I do best."

I push the *End* key on my phone and tread back to the hall. I take a gander at Sam and it's clear from the car keys he's rustling that he has accepted we are done here for the night.

"You look scary," he informs me.

I wrinkle my nose. "I feel scary."

He examines me with his practiced physician's eye. He was, until he won his first election eight years ago and gave up his practice, a family doctor. "Do you really know this man?"

"Yes. No. Not well." I had known Jones for a few days, worked with him for what added up to only a few crucial hours after he had crawled over my garden wall like a crab, invaded my house, my life, my mind, and helped me find a murderer and a group of conspirators and another would-be murderer.

"Carly, if you want my help, I can stay."

I don't even consider it, not taking any chances with Jordan's welfare. "No, I'm good." I replace the phone in its cradle on the hall table. "Thank you."

"Well, okay, your call. But whatever that is about," Sam says as he buttons his jacket and shoots his cuffs, "I hope you know what you're doing."

I walk forward, grateful, but a mite put out at his men-know-how-to-deal-with-crap routine. Still, I put a hand up to his cheek and he leans over to kiss me sweetly on the lips. This time the heat is gone, and expediency—so often a politician's companion—has set in. "Next time we do this," I vow, "no interruptions."

He chuckles and kisses me hard and quick. "For a long, hot time."

"Wowza." I laugh and peck him back. "I will hold you to that."

He draws me into a bear hug. "Makes two of us holding each other to bigger and better things." I like the sound—and the feel—of the living proof of that.

I groan. "You had better get out of here."

"Mmm-hmm. Or I won't go."

I grimace. Whatever lies outside my garden gate, I definitely do not want Sam's help or knowledge of it. We're not that close. Yet.

He reads my body language on that, I guess, because he says, "Okayyyy," and steps backward. "I am, as they say, so gone."

And like lightning, he is.

I shut the door and call upstairs to the girls. Within two minutes, they trot out the door and clang-sputter-and-putt down the street in Reiko's clunky old Toyota.

"Happy Saturday night," I bid my empty house as I twirl both locks and kick off my shoes. Hate them anyway. High heels were made for men who like to view women's legs in the pointy contraptions. Besides, my legs don't need the length. They already, as my ex-husband used to say, reach my armpits. "Without destroying your C-cup." Leave it to Len to come to mind when I am trying to deal with his and my daughter. He's the one who serves as her role model to act like a royal pain in the keister. Meanwhile, where is he when I have a challenge with Jordan?

Not here, that's for sure. Never was. That was one reason why years ago I divorced his sorry ass. Len Underwood does not do children. And to give you an idea of his graciousness and availability, he has only one. Jordan. While he is currently on wife numero quatro. That's right, number four.

Reciting this litany of woes against my ex, I march myself into my family room, pause at my French doors, and run my palm down the slider switch to dim my garden floodlights. God forbid Jones should not have privacy. I punch in the access numbers in the code box to kill the house alarms, unlock the two doors, and pull them wide. I take the flagstone path to my garden wall, a stark white, brick, eight-foot-tall expanse mellowed in the June moonlight. Silhouetted against its bulk are the twining vines and lush flowers of my wild English garden. When I met my caller the first time, he slithered over my garden wall. Tonight, he appears here again.

And this time, he's got my daughter in tow. My twelve-year-old daughter. And she definitely does not take garden walls like a crab.

I lift the barrier bar from its socket, turn the handle on the huge oak gate, and haul it open. Then I stand aside and in strolls Mr. Jones.

two

Jones, Jones, Jones. No man can compare. Though many should try.

He's a man most women would never leave home alone. A man most women would never be able to leave alone anywhere. In bed or out. An early-thirtysomething dude many women my age could imagine shucking their clothes for. And to me, he is one of a kind. All five-foot-eleven or more, maybe two-hundred-plus pounds of him, with honed, no-apologies muscle. With a form like Michelangelo's *David*—including the big hands (and you know what that implies, ladies)—Mr. Jones is a visual roll in the hay. And if the body is beautiful—well, then, let me testify, the face is absolutely arresting.

He is all-American melting-pot gorgeous. Prime-grade, Triple-A-rated man. Anglo, Asian, and African-American, this guy inherited the best of them all, with granite jaw, sculpted lips, square cheekbones, and dreamy half-lidded eyes that glow, swear to God, like silver neon lights. In fact, they gleam so brightly that even in this moonlight I have to squint to look into them. Especially behind the wire-rimmed spectacles he's perched on his noble Roman nose.

"Evening, ma'am." He nods in greeting, no smile, all business, severe as I have never known him. "Come on, Jordan." He urges her out from behind the garden wall.

I turn to watch my daughter enter—and I examine her closely for a clue to what the reason might be that Jones, of all people, has plucked her from a party in Maryland and brought her home. She's dressed as exactly and as neatly as she was when she left here tonight. Jeans, pink T-shirt, black hooded sweatshirt, new sneakers, mahogany tresses tied back at her nape in a black velvet hair band. At twelve, she's a willow, nearly as tall as my five feet ten, with the same tea rose skin and big baby browns. I let her use mascara and lip gloss, but she argues with me lately a lot about wanting to wear eye shadow and liner. And black. Black clothes, black hose, black nail polish, you name it.

At the moment, her attitude is black.

But not as dark as mine.

I tilt my head toward the family room. "Go inside."

Jordan begins to object, but I give her my stare. Some of my staff say I can kill someone with it. I might. One day. Right now I'm interested in answers. Once I know who to vent my wrath on, that'll be another story. "Go," I instruct her and Jones.

She flaps her arms and stomps away.

But he's scanning the rooftops and the top of my garden wall. Wondering what he's searching for, I shiver. But definitely what he looks like he's doing is protecting us.

And damn if he doesn't confirm it when he does a three-sixty turn and search, then gestures with a hand toward the door. "After you, ma'am."

I precede him. And I am wise enough to his ways and devoted enough to my need for security not to ask him why.

I drop into my easy chair near the French doors, commanding the room like a don who sits in the best seat *always.* Crossing my legs, I note Jordan has decided to sit on a stool at the kitchen breakfast bar. Jones, meanwhile, is doing what I call the man-of-the-house thing, locking the French doors behind himself, circling the downstairs into the dining and living rooms, checking the window frames and latches.

As he darts in and out of my sight, it dawns on me he has a lush crop of hair. Where once he shaved his head Marine-bald, he now sports enough chestnut curly stuff to do a shampoo commercial. Even his face has hair. A mustache. A big, bold brown brush that any cowboy from my home state would be proud to comb. And many women would itch to feel against their lips.

I lick my own and sit straighter, noting his clothes define a new disguise, too. Gone is Batman in a body-hugging black latex-type number. Hello to Mr. Tailored Yuppie in relaxed-fit jeans and a plaid button-down in greens, with spit-polished Italian loafers, all lending him the air of a Washingtonian, suburban style. So that leaves me silently admiring and inquiring, *What is he dressed for, that he has forsaken his sleek cat suit for middle-class weekend attire?* And what would the Montgomery County Police know about him that they would so readily release my daughter to him?

But while I'm getting chills cataloguing his wardrobe change and guessing what his new gig might be, Jordan twirls her hair. Downright bored.

Finishing his lock-up routine on a window, Jones peers at me. "New security system?" He jerks his head toward the little white box on the wall by the French doors.

I nod.

"Useless."

"Now, hold on, there." I paid two thousand dollars to have five men traipse around the house, infuriating Ming with their crusty old boots, drilling holes in my window frames, and leaving little piles of wood dust everywhere, just to hear this man inform me all of that is useless? "This system is supposed to be the best."

"Yeah, well . . ." He is drawing the drapes closed so securely I wonder if we have regressed to London in the Blitz. After all,

my garden is totally enclosed and no one can see in. "Don't believe everything you hear."

"The system and the installers came well recommended," I
inform him, proving my case.

"Sure they did," he states, flat as yesterday's beer, then takes up
position by the French doors in what I call a John Wayne stance.
Legs braced wide, arms folded, he appears more a Colossus of
Rhodes than a hi-tech bodyguard. He fixes Jordan with a no-
nonsense stare. "Okay, Jordan, you're on."

Mirroring his strength, she folds her arms in defiance and
shoots back, "You two seem to know each other well enough,
why don't *you* tell her whatever?"

Jones has gone to stone. It is not nice to mess with a man who
has had training so Special Ops, so psy-ops, so very mercenary
that I never could learn if it had been Delta Force, SEALs, or
FBI. One thing for certain, wherever he has been, whatever he
has done, his training made him agile, clever, and, dare I say, invincible. And though I know from past experience that he also
possesses charm and wit, none of it shows at the moment.

Works for me. In this Mexican standoff between Jones and
my child, I sit and patiently wait for Jordan to comply. She will,
I wager, because she is such a good girl.

Why do I say that? I trust her. Always have. And with good
reason. I tell her all the news that's fit to print and almost all that
she can understand about my job, our constituents, my life and
staff. No, I do not tell her about my hormone levels and my desires for Senator Sam Lyman. Nor have I ever told her about my
relationship with Jones two months ago. I never revealed his appearance or my dependence on him.

He eyes her now—and in those glittering depths, he shows
zero tolerance for her attitude. "Never let someone get the right
of first impression, Jordan. Be there first. Whenever you can."

What's this? A second-story man with a public relations
strategist's mind? I turn back to Jordan and arch a brow.

She's crossing her arms, glaring at him, but talking to me. "The police came in about ten o'clock and started to check the admission records for everyone who logged in tonight. I didn't see them, just heard from a few friends they were there."

"You were at the conference center at the Days Inn?" I ask her.

She nods.

Okay, she was where she was supposed to have been. Had she stayed with her friends with whom she'd gone to the party? "Were Nicole and Nicholas there, too, with you and Sherry?"

"All there," she confirms, her gaze darting to me. She's disgusted with this line of questioning. "Just like we said we were."

"And?" I ask.

Jones gives her the coach's rev-it-up sign, circling a finger in the air. "Keep going."

Jordan smacks her lips. "Some of the players were smoking while they were playing."

"Smoking," I repeat.

She makes a wry face. "Blunts. Weed."

"Great." I'm so thrilled I could scream. I had known that one of Jordan's friends smoked marijuana, but he no longer lived in Washington. "Were you smoking, too?"

"No, of course not," she fires back.

I ignore her sass for now and look at Jones. "Were the police arresting players for possession?"

"Yes." His closed expression tells me I'm cracking a tough nut.

Okay, I can deal with that. "And you feared they would arrest Jordan?"

"That's right." Ditto on closed.

He's never tried to jam me up like this—and I can't let him. "What about Jordan's friends? Did they arrest Nicole or Nicholas Deeds? Or Sherry Bunting?"

"No. I got them taken home early, as well."

That shocks me. I stare at him. "By your friends?"

"Yes," Mr. Cryptic responds.

I'm going to have to pry details out of him with a grappling hook. "Your co-workers or the police?"

He fixes me with his own high-wattage stare. "My associates, ma'am. I have many."

His tone implies he's ticked my questions about his story are so precise. His obstinance calls for a more pointed debate, the kind that requires bamboo up the fingernails. His.

"Jordan," I order her, "go to your room. You and I will talk more later."

"Right. Send me to my room," she grouses. "Get me out. That's tight." She jumps down from her stool. "Well, you know what? I think you need to grill him. Like who the heck he thinks he is, that he can just bargain for me like I'm a sack of po-tatoes. My other friends looked at me like I sprouted three heads. A snitch. That's what they'll call me. I did *not ask* for him. I would've gone to the precinct, no problem. But this guy comes along and, smack, picks me out like I'm in a lineup."

Jones listens, arms folded, eyes on Jordan—and absolutely no expression mars his perfect, manly brow.

For the favor, am I grateful? Am I pleased? Am I livid?

Oh, simple. All of the above.

I gaze at my daughter. Is she telling me the truth? What used to be so easy to discern in her has become more difficult since her best friend moved to Arizona two months ago. "Jordan, do as I say. We will talk after I discuss this with Mr. Jones."

"Jones. What kind of a name is that?" she barks. "I'll tell you. It's fake. Cuz he's a narc. Did you hire him to tail me?"

I recoil at her vehemence, and I'm sad that she thinks I would have her followed. "Why would I?" I retort.

She rolls a shoulder, ignoring my question and venting her own indignation. "Whatever. I've still got to explain to my friends why the Feds've been hawking me."

Abe, who has sat silently in his cage listening, suddenly jumps up and rattles the bars of his cage. Damn if this whole scene isn't rattling mine.

I dart out a hand, palm up to him, my rarely used signal that I am top banana in this tribe. "Quiet, Abe!"

Jordan starts toward him.

But I stop her. "No, Jordan. Abe stays here."

She halts, stunned that I would deprive her of the companion she has loved since he first showed up in our garden years ago, lost and forlorn. "But—"

"No," I insist. "Go."

If she were more of a rebel, she would argue with me. But she turns for the hall, some of the wind gone from her sails. "I'll never recover," she gripes. "I'll be zeroed out. The one with the mother with the shady dude who nabs you from the cops."

I watch until I hear her footsteps on the stairs, and then I glance up at Jones.

His X-ray eyes are making a journey from my bare feet along my calves to the thigh-baring black crepe dinner dress, the waist, the breasts, the cleavage, the throat, lips, and now . . . *hello-o-o, libido* . . . my eyes.

His own do a lockdown on mine and ever so slowly warm with the remembrance of a relationship that was as intense as it was restrained—and proper, too, for a lady of my status.

I run my tongue across the bottom of my teeth, drinking in the compliment of a younger man's regard. I swallow. Brush a hand down my skirt. And return to topic. "Okay, she's gone," I offer. "Drama queen time is done."

Humor playing about his face, he removes his glasses and puts them in his jacket pocket. "She's a handful."

"Not usually," I clarify. "Want a seat? You might as well get comfy." Plus, I prefer us on equal planes. That way, I feel as powerful, less girly, especially important when I deal with Jones.

"Thank you, ma'am." He grins at me so broadly that my hormones, already working on one man—and badly interrupted—jump up like cheerleaders at halftime. "But I'll stand."

The female in me wonders if he is purposely keeping his

distance—and she bristles at the rejection. The politician, however, feels just as foiled, yet goes for the prize. "Have it your way,
then," I say, opting for a bit of verbal graciousness. "But I'd like
to hear the whole story now, Jones."

"You heard it, ma'am," he tells me with such hot interest in
his gaze that those cheerleaders are chanting at me, *Hey, let's go,
come on, let's go!*

I do a mental shake of my head. "I doubt that."

As if he reads my mind, he examines my mouth and whispers,
"Why's that?"

I order those crazy cheerleaders back to their benches and
root around the field of battle for my logic. "You mean to tell
me that the sole reason the Montgomery County Police force
raided a computer gaming party of teenagers is because they suspected some of them were smoking marijuana?"

"Yes, ma'am." He nods, smiling.

"Jones." I beam at him.

"Ma'am," he drawls in a long low timbre that strokes my
senses and my far-too-fond memories of how he helped me,
even when I spurned him.

"If I believe that story, what do you assume *I* am smoking?"

His body stiffens.

I declare what instinct says is true. "You are on a job. You
are"— I let my eyes take a tour down his temptingly toned torso
to his long legs and big feet—"undercover. As a what? Suburban
home owner?"

"Computer technician."

I purse my lips—and when his eyes absorb the contours of
them, I scour my brain for my next ploy and ask, "So . . .
you . . . went to tonight's party just in case some children
needed help?"

He nods—and smiles in a let's-get-naked mode he surely
learned in some spook class I bet they titled James Bond 101.

He must've gotten an A, because I'm yearning for a cold

shower—and some logic. "Jones." I try to clear my throat. "What is the real reason the police are interested in this gaming group?"

"You heard it."

I shake my head. "Not even a little piece of it."

Judging from his scowl, he's real unhappy now. "Whatever you say, ma'am. I did you a favor. That's all you need to know. The only thing you need to do is keep the rest of the bargain."

Do I? And at what cost? "It was your bargain, Jones. Not mine."

He steps forward so that he is looming over me. Up close and personal, he is delightful to look at, but one stubborn pain in the butt to deal with. "I insist, ma'am. Do not pursue this."

"Because your client won't let you?"

He gets this wry look to him. "Now, ma'am, you know that I never know who my clients are."

"Well, *whoever* they are"—I pick an imaginary piece of lint from the skirt of my black dinner dress—"they'd be surprised to learn that you are moonlighting on their time, wouldn't they? Doing favors for others on their clock?"

"They won't know."

"Unless I go to the press."

He rolls his eyes around the room. "What's in it for you to blow the whistle on this?"

"Honesty."

"Ma'am, quit yanking my chain here. If you go back to the Monkey County Police and create a fuss, you get police in trouble, your daughter, her friends, and as an added little bonus you win yourself the jackpot—negative media."

"And if, in spite of your assurances, this tasty item comes out anyway, what do you think my media prize will be then?"

"No leaks will happen from my end."

"You are so confident."

He squares his jaw so tightly I fear he'll need dental work. "Totally."

"Pardon me if I can't get up the enthusiasm to applaud your confidence. This town is filled with folks who'd sell your good name for a nickel and the chance to be on page one of *The Washington Post*. Me? I am creating a new profile since April's romp through the homicide department of the Capitol Police. It's called shy and retiring."

Jones has the utter audacity to snort. "When you become shy and retiring, call me. I'll take you myself for the psych eval."

"Jones," I chastise him with the pose I call look-down-my-pretty-Texas-gal's-nose, "there is nothing here to joke about."

"And nothing to fear, either. I tell you, we're good."

"Words are so fleeting," I mourn.

He curses under his breath. "But you've had more than words. After Alistair Dunhill's murder, you had proof I can be trusted!"

I almost blurt, *That was months ago*. But gratitude and good manners stop me.

"For this"—he sweeps an arm toward the stairs—"you're gonna tell me you're not grateful?" If he were any angrier, smoke would come out his ears. "It is no small thing to pull out one daughter of a congresswoman, one of a senator, and the twin children of the most revered judge this side of the Mississippi."

"I agree." And I wonder what the other parents are saying at this moment to their children—and their saviors of the evening. "But just like the media found out a few months ago that a White House aide ran a few traffic lights and the District policeman let him off without a ticket—"

"I am *not* the D.C. Police, ma'am."

"Oh, I am clear on that point, Jones. But how does that help me? I seem to be able to learn what you are not, but never quite what you *are*, who you are, and who the hell pays your tab!"

"That does not concern you."

"It did two months ago—and for that little set of services, I *still* have not enjoyed any sticker shock!"

"Is that so? Well, hey"—he relaxes, peaceful as a fly on a cow patty—"maybe there is no bill."

"Yeah, and maybe I'm the president."

"Look, you wanna fret over that"—he's torqued again—"go ahead. I can't change the past. But tonight I did you a favor, nice and simple. I saw Jordan, recognized her from my prep for the job I did on you in April. I knew she'd come with her three friends and I had them extracted, too. End of story."

"Hardly."

"Ma'am, I did this for you. Call it for old times' sake. All I ask is you keep it to yourself. Jordan and her friends, too."

"Or what?" I fear the answer here. Do we get rubbed out? Excommunicated? Struck out in the ninth inning with bases loaded?

"Or I'll say that's no way to repay a favor." He leans in to me now, his face aflame at the injustice of my ingratitude. "For keeping your daughter's name—and her friends' names—out of the police reports, *yes*. I think you do owe me. Big-time."

"And what is the nature of that big-time payback?" *Oooo, baby, do I want to hear this answer?*

"Thank you, ma'am. You can say thank you."

I wish I could. I wish I might. But being polite, I could choke on the words. "And if I can't?"

"Then I'll have to say I am sorry I intruded on your evening, ma'am." His mouth droops. His electric eyes fade to gray. He is sad. Sad, mad, and dangerous. "I'll be leaving you." He faces the French doors. Unlocks them.

I reach out—but snatch back my hand. I can't—mustn't—give in to remorse that he's going without so much as a token of my gratitude. I rise from my chair. "I didn't get where I am, Jones, by accepting favors from others. I earned everything I've gotten by my lonesome."

He turns, stormy and sorrowful. "Maybe you think that's true, ma'am. But you're deluding yourself."

I bite my tongue. Why does this one man make me so crazy?

So conflicted? Why should I be warmed all over, as Sam Lyman's attentions have never heated me up, that this man would rescue my daughter and my reputation from the hopper, just by plucking her from a party gone bad? Why do I hate it that he has that power?

I give him what I can. "I am sorry, Jones."

"So am I, ma'am." He shakes his head and goes to granite when he adds, "But believe me, from now on"—he steps to the threshold—"I will do you no favors."

Bipolar as I once thought I was, two reactions hit me simultaneously.

No favors?

Ah. My fondest wish.

And a surprising new regret.

Half a heartbeat later, I follow him out to the garden, but he has disappeared, like invisible ink.

"So much for favors I want to refuse," I murmur, and drop the bar across the gate, scanning the rims of the wall and wondering if he left by scaling it, as was his habit. "Who cares?" I ask the night, ruing the fact I know the answer. Then I hurry back inside.

Jogging up the stairs to the third floor, where Jordan's back bedroom commands a view of the garden, I linger outside her closed door and collect myself. Determined to avoid a confrontation, I knock twice and wait for her permission to enter. House rules here are that no one breaches your privacy without consent.

"Come in," she calls, and I can tell she's still irked. As I open her door, her gaze meets mine. She sits on her bed, sulking and painting her toenails. Black.

"Rebellion comes in darker shades nowadays," I tell her matter-of-factly as I step over her clothes strewn on the floor and take a seat in her easy chair. "Mine always came in shades of red. Cherries in the Snow, I liked for lipstick and polish. With my hair"—that is the color of merlot—"I looked like I needed either a good meal or an undertaker."

She ducks her head, hiding her laugh and continuing her paint job. I glance around and note her computer is off. A smart move for her not to push her luck. "Whenever you're ready," I instruct her, "I'm here to listen."

She shakes her head as if to say, *Why should I?*

I examine her leisurely. Let her think and stew. After another minute goes by, I begin to lead. I'm used to that. I do it well. "Okay. Let's start with a few simple yeses and nos," I command more nonchalantly than I feel. "I took you to the Deedses' early. Nicholas and Nicole seemed happy to see you. Were they?"

Jordan nods.

Good. Lately, I have not been pleased with Nicole Deeds's rudeness to her parents, especially her stepmother. But Nicholas is just as kind as he has always been since a young boy when we first met him and his twin sister the day we moved into this house.

Without any further indication that Jordan wants to talk, I continue. "You all seemed happy to be going. Then Sherry Bunting arrived with her mother a few minutes before I left. Was she pleased to go, too?" I'd detected that Sherry, more petulant than usual, was having a bad day.

Lately, this fourteen-year-old had many of them. Sherry, the daughter of Senator Henry Bunting of Kentucky and his second wife, Norreen, had transformed recently from a sweet child to a black-clad harpy with a smart mouth and a badass attitude toward anyone except Jordan, Nicole, and Nicholas. Sherry is Jordan's role model for all the black she wants to wear—and I hope both find a new craze soon.

"Yes, we were all really psyched about it." Jordan throws this out with a bored insolence I am determined to eradicate.

"And Sherry's mother drove to Rockville, as planned?"

Norreen Bunting had read about these PC gaming parties a few months ago and, checking out their security for preteens, had recommended that the four friends go together. Security guards were posted at the hotel sites—and I had felt confident allowing Jordan to attend, until tonight.

"Yes." Same tone. Same clipped delivery.

I continue, "And she helped all of you register and set up for the game?"

"Yes." Same silent gap in the conversation.

"The computer they assigned you was running well?" I persist.

"Yes."

The vacuum in here is getting monotonous.

I learned long ago when I was a radio talk show host in San Antonio that all roads eventually do lead to Rome. So when interviewing anyone in congressional hearings or in my office who may not be as open as I wish, I travel the lane most dear to them—and when the opportunity arises I swerve to the topic I want. So I counter with, "Did you bring home your DVD game disks?" The organizers were always very helpful, giving kids duplicates if they damaged or lost theirs.

"I almost forgot them, but your narco friend there got mine for me."

Another favor I owe Jones for. "Were any other players taken home besides you four?"

"Dunno." She frowns. "I bet your friend knows. Why not ask him?"

Ah, surely I would if I could, but contacting Mr. Jones is like conjuring a body from the other side of the River Styx. He has no ordinary phone number—and no regular phone, but a matchbox-sized gizmo that operates on a different frequency from the technology the rest of us humans use. And when its usefulness is over, he can simply blow the damn thing up. Worse for anyone who might need to consult him, he has no office—or at least none he revealed to me. He claims no boss, no client, only a case and job. A more inscrutable man I have not met since . . . well, my father.

I shift in my chair, unnerved that my answer will reveal the little I know. And it chaps my hide sorely that I have to start with a negative. "He is not my friend, Jordan."

"Come *on*, Mom," she chastises, widening her big brown eyes at me. "I may be twelve, but I'm not a cretin. Geez. He didn't do this just cuz he decided to pick me out of the crowd. Or cuz he saw you in the papers. He *knows* you. Really well. So well, you let him check the house. God. Even Abe knows him!"

I nod at her perception. True, Abe did not object when Jones came in. And Abe—our veterinarian warns us regularly—is not only capable of tearing a human limb from limb if he meets a stranger who threatens his favorite people, but he is genetically predisposed to attack—and to win. "You're right," I concede, "Abe knows him."

Jordan throws up her hands. "I *knew* it! Now I gotta ask you, how can *that* be? Old Jonesy has got to have been here before for Abe to sit there in his cage and not go crazy to get out and clobber him. So that means, when *was* Jones here, huh? I can tell you—when *I wasn't,* that's when. And how does he know who I am, what I look like? That is double weird, Mom. Double weird. And I don't know him? Never met him? So I see what happened. The guy likes you—"

No, I want to object, startled at her insight. But I don't voice it because maybe then the lady would protest too much. So I sit very still while Jordan rails on.

"Yeah. I saw it. He likes you, has to. Why else is he gonna go up to the cops in the room, take them aside, and single me out?"

Right. And just how did he arrange that without creating a ruckus?

"You aren't gonna tell me, are you?" she digs away at me.

Like I have an answer. "Look, Jordan"—I can't let her put me on the defensive any longer—"because of my position, there are some things you cannot know. Should not. I have often told you that—"

"Riiiight," she interjects, and stares down as she slathers more polish on her big toe, then caps the bottle. "So here's a time when you need to come clean with me."

"Listen, young lady." *Uh-oh, wrong tactic, Carly.* I cannot help myself, though, and like a lemming to the sea, I march right over a cliff. "Jones is not a narc." Or I don't think he is. Or was. "He's a security man."

She grunts. "Mom. He wasn't pulling security duty at the gamesters' party. He didn't have a uniform on." She brushes a hand out toward the stairs. "Then I overhear him tell you he's pretending to be a computer technician."

This tidbit means she crept down the stairs to eavesdrop on Jones and me talking. Well, am I surprised? She's young and scared—and some dude has scooped her up out of a video game party of maybe a hundred teenagers and brought her home on the QT. In disgrace. If I were she, I'd listen in from the stairs to my parents' conversations. God knows, I'd done it myself when I was a kid. Often. To my shock. And sorrow.

Fighting back ghoulish memories of my parents' biggest door-slammers, I return to the topic of what little I know about Mr. Jones. "He's operating undercover. He's a security professional. A bodyguard. A detective."

"A spy?" A wave of admiration crosses her features.

I shake my head. "Not quite." Or at least I don't think so.

Her expression falls and she starts to examine her finger-nails.

Wincing at the prospect she'll paint those black, too, I try another tack. "I'm glad he helped you get your gear. It saves you buying a new DVD—or getting a copy from the organizers—doesn't it?"

She mashes her lips together. "Sure."

I march onward. "It's all very expensive. Free copies or not."

She doesn't remark. Doesn't have to. We both know I'm right on the money. She'd worked hard to earn it, doing more chores at home. I don't pay her to earn good grades: That's her job, period. But I value her help here—and because Ming is in college, we need all hands on deck to keep the house a home.

"Sooo"—she looks curious—"that's it on Jones? That's all you're gonna tell me?"

I nod. "All I know."

She narrows her eyes at me. "But he was involved in Congressman Dunhill's murder case, wasn't he?"

"Yes."

"What did he do?"

"He helped me find the real murderer."

Awe mixes with arrogance as she asks, "How did he do that?"

I lift my brows. We are way off subject here. "Very carefully. But Jordan, we are here to discuss what happened this evening, not my past relationship with—"

"Relationship?" she croaks. "Okayyyyyy, then."

"It was not like that." Her tone says Jones and I were more than acquaintances.

"No?" She pins me with her determination. "Then why did he do this tonight?"

Seeing my main chance, I go for the biggest buckle at the rodeo. "Are you glad he did?"

"Course I am."

"Why?" *Tell me why, dammit.*

"Because I don't want a rap sheet."

"I see. Who would, right?"

"Right! I'm too young!"

"And are you innocent?"

She guffaws. Not quite the reaction I expected, but I conclude from her blush that she interprets my question to imply some sexual connotation. Then she proves it when she says, "Course I am! I don't want to do any of that stuff with boys."

I go with the topic. "Are there some in your crowd who do?" Is this group of kids engaged in sexual activities?

She wrinkles a brow. "Not as far as I know, no."

Phew. A vast relief. "And *you* are not smoking weed."

"No."

"Sniffing?"

She laughs. "God, no. Hate the stuff!"

I blink—and so does she at her revelation that she tried sniffing glue and getting high. "Okay." Making a note to return to
that topic, I move on to, "Are any into acid?"

"Not that I know of."

"Alcohol?"

She sticks her tongue out. "Nooo."

"Pharm parties?"

She looks confused. "Farm parties?" A smile plays around her
lips. "Do Babe and Lassie get invited?"

She and I both grin at her humor.

"Pharmaceutical parties," I explain. "A new craze where kids
collect drugs in the house prescribed for their parents and sib-
lings, mix them up, and try them all out."

"Whoa! That sounds really ug-lee."

"I think so."

"No," she says empathically. "I don't do that. Who does that,
really?"

"A lot, evidently. I read it recently in a report summary from
the FDA," I tell her.

"FDA," she repeats, looking for a definition. "Alphabet soup
again."

"Food and Drug Administration," I provide, and go on. "Were
there any new people at the party tonight?"

"Can't be sure."

"Anything unusual you noticed about the event tonight?"

"No, not really."

"Did you get to play any segments at all, or did the police enter before it started?"

"Yeah, we played three segments before your friend came over
and tapped me on the shoulder."

"All right, Jordan." I rise, out of ideas, and head for the door.
"Get some sleep. We'll talk again tomorrow morning." Turning

the knob, I stare at her—and like my staff, she knows not to mess with me when I do that. "I will learn what happened in Rockville tonight, Jordan. Either you will tell me what you know or I will find out on my own. Decide which. But until I learn the truth, my dear"—I smile, but I offer no solace in my look, only Mom Invincible—"you are grounded."

three

Why some couples get married boggles my mind. You have friends, or family, or colleagues, and you constantly wonder, *What is it with these two?* They're mad for each other, and yet mismatched in every way. He's a hunk and she's a lump. She's a rocket scientist and he's dumb as a stump. One has the funny bone of a one-armed cheerleader and the other couldn't get a laugh out of a coyote at a roadkill barbeque.

The Deedses are like that. Inscrutably mated. He's a few inches shorter than I, about five-eight, toting three-hundred-and-fifty flabby pounds, while his wife, Marie, is an anorexic one-hundred-zip. Marie—numero dos for Goodwin—stands at five-four and packs into that tiny space as little personality as she can. I mean, this woman may sport the hungry mien of a *Vanity Fair* cover model, but her personality is bland as a prune. The black hair, black eyes, and mannequin-white complexion are striking, but compared to his first wife, Marie is as exciting as drywall.

It's eight A.M. Saturday, sunny and breezy in D.C. but dark and dreary in my mind. Without much sleep last night, I rose at dawn and tried to do my morning tai chi for naught. I have left Jordan at home alone on her honor to remain there and marched myself two doors down the street to now sit nursing a mug of coffee at the kitchen bar of Judge Goodwin Deeds and his wife. And for the life of me, I do not get why the Good Judge (as media nicknamed him long ago), who has the no-nonsense poker-up-the-ass personality of Gary Cooper in *High Noon,* and his second wife ever got hitched. True, he'd been lonely after his first wife, Jane, died of cancer. Jane was a beaut, built like a Dumpster, homely as sin, but sporting the personality of Auntie Mame. After she died, Goodwin packed on the pounds like a jet-liner taking on fuel. Where or how he'd found Marie beats me, but he never stopped shoveling in the goodies after they met. But hey, if I were married to Marie, I'd eat out of boredom, too. Reminding me of the Kewpie Dolls in the barkers' tents at the beach, Marie is as lovely as china. And so quiet you can hear her hair grow. The answer, I figure, to his initial attraction to her had to be her looks. And he'd had them once, too, now long gone to blubber. Their continued amusement with each other has got to be because he's got prestige and buckets of Old Washington money she couldn't earn in five lifetimes—while she had looks he'll never attract again.

But who am I to critique others' relationships when I can't get past kissing?

And my challenge right this minute is to get them to discuss what happened last night—and they are reluctant to go there. Ahh, and how do I know this?

So far, we have jawed about the weather. Divine. Their beach vacation. Soon. His docket. Crammed. The benefit auction dinner dance Thursday night for Marie's employer, the largest hospital and health care system in town.

"You are still coming, aren't you, Carly?" she asks, coming alive to contribute to the conversation for the first time this morning. "Our director is just thrilled to have the chance to meet you. He's got you at the head table with the vice president and us."

"I never miss a chance to dance," I tell her. Or schmooze with the administration, even if they are from the opposite party.

"Who's your escort for the evening?" She grins, and I wince at her put-on interest.

I see my chance to turn the tide my way and go for the gold. "You know, with everything that happened last night," I tell them, "I forgot to ask my friend."

"Senator Lyman?" she asks. "Jordan told us you were out with him last night. Why, he is so handsome, isn't he, Goodwin? Good potential for running for president. . . ."

I let that media hype die a natural death. "I might attend alone, because I'm not certain if Sam's in town or going home early for the weekend. Travel's a perpetual challenge."

"You have to go home often, don't you?" she coos. "Taking care of business."

"True, it's good to keep the folks remembering my name and face—and what I've done for them lately." I grin, stating the god's honest truth of a representative's demands. "But let me get to the reason for my visit this morning. I want to clarify what happened last night at that party. I dislike preferential treatment—for anyone—and I am considering calling the Montgomery County chief of police to discuss him letting our children come home. But I need to know what you think because we're all in this together."

The two of them look at me like I have snakes growing in my hair.

Shocked that this judge—who to millions of Americans embodies more of truth, justice, and the American way than Superman—remains silent, I pursue the subject. "I am concerned that they were brought home but claim not to know much about what happened there."

The Good Judge scratches his jowls and they wiggle like pudding. "The twins say they know nothing."

"Not even that some of the kids were smoking pot?"

"No. They didn't tell us that." He scowls, as if he wants to end this discussion here and now, then raises his brows cheerfully. "Maybe Jordan knows some who do."

Really? Why do I feel that you are pushing blame to Jordan? I can't imagine Goodwin just sitting around waiting for the sky to fall.

But then, the Good Judge doesn't have to worry about elections, does he? He's appointed to the bench for life. The Hill chatter that he's on the fast track to the president's short list for the next opening to the Supreme Court should make him think twice, however, about obstructing justice in his own home. Shouldn't it?

"Okay, I wonder"—I charge forward here because my neck and Jordan's are in nooses—"could I ask the twins a few questions?"

"Sure," Goodwin says, and points his chubby finger at Marie. "Go get them, please, honey."

Marie scurries off so obediently, I wouldn't have been surprised if she'd knocked her head on the floor, kowtow style, before disappearing up the stairs. When she brings them before us, however, her doll-like face is set in the red, rigid lines of one who has recently had an argument. And Marie has had it, clearly, with the twins, who come before me here like innocents to the slaughter. The two of them slink onto chairs at the kitchen table, hands hanging between their legs, pale heads bowed like penitents. To their father's inquiries, they only grunt answers of one syllable. Worse, watching Nicole, I get a big whine of sound and fury—and that signifies something. Just what, I'm determined to learn.

"Dad, honest," she claims for the third time in as many minutes, "we did not do anything that we need to tell you about." She glares for one flashing second at her stepmother. "For real."

The Good Judge sits, flowing over his kitchen chair like pie dough over a plate. Facing his children, hands wrapped around his own mug of coffee, he gazes with compassion on his daughter. Yet his words are harder. "Nicole, please describe for Jordan's mom what happened last night."

"I already did."

"Not from the time you got there. No. So, let's hear it again, Nicole," he insists.

"Yes, Nicole," purrs Marie in a meow I'd swear was perverse satisfaction, "let's."

With a chin-up look to her stepmother that we'd say in Texas means *Eat dirt,* Nicole crosses her arms and delivers a few sentences of pap. Nothing she says about last night is new to me.

When she finishes, Goodwin takes on a pleading tone that to my ears lacks any paternal power. "So, Nicole, nothing unusual went on at the party?"

"I guess, but I have no clue what." Nicole sticks out her lower lip and pushes a long blond lock of hair from her cheek. "And whatever it is has nothing to do with Nick and me." She locks eyes with me. "And far as I know, nothing to do with Jordan, either."

That last sentence comes with more conviction than the first, and I tend to believe her. So why, I have to ask myself, does Jordan act like she *is* hiding something? "Jordan tells me that some of the participants last night were smoking marijuana." I leave Jones's statements out of this discussion. After all, I'm on a fishing expedition here. "Do you know anything about that?"

"No. But if Jordan says so, then maybe it is cuz she knows more fan boys than I do—and more than Nick knows, for sure."

"Nick?" I ask her brother, who sits, hands folded, fine blond hair dangling across his forehead. "Did you know anything about use of marijuana?"

He shakes his head and avoids my eyes. Of the two, Nicholas is the more shy. Right now he is white-knuckling this interview, his hands clasped tightly together before him. A sad trait, for a boy to be timid. I wonder why.

"Son," the judge asks with tenderness, "please look at us when we speak to you."

Nicholas does as he's told—and raises his face to his father.

A hip-hop song in tinny tones breaks into our discussion.

The judge scowls at his daughter. "Really, Nicole. Turn that off—and leave it off or I take it away."

Oh, brother. My child is confined to her room without TV, radio, computer, and games—while Nicole still has her phone? Do these parents not care what happened last night? Do they not *want* to know?

"Thank you," says the man who has been praised for his stern treatment of some of the most reviled white-collar criminals ever to face trial. Yet to watch him in action with his own children is like witnessing Spider-Man disrobe and become a puny boy. Clearly, the Good Judge at home is a wimp. Jane and he used to run a tight ship here. Now neither he nor Marie knows how to elicit respect or even demand it from the twins, and this raises a red flag I tell myself I must not ignore. "Now," the judge continues, his tolerant gaze going from his son to his daughter, "tell me who was winning last night."

I try to hide my displeasure. *Where is he going with this segue?* For a man who'd sent famous white-collar criminals way up the river without cushy Club Fed prison digs, Goodwin sounded more to me like he was treating his kids to a free ride.

"We were." Nick is the one who answers his father. "We needed it, too," he states proudly. "We lost two weeks ago *major,* so this was cool that we were getting back on the board with big strikes, you know?"

"I do." The judge flashes his perfect teeth, showing all pearly, dentist-straight, and really rather tiny. Still, they're his best feature, in what is an ordinary face encased in flesh. He turns to his daughter. "Any problems last night with the group from Frederick?"

Nicole shakes her head. "Well, nobody flamed us last night, if that's what you mean."

I blink. The lingo of gamesters makes me run to keep up. And I have no idea who this group from northwestern Maryland might be. Jordan has not mentioned them.

"They were quiet last night, which was a-maz-ing," Nicole continues, lapsing into a bored nasal tone that might make me cringe if it weren't for the fact that I know my southwest Texas twang can take a few people aback. "No spam to our OS."

"OS?" I have to ask.

"Operating system," she informs me flatly. "Sometimes other groups figure another group's gonna win and they try to shut you down by sending spam to overload your system and weigh you down. Your challenge is to remove it and continue."

"I see," I say, but don't really, having played a few video games with Jordan and decided I don't have the perseverance or time to master them. "And this has happened often with this group from Frederick?"

"The Eagles? A couple times, yeah. But not in a while."

"Do they do anything else to harass you?" the judge asks.

Nicole thinks about that. "Nope, not the last couple of weeks. They're more into cheats lately."

"Cheats?"

"Sure. You know, like, the way they say they won, but didn't and try to scare you into thinking they're solid."

"I'm sorry, I don't understand that."

Nicole raises her brows and sighs, barely tolerant of my ignorance. "Cheating is, like, a way of life to win, you know. These guys just do what everyone else does—only better, cuz they win."

Terrific. Cheating as a way to get ahead. I really do need to limit Jordan's game time. I go in again with another angle. "Are they the ones who were smoking pot during game time?"

"Dunno," she says, face lax with disinterest.

"The . . . fan boys Jordan knows," I ask her, "were they the ones smoking pot?"

She rolls a shoulder again. "Not sure. Ask her."

"I will."

Minutes later, I watch them walk away to their rooms and Goodwin asks me what I thought of that discussion. "Interesting," I tell him but think, *Not especially helpful.* "I'd like to try to get Senator Bunting on the phone and see what his point of view is on this issue." I hold my breath, waiting for Goodwin or Marie to volunteer to join me—and when I see Marie frown, I give it one more try. "I believe acting in concert on this with the senator and with the chief of police will make the most valid impression."

"Right you are," Goodwin says, shocking me to my toes as he reaches for his phone at the end of the bar. But if he pussyfoots with Bunting like he did with his kids, I'll know where I stand. Out on a limb. Alone.

"More coffee, Carly?" Marie slides from her stool to get the pot.

"A half cup, yes, thank you." I watch Goodwin dial up Henry, whom I know only from across a crowded conference room—and believe me, none of those occasions has been delightful. Henry, in the Senate now more than ten years, is a warhorse for our party, a diehard stick-it-to-the-opposition kinda guy. No matter the bill, he stands on the only planks the leadership provides—and sometimes, even when the bill tanks, he walks the board right into the drink. He resembles a jolly old elf—and acts that way, too—until you don't do things his way, then from behind that façade of Santa's helper emerges Scrooge. Talking to him about his daughter Sherry receiving a favor from the police makes me leery of a sane discussion. I have heard from Jordan that he is a harsh disciplinarian—and because of it, I fear Sherry may permanently become a fruitcake.

"Good morning," Goodwin begins. "Senator Bunting, please." He mouths to Marie and me, *The maid,* while he waits, and then says, "Hello, Senator. Yes, how do you do? Yes, would love to meet you, too, I hope, sometime soon. I know Marie has told me what a wonderful friendship she and your wife are developing. Yes . . . super. Super." And they go on making nice for a minute more, when he tells Henry I am here and we've just had a "useful discussion with Nicholas and Nicole about last night's events and—"

Interrupted, Goodwin looks at me. "I agree, but Congresswoman Wagner and I and my wife have talked this over, and we wondered if you would give us your view on talking with the police chief about—" Silence settles over Goodwin as he grimaces and tries to get a word in edgewise.

And obviously Henry won't let him, because Goodwin reaches

out to hit a button on the wall phone fixture. The room fills with the stentorian sounds of Henry Bunting filibustering us. "No, sirree," he says in his Kentucky Colonel bluster. "No, sir-ree. I do believe my daughter, Judge Deeds, I do. If she says nothing went on there that I need to be concerned about, I see no need, sir, to talk to the chief of police."

"Senator," I interject loudly enough so that it reaches the wall receiver, "Congresswoman Wagner here. Sir, I *do* feel the need. The man who brought my daughter home to me, sir, did not provide comfort or assurances. And so—"

"Well, Congresswoman," utters Henry bluntly, *"I am totally satisfied.* The gentleman who brought Sherry home to us had manners and a badge."

"How about a number?" I ask, needing anything I can hang on to and trace, if need be.

"Pardon me?" Henry has taken umbrage at my stubbornness. *Tough.* "Did he have a badge number, Henry?" I figure if we're gonna get down in the dirt and wrestle, we should surely get down to a first name basis.

"Carlotta," he calls me, and I know he mistakes my name on purpose to rile me.

I pursue him. "A name, then?"

"Yes, he had a name. Wilson. Brad Wilson."

Brad Wilson. For ingenuity, it certainly does beat plain ol' Jones. But if Brad Wilson is the man's real handle, I'll eat my Stetson. Hell, if he really is a patrolman, I'll eat my boots. But it was mighty intriguing that a man who portrayed himself as a policeman had taken Sherry Bunting home, while the man who brought the twins home to their parents was a plainclothesman who showed his badge as a private investigator with a Maryland license. And me? What had I told the judge and Marie about who'd escorted Jordan home? Well, part of the whole truth. I'd said he was an undercover policeman whom I had met some time ago—and it was he who instigated this removal of the four youths from this game party. Okay, so I fibbed. I can't very well tell the whole truth to the judge, can I? Not when that would take days—and we certainly do not have that kind of time before the media makes you-know-what hit the fan.

While I'm thinking, Henry's been steaming along his path toward indignation. Marie pipes up and asks for Norreen, but Henry cuts her off with, "Not here. Out on errands." And that's when I give Goodwin the cut sign, fingers slicing across my neck.

Goodwin raises his index finger to me as Henry winds down. "Thank you, Senator, for your time. I want you to know that Congresswoman Wagner and I are going to talk over going to the chief."

"You do that, Judge Deeds. You do that. But do not include me."

Goodwin scowls and tells him, "Think nothing of it, Senator."

"Clearly he doesn't," I snort after Goodwin bids Bunting good-bye and hangs up.

"What a waste of time," Marie complains. "I just wish Norreen had been there. Maybe she and I could've reached an accord." Marie smiles at me so sweetly I'm getting a sugar high. "Norreen and I have become good friends, you know, sharing our car pool duties."

Feeling like I've been attacked from the rear, I examine Marie with what I hope is placid acceptance. A nitpicker, she has given me grief over car pool duties for gaming and Girl Scouts—and part of my need for the full-time assistance of Ming is so that I can do my share—or Ming can—of the parental running back and forth.

Her husband nods sadly. "Done now. Sad. I thought he'd be more agreeable."

"What made you think that?" I ask.

"Aren't you folks up on the Hill supposed to be the ones who find common ground?" he asks rhetorically, clearly not expecting any answer.

"Some of us do, some of the time."

"Ain't that the truth," he retorts. "What a self-centered ass!"

His wife reaches to put a napkin to her mouth, feigning catching herself from spitting coffee across the room. "Goodwin!" she chides in fake delight much too good-naturedly to be stomached. "You never criticize anyone!"

"Today's my day, Marie." He gives her a disgusted look as he punches numbers on the phone, leaving the conference call button pressed, so that when the receptionist answers, I know he's called police headquarters. Call me stunned. I never thought he'd budge. I'm admiring Goodwin, and chastising myself for my bad judgment, when he asks for the chief. But he's told the man is out on sick leave suddenly and won't be back for two weeks.

Goodwin and I look at each other like mourners at a wake without a stiff.

"Well, damn," I groan, "that puts us in a pickle." In my head, my wheels are spinning. Can't talk to the lieutenant because he might not know Jones . . . or how and why the chief wants to handle it—or not.

"Well, I have an idea," Marie perks up—and inside my tummy turns because I have a sick feeling she's playing her own game of chess. "Why don't I call Norreen later and talk, just us girls?"

Oh, *that* makes me happy as a chicken in a stew pot. The girls can accomplish *precisely what* to cure this ill?

"Then, Goodwin," Marie says, "you can call the game organizer."

I want to do this on my own. "Vickie Enrici?"

"Yes." Marie nods, looping her arm through Goodwin's, doing a cuddle-up to her hubbie, which he, judging by his ramrod posture, is not reciprocating. "What do you think, Goodwin, hmmm? See if she knows anything? If we investigate what it is that the police might have been after, then at least we might have an idea of how delicate this investigation is. After all," she says with more severity, "your children——" She blinks, realizing her faux pas. "Our children say they have done nothing wrong. And we have no reason not to believe them." She smiles at me—and I swear I can hear her declaring checkmate.

Goodwin nods slowly. "Maybe so. Maybe so. Good thinking, Marie."

By whose yardstick? This doesn't solve our problems. We could still have last night's events come back to bite us in the ass. Finding out about whatever the police were looking into doesn't mean we are absolved of accepting a favor. What is Marie thinking? And what is Goodwin doing humoring her?

No answers magically appear before me.

But whatever they are, I'm not sure they're my business. My only goal is to save my own skin after I save my daughter's.

Making a beeline to the front door, I depart with polite thanks. So much for the good deeds this judge has done. His reputation has outgrown him. You see, to my mind, good deeds begin at home. With spouses and children. And yet, for cloudy reasons that are nonetheless none of my business, this good judge has failed them all.

As I walk the two doors down the sidewalk back home, I mentally pinch myself at the hollow results of my morning's endeavors. Astounded at Goodwin's actions—or lack of them—I decide to track down the Montgomery County chief of police myself.

Back home, standing in my hall, tapping my impatient fingers on my table, I dial up police headquarters. More than twenty minutes later, when finally I get the chief, after being transferred from one of his phones to another, he quickly disavows any knowledge of any undercover or plainclothesmen who reported extracting my daughter from a gaming party last night. The chief's virulent case of amnesia means Jones is into an investigation that everyone prefers to keep hidden.

Except me.

So why would one of the most respected lawmen in the

country do that? He's covering something. Just like Jordan is. Probably the twins and maybe Sherry, too. And why is Goodwin suddenly such a wuss at home? And Marie even more simpering than I recalled? Has everyone changed but me?

The only thing that springs to mind is a niggling memory of news about Goodwin that I read very recently. I snap my fingers, remembering I saw it online.

I march into my den, fire up my computer, and open my e-mail, where I subscribe to the *washingtonpost.com* daily digest. I find the old e-mail, click it open, hit the link to the *Post* site, when *wham!* an instant message box flashes onto my screen. Mind you, I get IMs only from Jordan and I know she cannot be online, but I don't recognize the e-mail address, either. Call me a glutton for intrigue, but I open the damn thing.

And there before me—in full color—is the livid face of Jones. "Ma'am!"

"What the hell are you doing on my e-mail?" I squawk at him.

"Ma'am!" he repeats, and moves his face closer to the camera-phone-e-mail thingie he must be using and I instinctively draw back. "What do you think you're doing?"

"Pardon me?" I enunciate with all the grandeur of a five-time-elected gal from a state where we shoot intruders first, chew the fat last.

"You heard me," he growls back.

"I am on my e-mail." I put my finger on my mouse, ready to flick him off.

"You were down to see the Deedses."

"I can go where I want."

"I told you to leave this alone."

I move in to gander at my screen more closely. Backed by a wall of machines with techno blips and lines and flashing lights, he's got a black polo shirt on today and a monitor screen behind his left shoulder shows the front door of . . . the Deedses'? "Where are you?" I ask, predicting I'm gonna get a spook's empty answer.

"Close."

Concentrating, I relive my walk down the street from the Deedses' . . . with the usual cars and an unusual van parked off to the left. Residents of Georgetown drive BMWs or Mercedes, sometimes Volvos. My own Tahoe sticks out like a sore thumb. Come to think of it—now consciously—so did this van. "Casing Q Street, are we?"

"Ugh!" he scoffs. "Me to know and—"

"Me to find out," I finish in our old repartee. "This is a free country, *still,* Jones. And where my daughter is concerned—"

"Mom?"

I spin in my chair to find Jordan walking into my office. Wonderful.

"Heyyyy. Jones!" she sings, bending over my shoulder. "How cool is that? He does IMs! Gee"—she sidles up to the screen—"where is he?"

And like Houdini, he disappears.

"That"—she straightens, eyes shining like she's seen heaven— "was awesome. What did he want?"

I grind my teeth. "Nothing."

"Oh, come *on,* Mom—he—"

I sputter, "Like I said, Jordan, nothing to concern you." I power down my computer. "I'm going in to work. Stay here. I'll lock up. Ming will be here shortly."

She presses her lips together. "Sorry."

"Yeah, I get that. Want to make it all better and tell me what I need to know?"

She shakes her head. "Can't. Wish I could."

"Makes two of us." I stand up. "Okay, then. I think I will try to invite Senator Lyman for dinner tonight." I need a change of pace. Some fun. "Set the table for four."

"Sure, not a problem. If he comes, that would give me a chance to apologize for interrupting your date last night and show him I'm not a loser."

I'm thrilled she has recovered her manners, but I'm not ready to be less than stern with her. I walk around her. "Gonna change my clothes and drive in. Get your homework done."

"Sure. Nothing else to do." She flaps her arms to her sides.

I examine her. I'm putting a guilt trip on her, but guilt is a very good thing to have, especially when earned. "Secrecy does not become you, Jordan."

She winces. "Did the twins say anything?"

Does she want to know if her own stance is now moot—or does she need to know how to cover new tracks?

"They know nothing. That is their statement and their parents believe them."

She nibbles on her lower lip. "Okay. Thanks."

"See you later this afternoon," I tell her, and put an arm around her shoulder to draw her near and kiss her forehead. "I love you."

"Love you, too, Mom."

She marches off—and I call the one man every congressperson swears knows more about them than God and the FBI. My AA, Aaron Blumfeld, has endured me for nine years—and loves the challenge. When I describe my newest for him this morning, he doesn't question it. "Learn what you can about Judge Deeds" might possibly even sound harmless.

His *Yes, ma'am* is short and sweet so that I can change and drive myself to Capitol Hill, tormented for fifteen long minutes by my charming choice between the snake that lies under Rock Numero Uno—or under Numero Dos. Do I call the *Post* and fess up, frying with me a federal judge and a senator, plus their wives and children? Or do I twiddle my thumbs and silently wait for Armageddon as a party of one?

Driving around to the members' garage entrance of Rayburn, I idle while the Capitol policeman at the barrier pulls out his undercar bomb detector rod and runs it around the perimeter of my Tahoe. With thumbs up, he directs me through and I quickly find my assigned space, park, then take the elevator up to my floor.

Saturday means few of my colleagues are in town—and fewer in their offices. The wide, glistening halls echo with my footsteps. But when I open my office door, not only do I see Aaron wave at me from behind the glassed-in cubbyhole we laughingly call his office, but I see two of my legislative aides and my press aide. "Good morning, how are all of you?"

They all quickly stand and bid me hello. Aaron hurries out and smiles at me. A nice Jewish boy from Silver Spring, Aaron sports a fit but stocky body, male pattern baldness, and a rapier mind.

"How are you, ma'am?" he asks, and walks with me toward my inner office, scooting ahead to open the door for me.

"Thank you, Aaron. I've had better. And you?" I put my purse down on my credenza and walk to the window to pull up the blinds, letting the light brighten my work space—and my dark mood.

"I'm very well," he tells me as he closes my door and comes to stand before the broad desk that I bought a few years ago because it gives me a feel of history and heritage. Old—early Johnson, Andrew not Lyndon—its vast expanse gives me the impression, false though it may sometimes be, that I am the master of my ship.

"Good." I try to be congenial, though I am wound tighter than a two-dollar watch. Once here in my inner chamber, I always feel powerful—and safe. Only once have I felt its sanctity violated and only once changed the décor. After Alistair Dunhill was murdered in my office chair two months ago, we had my desk chair reupholstered. (Alistair kind of . . . well . . . leaked on to the damask as he died, poor man.) And we've also had the room recarpeted. A few glass fragments had become embedded in the tufts during the commission of the crime, and Capitol Police forensics boys cut holes in it, crude as Big Bend's boulders. I needed it replaced. Physically. Mentally. Hey, call me fussy. Call me wussy. But I wanted a clean sweep after the tawdry murder of my party's second most powerful man here in my domain.

"News?" I ask, getting to my point without shilly-shallying.

"Yes, ma'am. Some."

I roll out my chair, sit down, and cross my legs. "Tell me."

"Goodwin Deeds. Age fifty-five. Old Washington money and family. The Good Judge is descended from the Riggs banking family. His first wife, Jane, brought him more blue blood, a distant relative of the Lees of Virginia. His second wife, Marie, is more worker bee. Vice president of accounting for Metro Hospital and Health Care Group. She worked her way through Trinity over in northwest. Her dad was a carpenter and mother a clerk at the old Woodies Department Store. Twin children, age twelve, from the first wife, who died of cancer." He smiles serenely. "But you know all this."

"Most." I note he is reciting this, nothing written—no trail on this, then. "Good detail. Anything else?"

"Mmmm, some."

"Like?"

"Two of his colleagues on the bench don't care for him or his new wife."

My eyes widen on that one. "How did you learn that?" Aaron had worked on the Hill eight years before he came on board with me—and I've often conjectured he knows as much as any director of the CIA.

"Cocktail party talk. One of my neighbors clerks for another judge on the same court as Goodwin."

"I'll weigh the source," I decide.

"Do," he agrees. "One other thing."

I can tell by the gravity of his tone this one's a doozy. "What?"

"His big headline-grabbing convictions a couple of years ago of the two corporate execs who bilked their companies?"

"Yep, I remember those." Goodwin had heard the cases of two different presidents of two large weapons manufacturers whose headquarters were here in the capital. While Aaron recites details I know about their verdicts and how Goodwin had thrown the book at both, I'm sitting straighter, recalling that I know someone who had been friends with both men. My ex. Leonard Underwood. I tilt my head. "What about them?"

"One got out on parole last week. Paul Turner. His wife, Barbara, who went into a major depression after his conviction, just got out of a rehab, went home, and then he came home . . . and suddenly she's not doing too well. She attacked her husband last week and he had to commit her again."

"That's a shame." I know the terrors of living with someone who is volatile. My mother has always had a hair trigger—and from her example, I learned how to control my own.

"Worse. Goodwin had him arrested Thursday night for trespassing at his home."

I fall back, stunned. "I didn't know that. Was it in the papers? Did I miss it?"

"Maybe you didn't read all your news briefs yesterday morning? You had that eight o'clock breakfast for Kirk Crandall over at the Marriott—and you wanted to drive yourself, so you probably never finished." He chides me often these days for not letting him or other staff members drive me to events. "But there's more. Goodwin slapped a restraining order on him."

Amid the tension I felt in their kitchen among the four of them, the probability that it was caused by an external problem didn't spring to mind. "That's terrible." I sit for a second. "Anything else I should know?"

His eyes lock on mine. "Only if you want to tell me what *I* should know about why we're interested in Deeds."

"Ah, yes, I am thinking about that, Aaron. Something happened last night at home that I have a challenge with and it involves Judge Deeds and his children."

"And Jordan," he adds with certainty because he makes it his business to know my schedule and hers.

"And Jordan," I confirm.

"I see your dilemma, ma'am."

I offer him a wan smile.

He walks to the door and turns. "I'll see what else I can learn for you."

"And quickly, too," I urge him. *As if*—I rebuke myself—*as if* such odd facts about Goodwin could save me and Jordan, if or when the media crack this little nut wide open.

But deciding to not obsess about my troubles and have fun are two different things. Witness the past hour or more when Sam Lyman and my daughter sit at the dining room table but walk around each other verbally like two cowboys itching for a bar-room brawl. Try as I might to smooth things out, the two of them are not getting any closer to resolution. Me, I'm getting tense as a plucked chicken.

"Okay, Jordan, why don't you take your plate into the kitchen and I'll clean up tonight? Ming"—I gaze across at her—"you may leave, too, if you like."

"*Shi, shi, Taitai Wagna.* Thank you, Mrs. Wagna," Ming explains her Mandarin, and nods in deference to me and to Sam. "Sen-ta Lyman. Reiko and I will go out later. Okay with you?"

"Yes, Ming. The senator and I are here for the evening and so is Jordan."

"Yes, she is on the ground."

I grin at Ming's attempt at the Americanism. "Grounded. Yes, she cannot go out."

"Very good, Taitai. Thank you for steak. I like every much. Cay-gin is much like Szechwan. Hot to burn mouth." She grins. "You like a lot, yes?"

I nod. "Too much."

Many minutes later, Sam tells me, "I like Ming." I'm dropping the grill racks in the sink to soak in soapy water and he's drying the salad bowl as he continues, "But Jordan and I have a way to go."

"Yes. I don't understand her attitude toward you. She is usually very polite."

"Carly, she was never rude tonight. And she did apologize for last night's interruption." We grin at each other. "Tonight during dinner, she was testing me."

"I suppose," I say as I wipe down the counters. "She's been pulling away from her father these past few months. Maybe she's reexamining what she wants in a role model." The light in her eyes when Jones was on the computer screen springs to mind and I shake it away, knowing Jones is the farthest figure from a father any child could imagine.

"I gather Len is not Mr. Personality when it comes to children."

I huff. "Right on. On their trip to Japan in April, he managed to alienate her by denying her the right to come home to be with her friend."

"Alistair's son, right?"

"Yep. Zack. Great kid. Anyway"—I wring out my dish cloth and wipe down the sink—"Len was more devoted to getting what he wanted from the Japan trip than accommodating her need to show sympathy. He may never be able to get her affection again."

"As long as she doesn't judge all men by his measure."

Seeing how her attitude toward Jones had changed, I could easily assure him that. "I think she'll differentiate between the two of you."

He walks forward and wraps both arms around me to draw me close. "I hope so. Like how some of us have really hot lips."

"Mmm." I lick mine as I examine the lush contours of his. "From the Cajun spices, huh?"

"And wondering if I can use them on the hot cook." He grins.

"Oh, I do hope so."

"Really?" He arches a blond brow. "Sure of that?"

I narrow my gaze on his mouth. "Try her and see," I whisper.

And so, dear friends, he does. And so, be still my heart, he gets me revved. And himself, too, I am certain, because I can feel the hard proof against my tummy.

We move to the couch. We slide down to the bottom. We experiment with a little of this and a lot of that, and just as we are about to make major decisions concerning the suitability of removing one bra from beneath one blouse and unzipping flies, a loud scream blasts into the room with the French doors slamming open and careening off the walls. And Jordan—who should be upstairs, mind you—stands wide-eyed and panting on the doorstep, moaning, "Oh, god, oh, god, Mom, Sam. Oh, god. You have got to come!" She rushes over to me as I struggle to stand. "Hurry, Mom. He's bleeding!"

"Who?" I croak, wildly disoriented.

Sam pushes his hair back from his forehead and rearranges his belt buckle. "What are you talking about?"

"Judge Deeds, Mommy. He's dead." Sam and I run out the door, with Jordan right behind me.

four

Death is never pretty. Even when it comes softly in bed
at an age when few regret the loss, death looks wrenching. And
Judge Goodwin Deeds looks like he met his maker after someone dragged him through hell backward.

Sitting in a chair, head down on the keyboard, he faces the
three of us as we rush into the room.

Sam and I skid to a stop, Jordan on my heels.

With his eyes half open, mouth lax, tongue lolling, chubby
cheeks draping over the keys, the good Judge looks like he's be-
gun his journey to the great beyond with a few itty-bitty problems left behind.

For one, the cord to the mouse looks like it was the not-so-
massive weapon of his destruction. Wrapped around his neck,
the black plastic-covered cord lies taut against his throat and the
skin around it is red from strangulation. His hands hang limp at
his sides, knuckles grazing the parquet floor. One hand is badly
bloodied, as if . . . someone has dug flesh out of it.

"Damn, damn," Sam curses as he rushes forward, bends, and
presses fingers to Goodwin's carotid to find a pulse.

"He's dead, Sam," I manage through a dry throat.

"No!" Sam is working feverishly, pushing Goodwin's chair
back from the table, pulling at his limp body. "Never say that till

you're sure!" But he turns Goodwin's head and moans, "Oh, god. Someone bashed him." Sam raises two fingers to show me blood. "Call 911."

But my feet are rooted to the floor. Paralyzed by the sight of my neighbor murdered, only my eyes slide to the floor near Sam's feet, and there, upside down, broken and coated in bloody gore, is another keyboard that I'd say someone clobbered him with. Why they'd have to double their insurance by hitting him in the head *and* strangling him beats me, but then, you know, I'm not a killer.

Sam, however, will not be deterred. With the instinct as well as the training of a healer, he's set on saving Goodwin. I peer at him as he rushes around the judge like a wet nurse at a still birth. Damn if I don't know dead when I see it. Animals and people. No matter the means by which life is lost, death is sad and ugly.

"Carly, help me!" Sam's tugging at him. "Help me get him down."

I do not see the point. As we speak, Goodwin is passing the pearly gates. Minutes have passed, it must be, since Jordan screamed her way into our family room. Like a flash of lightning, Sam and I bolted out the door. Jordan followed us, I don't know why. Curiosity might have propelled her back—along with the fact that I was running here, too. She's just a kid, older by two years than I was when I first saw a dead man—*so of course, Carly, she's freaking out.*

"Carly! Snap out of it! Help me get him on the floor," Sam urges me. "And Jordan, call 911!"

With my arm circling Jordan's shoulders, I push her toward the phone to dial emergency. I step further into the Deedses' first-floor computer and game room. Crammed with four personal computers, plus five gaming consoles—one Wii, one Nintendo, and three Xboxes—and god-a-mighty who-knows-what, chairs and boxes of games, floor to ceiling, the room looks like a yard sale gone deadly.

"Carly!" Sam demands.

"Coming." I rush over to help him. "We shouldn't be moving him, Sam. I mean, the evidence—"

"Screw that. If I felt right, he has a thread of a pulse. I might be able to do CPR if I can get him laid out."

"I hear you." I kneel in front of Goodwin and try to circle my arms around Goodwin's waist. But he surely should have met Jenny Craig and friends, because all I'm doing is clutching rolls of blubber and huffing and puffing like one of the three little piggies. His face falls forward so that his forehead is on my shoulder. I cringe, but Good Samaritan that I am, I tug some more and get no results.

Sam, who's wheezing from exertion like I am, tries to leverage the body off the chair, but the armrests obstruct any movement. Goodwin sits like Jabba the Hutt, wedged in the chair, tight as tuna in a can.

With my shoulder, I push hair back from my perspiring cheek and repeat the obvious. "He's a dead weight, Sam. We can't—"

"We have to, Carly! Come on, heave-ho." Sam rolls the chair farther away from the table and a stack of disks clatter to the floor. With one sweep of his arm, he shoves them away. As they skitter under the desk, he clears a path. "Okay, quick, Carly. Let's lower him to the floor."

We get him down, but, still in the chair, he rolls to one side.

"Just get behind him here," Sam tells me. "Push on the count of three. Ready?"

"Right." One, two, and three, we ooze him over like a slab of bread dough. He slaps to the wooden floor, face up, still in his chair, legs bent, feet dangling. His hands up now, I see I was right about his wound. I swallow bile at the sight of raw flesh, gouged out from Goodwin's right palm between thumb and forefinger.

Suddenly fluid gurgles in his mouth. The sound echoes in the room like a fish tank's bubbles.

"Oh, gross!" Jordan clamps a hand over her mouth and gags.

I'm tempted to do the same, but instead instruct Jordan, "Get the phone, Jordan. *Now.* Call 911. Hurry."

Sam sweeps Goodwin's mouth with his fingers, extracting liquid and something I can't see that he tucks in his shirt pocket. "He's so fat," Sam is muttering. "I don't know if CPR will do any good. But I sure as hell will try!" He bends over Goodwin to begin pressure against the chest.

I shimmy up next to Sam, still on my knees. "Need anything?" I ask, feeling useless. But he can't answer, so I look around the room, taking mental notes just in case I need to remember things.

For certain, someone had a helluva party here—and I don't mean gaming. I mean a knock-down-saloon-worthy romp. Disks of black and blue run all over the floor, the desktops, the workstations. The Xboxes and the Wii stand, I would say, untouched. But the PCs looked like casualties in a fistfight—one screen face down, its keyboard missing. Another with its DVD drive open, its light blinking. Only the one in front of Goodwin seems untouched. Intact.

The rest of the room is a shambles. Chairs sit askew as if someone threw them this way and that. One wire basket sits on its side, its contents of disks spilled on the floor. One picture on the wall hangs by a corner.

Clearly, whoever instigated this particular scene had a rattler's temper and a coyote's impatience. I had been in this room exactly twice—and it had been as neat as a nun's lingerie drawer. Now it appears the devil himself had done the ransacking.

A wild thought occurs to me that that person just could not have been Jordan. *Could it?* I mean, just because she found him doesn't mean she did any of this damage.

Hearing her talk on the phone in the other room, I rid myself of suspicion. She's a good kid and at the moment she's hysterical in her demand that the ambulance come: "Please, now, now, hurry!" She gives our address, then tells them, "We're two houses away, on

Q Street. Yes. . . . My name? Jordan Underwood. No. . . . No, I'm twelve. I'm with my mother and her friend."

Good girl, I'm praising her, and following it with a firm denial that she would have riffled through this game room . . . or hurt Judge Deeds. She's not strong enough . . . but then, the judge was too overweight and out of shape to defend himself from anything larger than a bug. Couldn't even get out of his chair without a yank from a crane or a come-along. So whoever attacked him either knew that and planned for it—or just hit the jackpot when they came calling for . . . *what*?

Oh, brother. I run a shaky hand through my hair and tell Sam, "I'm going to talk to the police. They'll want an adult."

He doesn't stop, just kind of grunts a little as I shove up from my knees to march into the family room and put my hand out to Jordan.

"Give me the phone, sweetie. Sit down here with me." I point to a nearby couch, and I hug her as she buries her face in my shoulder. "Yes, hello. This is Congresswoman Carly Wagner from down the street. I am the mother of Jordan Underwood, whom you just spoke with. . . . The address here is . . ." I pause to calculate the house number and give it to her. "How long before they arrive?"

"Ten minutes, ma'am. Maybe more."

Anything seems like an eternity.

"Your name again, ma'am?"

I give it to her—and note the clock on the wall and the time we're talking: 8:21 P.M. Memorizing that, I disconnect, replace the phone in its cradle, and for the first time it occurs to me that Jordan should never have been here because she was grounded. Had she snuck out the front door when Sam and I were beginning to get friendlier on the couch? Unless she can suddenly fly, she had no other way to get out.

Suddenly I'm seeing red. Angry as a bull in a china shop, I stare down at her. She can't see my expression, which is a really good thing, considering she disobeyed me and now, as a result, she has stumbled into a tragic situation.

Sam is standing at the computer room door, sagging against the frame, as weak as if he were a puppy who'd swum through a gulley-washer. "He's gone."

"Gone," I repeat, confirming what I've known since we first ran through the door and I got a gander at Goodwin.

Jordan looks up.

Sam peers at me, kindly and sorrowfully, the doctor delivering the grim news. "He's dead."

Course he is. But then, because men always want praise for their insights, I bless him with, "But you were right to try, Sam."

"I couldn't help him. Too much fat around the heart to do any good with the CPR," Sam's rattling on to himself like the town fool, till I hear something that makes sense. "And out of his mouth"—Sam stares at me, a bit dazed for a doc who used to deal daily in life and death—"I got this." By index finger and thumb, he holds up a blue flash-disk.

Jordan stiffens.

"He tried to swallow that?" I ask him.

"Who knows what he intended," Sam announces, switching his attention from me to Jordan and back, "but he definitely choked on this disk—and then someone finished him off by strangling him."

And bashing him in the head, too. "Sad," I mutter, "very sad."

And the reality of what is about to occur with the arrival of the police and the paramedics hits me in the head, too. Suddenly my brain is doing the crazy-woman-running-through-the-haunted-house thingie, yelling like a banshee, *No, no, Carly, surely your daughter has not discovered a dead man. A murdered man.*

Surely she cannot be hauled in for questioning by the police.

Oh, but she can.

She will, Carly.

And what about you, Carly?

I am now in the presence of a dead man. Another *murdered* man.

And who on God's green earth has the misfortune to discover two dead men in two months?

Do I need to raise my hand? Can't I just quietly go to the head of this infamous class and then silently fly away like Tinkerbell?

No. Because this means now, not only is my daughter involved in a homicide case, but I—up for reelection, about to claim the limelight and deliver the keynote address at my party's convention, eager to rise in my party's rank and favor, delighted to have a higher profile with Americans from states in addition to my own—ah, yes, that means that I, Carly Wagner, am now that most unique of women.

A dead woman, walking.

I sit straighter, suddenly lucid as an owl.

Sam wanders over to me and Jordan, sinking into the sofa opposite ours in the Deedses' family room.

I allow him no rest for the weary. "Did Goodwin die of the whack on the head or strangulation?"

He scrubs a hand over his face and considers me a moment, probably trying to decide if I'm a ghoul or just plumb smart. "I'd say the keyboard weakened him, but the cord killed him."

"And the gouge on his palm? What's that about?"

He shakes his head, turns up his open palms. "Clueless on that."

Jordan pipes up with, "Judge Deeds had his electronic access codes implanted in his hand."

"Pardon me?" I croak.

She opens her hand and points to the webbing between thumb and forefinger. "Here. He opened all his techs with this. His garage door opener, his house safe, his computer."

I'm stunned, never having heard of such a device. "How? Why does someone do that?"

"It saves time," she explains nonchalantly, like everyone should avail themselves of one of these implants, "plus, you don't have to remember passwords and have all kinds of other gadgets. You just wave it at the infrared reader."

"So . . . someone would slice open his palm and take this device to open or operate whatever the judge could," I conclude.

"Right." She nods.

"Does Marie have this?"

She shrugs. "Don't know."

"The twins?"

"Carly?" Sam is running both hands through his hair. "Give it up, will you? The police will soon be here and we'll be going through this stuff all night long."

And what we know will contribute mightily to the entire investigation. "The more we know, the more we understand."

"Forget understanding this." He tips his head toward the computer room. "It's a mess. And we're in the middle of it. Nothing we can do about it now. Christ." He rubs his eyes. "If they can find this guy after the way I fucked up the crime scene, they'll be lucky." He looks up, his eyes falling on Jordan. "Sorry."

"It's okay," she tells him politely, making me think, *It's a hell of a time to bond with him now, kiddo.* "I know words like that."

What about what else you know? I'm about to be relentless in my dealings with my daughter. "Do the twins have implants like that, too?"

Sam scowls at me, not happy about my dedication to questioning, but too bad. This is my daughter and she is a tougher cookie than I thought. After all, she left the house tonight against house rules, didn't she?

"Jordan?" I pressure her.

"No, ma'am. They don't."

Ah. "Thank you." Her respectful address signals she knows on which side her bread is buttered. "And why did you come here tonight?"

She squirms.

I rise up and walk away from her. "Tell me now, Jordan. Before the police come."

She gazes at the floor.

"Jordan! A man is dead. Murdered. The police will not be as

kind to you as I am if they think that there is anything you are hiding that is important to this case." I walk toward her, bend over, put two fingers under her chin, and raise her face. Tears swim in her eyes. "Darlin', tell me so I can help you if there is something that is—"

"It was our usual game time. Saturdays at eight. For an hour."

This I know, so I wait for more that I don't.

Then she offers me fluff. "I had to come, Mom."

"I hear you," I say, and straighten up.

She swallows hard. "I figured the Deedses would let me in. They never ask anything about what's going on at our house, so I figured I wouldn't have to tell them I was grounded."

The self-centeredness of each member of this family was a fact I had noted but did not see as useful here, other than that my daughter thought she could pull one over on them as well as me. "Did they let you in?" I prod her to continue, wondering just how many minutes away the emergency crew might be now.

"No, no one was home. I—I came in through the garden gate and knocked at the kitchen door, like I always do. But when I knocked, the door kind of fell open, so I came in. I called for someone, but no one answered and I just walked in . . . and then I went in there." She tips her head toward the computer room door. "And that's when I saw the judge." With a frisson, she takes her attention from the doorway to me.

"Did you think he was dead?" I persist.

"Yeah. Absolutely."

The maternal knowledge that my precious child could consciously decide to deceive me saddens me—and makes me bold as well. "Why would you defy me and come here, Jordan?"

"I told you."

I shake my head once. "You told me a reason that sounds too much like a justification for something else."

Her big brown eyes swim with tears. "I wanted something."

"What?"

"It belongs to a friend."

I do not move a muscle as I wait.

"I promised I'd try to get it back."

I hear a siren in the distance, coming closer.

"A disk. Like that one that was in the judge's mouth." She nods toward the blue disk that Sam has placed on the sofa cushion beside him.

"What's on it?" I ask, my heart in my mouth.

"Pictures."

At the increasing din of the EMS truck as it comes down the block, Sam says, "Come *on,* Jordan. They're here."

"Pictures of what?" I demand.

"Sherry." She sucks in a big breath and adds, "In some stuff she bought at a couple of wiccan sites."

I close my eyes.

"And at Vamps Are Us."

I grope to sit down next to Sam on the couch.

"What's Sherry Bunting doing," Sam asks, hoarse with trepidation, "buying things from witches to vamp boys?"

"Vampires," Jordan corrects him, "not vamps. And wiccans are good witches."

He knits his brows. "Sure they are."

She shakes her head.

I sit back, trying to find a center of gravity in a spinning universe, and then I ask her, "How wild are the pictures?"

She clears her throat and that's about all the answer I can stomach at the moment.

Sam's mouth falls open.

I swallow hard. "Is she naked?"

Jordan's eyes narrow in bright pain. "No, but—"

"*What,* then?" Sam demands.

"She's making potions and . . . um . . . casting spells."

A creature who believes in better living through chemistry, I nonetheless doubt the efficacy of Sherry's concoctions and curses. "You don't really believe she can *do* that, do you?"

"Oh, *yeah,*" Jordan says in awe. "She made Corey Winthrop

get the flu last week after she drank Sherry's super stew—and her hex on Mason Carlyle made him fall down the stairs outside the gym and break his leg."

Those two schoolmates of Jordan's and Sherry's had missed the last days of classes for health reasons. "Jordan, I doubt that Sherry could have that power."

"Why?" she asks, totally believing her friend's capability to hurt others.

"Are those hexes on this disk?"

Jordan fidgets. "These are new. Heavy-duty. She's hexing the gamester team from Frederick and . . . um . . . her daddy's opponent in the fall election."

Sam groans.

I glance around the room, searching for how damaging such a disclosure could be to Sherry, her father, Jordan, and me. But I'm overwhelmed by the greater importance of a man murdered, lying dead in the next room. "I can see how you wanted to get this back for Sherry."

"Because once Sherry knew she could do this stuff, she started to sell her chants and recipes. So she's making money."

"Oh, my god," Sam laments.

"Yeah." Jordan licks her lips. "Lots of it, turns out, and when people started to know about how good they were, she wanted to stop before her father found out."

"Or the media," I add on a whisper.

"I had to help her," she responds. "You see, right?"

Sure. I mentally survey the damage.

We have one strangled judge, one senator involved in mucking up the crime scene while trying to resuscitate him, one congresswoman with a penchant for finding murdered men, one twelve-year-old discovering a body while searching for a disk filled with tasteless files from another wayward child for which her proud, prominent, take-no-prisoners daddy is gonna whup her heinie something fierce.

Six people.

One massive scandal.

A murderer on the loose.

And who of all the people in all the world is the one person that—odds on, right now—knows more about this train wreck than me?

Right.

Jones.

But I insulted him, alienated him, and refused to thank him for keeping my daughter out of trouble. So he vowed he's never gonna do me any more favors. Even warned me to quit snooping into Deeds's affairs.

But the way I see it, chances of that are slim and none, because the minute Judge Deeds breathed his last, that boat left the dock.

five

Lawmen give me hives. Sheriffs, Rangers, and policemen all have the same effect. That's an old reaction from the botched investigation job they did when I was sixteen and my daddy walked out of our ranch house—and never came back.

I'm currently gazing at my newest acquaintance in the law enforcement profession, and my palms are beginning to itch something ugly. He's not, though. Oh, no. Detective Graham McGinty of the Metropolitan Police Department of the District of Columbia is a fiftyish flask of sharp Irish whiskey. Tall, very. Silver-haired, as in startling. Big, barrel-chested, and Black Irish bad. His gruff personality seems to be no put-on for us civilians in the room.

I bet beneath that exterior lies a sentimental sort who in private can break into a fine rendition of "Danny Boy," but for us—and the boyos on the force—he acts like the meanest bear this side of the Potomac. Growling at his forensics techs, barking at his patrolmen, he has interviewed Sam with cold indifference. I've watched him closely, not privileged to overhear him as he fires off questions to Sam in the Deedses' kitchen. But from Sam's body language, I see he gives it back to the detective in spades as they walk into the computer room, close the door, and, I would assume, review Sam's CPR attempts. Meanwhile, the EMTs and two patrolmen who were the first responders to our call have kept Jordan and me cooling our heels on the couch.

Since it is now midnight, I am none too sweet myself. When McGinty emerges and sends Sam home, he drags his hands back through his wealth of silver hair and comes to stand in front of me.

I still sit on the sofa in the family room area. Beside me, sleeping, lies Jordan, her head in my lap.

He pulls up a chair. "She the girl who found the body?" McGinty asks me, barely lowering his voice so she can continue to sleep.

He knows she is. His patrolman told him so—and so did Sam. I overheard that when he first arrived. "Yes," I reply with a precision that implies my dwindling patience. "We have been here all night, waiting for you."

"Thanks," he responds, black eyes floating over me, noting mouth, blouse, slacks, child, and retracing his steps to hair, eyes, mouth, eyes again. "You're the congresswoman."

"I am."

"This your daughter?"

"She is."

"Not too talkative, are we?"

Not too polite, are we? I inhale. "Not usually at this hour of the night, no."

"Thought you folks in the House were always talking." His attempt at sarcasm comes with a straight face.

I give one back. "I like to listen, as well."

"Well, I tell you, Congresswoman . . . ah—"

"Wagner," I supply to move this along, though I know he knows my name by now from his staff and Sam. McGinty is just trying to exert power. As a method of extracting cooperation, I understand it. I've seen it hundreds of times in my own hallowed profession. But it takes him down a few more notches in my rapidly lowering esteem. "Carly Wagner, Detective."

"Detective Graham McGinty, ma'am. Tell you what."

I stare at him.

Ha. Made him blink. So, he's not happy with my tenacity. "Let's wake up your daughter to get her statement."

I counter with, "Can't you start with me and let her slee—"

"No," he cuts me off. "I need to hear her story, and now."

All right. *Try this on for size.* "I will remain with her while she tells you what happened."

"I'm not crazy about that, Congresswoman."

"And I'm not crazy about you talking with my underage twelve-year-old daughter, Detective McGinty. So if you are not going to agree to that, then I will not allow you to interrogate her without my lawyer present. Take your pick."

His long-lashed ebony eyes narrow on me. "Have it your way." He looks down at her, raises his chin. "Wake her up. Now." I set my jaw, and get ready to do just that when he barks, "Come on, we gotta talk here. Jordan. Jordan!"

She stirs. I know her well enough to feel that she has been rousing herself since McGinty first approached me, but I bet she smartly wants to assess how this detective fares with me before she lets him have at her. I applaud her good sense but know time is a-wastin'. I smooth her hair from her brow and nudge her shoulder. "Sweetie, wake up and talk to the policeman. Sooner you do, the sooner we get home and into our own beds." I examine our inquisitor, who, arms akimbo now, is impatient as a flea. "She's had a trying night."

His eyes say, *Let's see, lady.* His lips say, "I understand." Then he flips out a notebook, whips it open, and reads a few things there. He leans forward and, elbows on knees, scratching the corner of his mouth, he says, "Okay, Jordan, awake yet? Right. Tell me what happened here tonight."

Jordan sits up and grabs for my hand, squeezes tight. She inhales, brushing hair from her forehead, and stares at him. But when she starts to speak, she's quick and logical, even emotionless—and her summary of how she found the judge, then ran to get Sam and me, leaves McGinty examining her for a very long minute with a totally blank expression.

"Why did you come here tonight?" He's going back to the start of her story and the motivation that I, too, noted she omitted.

"To play a game."

I dare not move, repressing my instinct to wince at her brevity. She's scared to death. I feel it in her trembling hand. If brevity is the soul of wit, it is also the essence of fear. My gaze strays to the sofa where Sam had set the disk. He must have picked it up when he rose. I would say he's probably given it to McGinty by now—along with an explanation of what it is. So the cat is well out of the bag.

But if McGinty detects anything other than her distress, he doesn't bat a long lovely lash and asks, "What kind?"

"Whatever we decided when I got here. We play on Saturday nights at eight."

"But they weren't home," he states.

"No, they weren't," she seconds him.

"Only the judge. Do you know where the rest of the family is?" he asks her.

"No."

He reaches into his jacket pocket and pulls out a candy bar. Snickers. "Want some?" he asks her, no smile, no compassion, no emotion of any kind. Just doing the job. I know this style of attack of studied indifference. Lethal to those who have something to hide.

Jordan shakes her head. "Don't like nuts."

I bite my lip so I don't laugh in his face. What is the deal with candy to a baby? Is this the new way to cozy up to young witnesses?

"Okay." He rips the wrapper. "You?" he offers me some.

"No. Thank you."

He munches his bar while he examines Jordan. "And you just walked in the kitchen door?"

"It was unlocked. It usually is. I knocked, but—"

"Wait a minute. Wait a minute." McGinty has a finger raised

and he's trying to swallow before he talks. "This back door is usually unlocked?"

Jordan says, "Yes. On Saturday nights. They leave it unlocked for me. For the game."

"This is Washington. Georgetown. Who leaves their back door open?" Ol' Graham McGinty is utterly amazed.

Truly a rhetorical question; nonetheless, Jordan tells him, "The Deedses have an alarm system like we do, but the judge hated it. The alarm was loud and hurt your ears. When they were home, they never had it on because it skipped and turned off their phones."

"Why didn't he have it fixed?"

Jordan says, "He did. But it kept breaking. Ours does, too."

With raised brows, McGinty reads my eyes to check out the truth of that.

I confirm, "These houses are so old that the electrical wiring in the windows and doors sometimes connects improperly and that can short out the alarm, the electricity, and the phones."

"Defeats the whole purpose," McGinty concludes as I silently agree with him—and recall Jones's criticism last night of my own security system. "So then"—he breaks off a piece of his candy bar and chomps away—"when you came over, the door was unlocked."

"And open a little bit."

"Okay." He chews on that idea. "And you usually just walk in anyway. So you think, hey, no biggie, right?"

She nods. "Yes, we're friends. I just walk in."

"What time did you come over?"

She shrugs. "Not sure. Five of, five after, maybe."

He turns to me. "Can you confirm that?"

"No."

His silver brows jump. "Why not?"

"I thought she was in her room."

He frowns. "Why's that?" When I tell him she was grounded,

he spins on Jordan. "Your mother didn't know you had come over to play a game?"

On a thread of guilt, she says, "No."

McGinty shifts to gaze at me and his black Irish eyes aren't smiling. "Why not?"

Jordan sighs and confesses, "I snuck out of the house. So, no, my mother didn't know I was gone."

He examines my reaction to that. "True?"

"True," I offer, and hold my breath, expecting him to ask her why she's grounded, because if and when he does, this interview is suddenly all about last night and Jones, his buddies, Sherry and her pictures—another giant can of worms.

He ponders a minute. "Playing games is so important you'd risk your mother's anger by coming here. Is that what you're telling me?"

"Yes, I am," she says with a conviction that chills me because she would defy me to save her friend. I can't condone that—and yet, while part of me approves of her loyalty, the other mourns her continued devotion at her own expense.

It also makes McGinty change direction. "You like the judge?"

"Yeah."

He waits and she does, too. "That's it?" he probes. *"Yeah?"* he mimics her.

I am unhappy with him, but Jordan is insulted.

She sits straighter and zeroes in on him. "I liked Judge Deeds."

"Sad he's dead?"

Jordan's eyes trail to the computer room door. "Yes. He looked . . . terrible." Her eyes flood with tears and I wrap an arm around her shoulders. "He was nice to me."

"All the time?"

"Most of the time." She sniffs, swipes at her cheeks. "Why?"

He stops eating. "I ask the questions here."

She narrows her eyes at him—and so do I.

"Okay." He nods when he gets a gander at our expressions. "How about Mrs. Deeds?"

"She's okay."

"Do you like her?" he shoots back.

Jordan tilts her head from side to side. "She doesn't talk much."

"Is that right?" He rolls the empty wrapper around his finger. "Why?"

"She's kind of afraid of kids."

I gaze at Jordan, astonished by her bluntness—and an insight into Marie that totally escaped me.

McGinty's unfazed. "Why's that?"

Jordan shakes her head. "Not sure. Maybe because she hasn't had any of her own yet to raise from babies. But you should ask her."

"Mmm." He's thinking and chewing on her idea as well as his candy. "I will. You are with her a lot?"

"She does car pools."

"She ever do anything you don't like?"

Jordan shakes her head. "Not really."

"How about the judge?"

"No."

"Sure?"

She knits her brows. "Yeah. Yes. Like what do you mean?"

"He ever yell at you or not let you play with his children?"

McGinty is clearly on a fishing expedition. "Detective," I interrupt him, "you are asking very specific questions. We could be here all night."

"Just trying to get a picture of how your daughter came here tonight and what she thought of the judge."

"She told you."

"Ma'am, you may have been involved in a murder investigation once before. . . ."

I pull back, offended and alarmed that the sad case of Alistair's death has branded me with the D.C. police as well as the Capitol force.

"And you may think," he continues, "that because of that and your elected office you know where this interview should go— or how. But I assure you, I am the one who is in charge here. And you and your daughter will answer my questions as I see fit until I think I am done. Are we clear?"

"Very," I reply. "But if you want her to talk about her relationship with each person in the family, you can simply ask her to talk about that. This cat-and-mouse bit is tiresome, especially at this hour of the morning."

"Well, then, let me see if I can get you both out of here in a reasonable time frame." He shifts in his chair and turns back to Jordan. "Why do you like to play video games?"

She shrugs. "They're fun. Fast. More interesting than TV shows."

He looks unconvinced. "Do you play sports?"

"Sure, in gym class. I'm not crazy about them. I'd rather dance."

"You take lessons?"

She nods. "Ballet."

I let him go on asking about her interests, school, her other friends, figuring McGinty is trying to build a profile of who she is.

"Why do you get together to play with the Deeds children?"

She blinks, confused at his direction. "They're my friends. And they're both super-good at it. Nicholas is the best."

"So . . . you learn from him, do you?"

"Oh, well, he practices a lot more than I do. Finger moves." She wiggles her fingers at McGinty.

He turns to me. "Do you like that your daughter plays these games?"

"I don't see harm in it. It's the wave of the future to be proficient in computers. Technology. We use it now to track people, to bank, to operate, to publish books, to fly to the moon. I think it's good for her to know this."

He thinks about that a minute and looks accepting. "Okay, thanks, Jordan."

I am astonished at his change of mood. Not certain if I can trust his intent, I tell myself to dig in for a long night. But he thanks Jordan and points toward the back door. "How about you go out and sit with one of the policemen in the back yard?"

Jordan checks my expression.

"Darlin', you go out there, but you do not answer any questions by any police, do you hear me? They cannot—are not allowed to do that without me present. Go ahead and wait for me." I shoo her along. "I will talk with the detective, and we'll go home soon." I watch her leave.

"Nice kid," he says when she's out the door.

His compliment indicates he's on another search mission. Okay. I'll help him out if I can. "Thank you. I am very proud of her."

"She ever give you a hard time?"

I cock a brow. "Are you asking me to describe if she is a problem child, Detective?"

His dark eyes are flat, waiting. "I am."

"She is wonderful. My challenges with her are few. Always have been. She is now twelve and bright, into ballet and Girl Scouts and gaming parties." Seeing nothing registering in his features that he wants to pursue this with me, I continue. "Her life is normal and she responds easily to the hassles of me being a congresswoman with long days and a hefty travel schedule. Maybe that's because she has never known any other lifestyle."

"And you are divorced."

Ah, so someone at the precinct had done some speedy background investigation of me for McGinty's use. "From her father, yes. Have been for six years. So Jordan is used to that, too."

"A smart kid, then." It's a question.

"She is."

He rubs a hand over his mouth. "And the black nail polish? What's that about?"

I grab a breath. "A bit of rebellion. Normal for her age to try her limits."

"Nothing else going on?"

"Like what, Detective?" To show my displeasure, I give him a long hard stare from my big baby browns. To a question wide as the Texas sky, I am certainly not offering up my entire lifestyle and Jordan's. This man deserves cooperation, but not a window into everything we are.

He shrugs. "Just asking." He slaps his hands on his knees and rises. "Okay, then, thanks, ma'am. You know the drill on murder investigations. We'll take your fingerprints in a few minutes and ask you to give us your clothes and shoes for analysis. Then give your phone numbers to the patrolman over there. Here's my card. You call me if you think of something I should know. Otherwise, I'll be in touch. Soon."

I rise. "Thank you," I say, but don't mean it.

To my right, two tall men in navy suits stroll in the kitchen door. With white shirts and dark ties—if we gave them sunglasses, both could be mistaken for Blues Brothers à la John Belushi and his gang. Both dudes look like they expect deference. McGinty gives 'em a nod and two words. "A minute."

Then he turns to me. "Okay, ma'am. No going out of town. Not even to your district. Not till I say you can. Hear me?"

"Right." Wondering who these two new guys are, I let that go, resigning myself to being captive physically. Captive mentally, too. What did Sam tell him about that disk? Where is it now? And how do I find out without getting myself charged with obstructing justice and my daughter charged for lying to the noble Detective McGinty?

After an hour or so of watching McGinty walk the Blues Brothers through the scene, I figure they're FBI—and they're debating who gets to lead the investigation of the murder of a federal judge. Though I know the Bureau should get the nod legally, McGinty wins. Or I think he does as I watch while Jordan and I are in the hands of the forensics guys for fingerprints and clothing swap. Finally, given blue shapeless gowns to wear home, we're freed by McGinty and walk home.

Standing at the hall stairs, I inform a worried Ming about where we've been all night and send her off to bed. Then, with a few assuring words, I go upstairs to tuck Jordan in to her own bed and make my way back down to the kitchen. Abe is asleep in his cage and he rouses briefly, but then lies back down in his comfy little bed.

Whim, whimsy, or cockeyed logic has me grabbing a ginger ale from the fridge and heading for the back yard. In my garden chair, I seek out a contentment that eludes me. Seeing unnatural death once more come to one of my acquaintances, I am unnerved by the evening's events. Jittery. Ragged. I close my eyes a minute and listen to the warm silence of the dead of night. Only the tinkling of my next-door neighbor's garden fountain punctuates the calm.

I inhale, do a bit of *chi* generation as I sit with legs crossed. That's the wrong pose to do that—but hey, call me a nonconformist. It relaxes me nonetheless.

I sigh.

The trees do, too.

And then I look up to that portion of my wall where the moon does not shine—and my patio lights never reach—and over the wall slides a long, dark shape that appears before me and squats down. The man I expected.

"Hello," he murmurs. "How are you?"

"Tired," I tell him. "Exhausted," I clarify. "Glad you came."

"Are you?" He seems a bit incredulous. In the shadows, his face is all angles and planes. He looks dog-tired. His eyes, dull.

"Of course. Who else would I welcome over my garden wall at this hour of the morning?"

"Or at the end of such a day," he adds.

"True. How'd you learn about Goodwin?" I ask, needing to know when and how. And most of all, why.

"Police bandwidth. When Jordan put in the 911."

"Ah. Were you surprised?" *Were you still outside monitoring the house?*

"Yes. Very. How'd it go with McGinty?"

Has he purposely changed the subject? I am too tired to jump on his case right away, so I go with his flow. "He's a bear."

"Yeah, well. His world is filled with more nasty crap than Sarge Brown's." Brown had been the detective on the Capitol Police force whom I had come to know well when he led the investigation into Alistair's death. "McGinty is jaded."

"He went after Jordan with a hacksaw."

Jones smacks his lips. "No excuses for that." He tips his head at the other patio chair. "May I sit?"

I grunt. "Does this mean that you want to share something with me?"

He clears his throat—and I note this isn't *yes* and isn't *no*, but maybe a *want to.*

I try to close the deal. "Last night you refused to talk and wouldn't sit. Change of heart now that a man has died, Jones?" *And now that you need to know facts from me?*

He works his jaw, doing a seemingly thorough exam of my garden. "Yeah. You could say in this round you hold a better hand."

Do I? How much better? "Then, by all means . . ." I tip my head toward the chair.

He plants his buns in it, and if I had more energy, I'd laugh at the way the graceful wrought iron makes him stretch his long legs out, black-clad cat-suit feet nearly touching mine. I can't help my wandering eyes, admiring his muscles in the body-hugging M5 gear, questioning why he has it on, where he's been, what he's done tonight that requires him to don the super-secret hi-tech fabric that neither fire, ice, knives, nor bullets can penetrate.

That, he's not going to share. But he does reach down inside the neck of his skin-tight shirt and pull out a lighter and a pack of cigarettes. He shakes two out, fires them up, and passes one over to me.

My brand, too. How kind he came prepared to humor me. "Bad for me," I object, but take it anyway.

He inhales, blowing smoke languidly into the dark night. "Got an ashtray out here, or are we killing your plants?"

I reach over, dig out a tin from behind a rock. "Knock yourself out," I say, then plunk it on the glass-top table and take a long satisfying drag. I can feel my blood pressure climb along with my curiosity. But damn if I am going to push him. He came to me. And for a recitation of what happened in that house.

Jones is not happy about having to ask for it, either. He's deep into pondering, too, how to approach it. "We had a camera on the front door."

I level my gaze at him. "I knew that from yesterday morning when you sent me that instant message. So what did you see?"

"Two people."

Two folks finished off Goodwin? Christ, that is sad. And terrifying. "Jones, if you know who killed him, you tell the police ASAP and get my daughter and me and Sam Lyman out of the spotlight."

"Trouble is, I'm not sure."

"Why not?"

"Because, dammit, I was not in the house. How the hell do I know who did it?"

"Well, if you know who went in—"

"Two people, I tell you, and I'm working on it."

"*What's to work?*" I know that's a simple question—and Jones, above all others, has too few simple answers. "Two in, two out. Or should be. Were there two out? Had to be, or the police would have found them while we were there. So, then, how did they come out? Angry? Running? Scared? What?" Now, I'm fried. He knows so much and for his spook's reasons, he's gonna keep the wealth to himself. "How?"

"Came out normally. No rush. No fuss."

How can that be? "You're sure?"

"I've been over the footage three times." He bites off his words, taking a drag of his cigarette in abrupt jerks that articulate his frustration loud and clear. "I'm certain."

All right. "So anyone in the back door? It was unlocked when Jordan got there."

"Don't know."

"Why?"

"Didn't have the opportunity to plant a camera there. We were going to sink it tonight, after the family all went to the beach."

"How do you know that's where they went?" Jordan had had no idea of it. What's *his* source?

"Goodwin talked about it today on his cell."

"I didn't know you could bug cell phones." I commend him with a nod.

"We don't. We have a piece in his clerk's phone."

My mouth drops open. "I suppose you have a court order for that?" I check his eyes. "Okay, so maybe not. Nonetheless, you guys get around!"

He looks sheepish. "Not enough, I guess."

I take another drag. "I'm with you on that one."

"And so," he says, "I came to make you an offer you can't refuse."

"Be still my heart."

"I tell you a fact about the case, you tell me about the body."

I close my eyes and open them again. Did I really just hear that or am I punchy with fatigue? "You show me yours first."

He blows smoke into the night air—and I hope he's not going to try to blow smoke up my agreement to his little deal. Then he announces, "We're not interested in the marijuana," and I conclude he had to try that as an opener, didn't he?

I drop my chin into my neck. "Oh. Come. *On.* Jones. I knew that was not what you're really looking for the second you told me."

He smacks those fantastic lips and nods his head. "Just clearing the air. Here's the job. We're looking into the sale of goods."

Holy moley. "What kind of goods?" *Potions? Curses? Spells? Pictures of senators' daughters in witches' garb?*

"Over the Internet."

That adds to my trauma. Pictures and text can transfer easily over the Net. I have to see if Jones will give me an inkling of what's on sale. "What is it? Credit card scam? Trafficking? Porn?"

"It's dangerous, that's what it is."

Okay, closed door on that one. I'll go for the other piece I have to work with. "Who went in that house tonight, Jones?"

"Two people, one I know, one I don't . . . but we're tracing him as best we can."

The second is a man, I note. "Do I know the one you know?"

Silence is my answer.

"Terrific." I use what I can, search for a flicker of agreement. "Was one of them Paul Turner? Or his wife, Barbara?"

Jones scowls. "You know about Turner attacking Goodwin the other night?" While I note he has not confirmed Turner's entry to the Deedses' home tonight, he has confirmed he knows about Turner's relationship with Goodwin. He has also revealed that Turner attacked Goodwin. That means either Jones has done deep background on Goodwin or he has researched both men—and for cause. "But why do you ask about his wife?"

I smile because this means Aaron could learn more than a security man with a team of helpers. "Barbara Turner went bonkers recently and her husband had to recommit her last week. Maybe she broke out of her newest rehab. Who knows?" It was a good card to play—and Jones absorbs it like new information.

After a second he asks, "Was the body warm when you got to him?"

How did *Goodwin's body feel when Sam and I turned him?* What I recall most is how damn heavy he was. And limp. When I found Alistair dead in my office one morning two months ago, he was cold, rigid, and turning green. But at that point, he'd been dead all night—and now, for the life of me, I could not recall how quickly a body cooled after death. But shouldn't Jones have an idea of when Goodwin died? "Are you telling me you don't know when he was murdered?"

"Assuming his wife and the twins didn't kill him before they left for the beach—and that neither of the two I saw did him in—he could have died between seven-thirty-five, when the last visitor left, and when Jordan found him. What time was that? Eight o'clock?"

I take another draw on the cigarette, and the garden spins around for half a minute. "I never looked at the clock," I tell him, figuring smoking is adding to my body's stress and making me dizzy. "Not when she ran in to get Sam and me—and not when we were working on him. So if you have the time of Jordan's call, that means Goodwin died between seven-thirty-five and . . . ?"

"Eight-fourteen."

"If Jordan had gone sooner, she might have run into the murderer," I state with a shiver and a silent prayer of thanks that she missed him.

Jones takes a drag, not bothering to agree with my chilling conclusion. Then he leans over, elbows to knees, and from here I can almost smell his brain cells burning with interest. "How was the judge killed?"

"Not able to ask McGinty?" *Don't all you folks work together?*

"Better if I don't. My case is private. McGinty has no need to know."

I can't resist needling him. "No 'associates' of yours on his force?"

My reference to his statement of Friday night makes him glare at me with a glint of humor. "Enough. But to ask them would take me time I'd prefer not to waste. And you are that rare creature—an eyewitness."

"I see," I say, knowing that I could refuse, but I need Jones's cooperation to survive this. He's given me a few clues. I'll equal him. "Goodwin was strangled."

"How?"

"By man and mouse," I respond, knowing I'm being cute and obtuse.

"Explain that."

"The cord to the mouse from the computer in the computer room. The murderer wrapped it around his neck. Also bashed him on the head with a keyboard."

"Anything else?"

"You mean unusual, because now I'm suddenly an expert on murder scenes?"

To my cynical quip, he tilts his head in consideration. "You cracked the case before with your logic and memory," he says, oozing praise all over me in that who's-your-daddy bass that would lull me if I were a woman with a lower public profile and higher romantic expectations.

To end the mutual eye-lock, I snort and take a puff of my cigarette, as much a diversion from Mr. Charm here as it is my need to stay focused. I do a mental inventory of the crime scene to give Jones something—anything—except the small blue disk in Goodwin's mouth. "There was something else." I raise my hand. Splay my fingers. "Someone tore up his hand."

Jones's eyes light up like a Christmas tree. "Really? How so?"

I describe the carnage.

"They did it to get into the computer," he concludes, then slaps his hands on his knees and rises like Proteus from the sea. "Hot damn. Okay. Great. Hey, thanks."

Me, I feel like the bride left at the altar. "Aren't you forgetting something? Like the identity of the man you know who was at the front door?"

"Nope. I told you enough. More than, actually." He exudes the pheromones of obstinate male. "I'm serious. We're talking murder."

"Death doesn't shock me, Jones. In South Texas, the living has always been hard—and so has the dying. But now we're talking my daughter here. Her *life*. And McGinty has a way of treating Jordan as if she might be responsible in some way for Goodwin's murder."

Jones gets his stern papa face on. "You let this go, ma'am. I am telling you straight. McGinty is good. Best there is. And so am I."

I purse my lips, tilt my head in question. "Really? And that's why you failed to put a camera on the back door?"

He curses, stalks over to me, grabs both arms of my chair, and bends down in my face. Anger flows out of him like lava. "You listen up, Carly Wagner. I'll make sure Jordan is cleared." If we were some other people, some other time, someplace else, the intensity of his words might be as intoxicating as they are gratifying. "We'll find out who did this to Goodwin, I promise you."

I stare, wanting to believe, needing to trust, dying to enjoy my realization that he cares enough to say the very best. But I am as stubborn as he. "Good night, Jones."

He blinks, shakes his head, steps back. "Ma'am. Do *not* meddle in this investigation."

"I'm in it knee-deep, Jones." I wish I had more to bargain with, anything to use to pry him open. But I'm stumped. "See you around."

He exhales like a dragon who's lost the fire-breathing contest. With a flick of his eyes and a slap of his thigh, he mutters a ripe unmentionable and dashes away to scale my garden wall.

I watch his deft brick-climbing exit, stub out my cigarette, and make for the house, opting for sleep—and some idea of where to start to unravel this mess.

I'm pulling open my French doors when my ace in the hole hits me—and stops me in my tracks.

And I can actually smile. I possess more means and more moxie than Jones knows I do—and maybe other facts that he could never learn.

Tomorrow I'll pursue it.

We'll see if I can surpass the feats of the dynamic duo of McGinty and Jones.

six

Three hours later, I'm up, mainlining coffee and picking up the hall phone. But I pause, wondering if ol' Graham McGinty had any reason last night to get a court order to tap my phone. Not a lawyer, I'm not versed in such intricacies—and I've watched enough *Law and Order* and *CSI* shows to be a danger to myself. I drop the receiver to head for my briefcase in my office —and dig out my cell phone.

Dialing up Aaron, I deliver last night's events with a three-sentence summary. Instantly awake and characteristically nonplussed, Aaron proceeds to earn his salary.

He jumps right in with an urgency that speaks of the dedication for which I value him. "What do you need?"

"Our discussion yesterday," I begin, searching for the coy words that give away nothing, wondering if cell phones can be tapped as well as stationary ones. "I need more info on all those related items."

"Got it. When?"

"You know me."

"Soon as possible, then. Will you be in today?"

"I have to be available if and when the detective on the case wants me or Jordan to go over the facts again. But if he doesn't call before I go, then I'm at Rayburn in an hour."

"I hear you. Do you want to write the statement for the media, or shall I call in Dana?"

My new press aide—my third in as many years—is so new she has yet to emulate my rhetorical style. While she shows more promise than her predecessors and knows grammar and syntax to a tee, I think this important statement demands brevity and precision she might not yet command. "You write me a draft. I'll finish it when I get in."

We're about to sign off when he halts me in my tracks with, "Reporters on your doorstep yet?"

"*Damn.* Sorry." I apologize to him because a Texas lady never curses out loud. "Hang on." And I go to my front window, push back my drapes, and stare at a tight flock of four who stand in a circle like a gaggle of turkey buzzards waiting for the prey to die. "Yes, for godssakes, they're swarming already. They're getting their money's worth with the crime scene only two doors down."

"I'll call the D.C. Police," Aaron declares, "and see if I can get them off your doorstep. What's that detective's name?"

"McGinty," I tell him while I peer at the crowd and try to figure out if I know any. "Graham McGinty."

"An Irish policeman in D.C.?" Aaron quips.

"Without any charm, let me add," I inform him. "Well, well . . ."

"*What?*" Aaron, alarmed, tries to come through the wire.

"Mickey G." Mickey Gonzalez works for the paper with the largest distribution in my district in Texas—and he hasn't ever loved me like he should, nor even like one of the South Texas *jefes* says he should. Most times that's okay, because I believe in freedom of the press, even if, in his case, I'd often prefer to push him through one.

"*Is he there?*" Aaron jumps at the name that makes him turn purple with frustration.

"No—and I'm shocked." But then, Mickey G. and I had had a tiff when Alistair died—and I'd warned him to stay well away from me while I cooled off. "Or maybe he's just courting my favor by being scarce."

"Or he'll show up at the office. Not to worry. I'll be on the lookout. Meanwhile, ignore the rest," Aaron orders. "Put on your sunglasses and back out of your garage like you have the devil on your tail."

"Bah. I do," I growl, then drop the drapes back in place and end the call.

I immediately hit the speed dial for the man I rarely wish to talk to. "Good morning, Leslie," I say when instead of my ex-husband I get his new wife of four months. "Carly here. I need to speak with Len."

Leslie is a talker. Why not? She's one of the local cable news channels' commentators, and I swear she was born to it with a mike in her mouth. This morning she wants to chew me out for my early call.

"Leslie," I say, interrupting a monologue that rivals a Victorian novelist's word count. "This is an emergency and it concerns Jordan. So just wake up Len and do it before he genuflects before the TV screen, will you, please?"

"Carly," he comes on minutes later. *"What's the emergency for Sunday at six in the fucking morning?"*

"Len. Listen to me. I have no time to repeat this and I need you to meet me at the Tidal Basin this afternoon to talk more." Then I let him have all the news, full-bore.

"Christ almighty, Carly!" he says, flying his traditional unsympathetic colors when I'm done. *"First you find a dead man. Now Jordan! How the hell does this happen?"*

Bad stars. Bad timing. No clue. "It did." I can't get mournful or self-pitying with Len because he would laugh right in my face. He claims I need no one, never did, so of course he has a way of avoiding the knowledge that with him, any wife had better be prepared to stand on her own two feet. But with his only child, he better be prepared to stand up for her, or I will nail his feet to the floor. "Just meet me. Let's say, at the paddle boat rental. Noon. If that changes, I'll call you on your cell."

I take a quick shower, praying on this Sunday morning for deliverance from Len. But he's my cross to bear.

Just like the Sunday funnies, I conclude with a sigh while I dress and watch the morning talk shows. The political gab fests do not amuse me. Instead, I'm listening and shuddering that the media have already launched their bombardment. The criminal and untimely death of Judge Goodwin Deeds is sound bite numero uno, with Jordan's discovery in the headline. Sam's rescue attempts come in second, but third on the hit parade is the story of how the three of us together entered Goodwin's house—and that this is the second murdered man Carly Wagner has discovered in as many months. Clips follow of Marie and the twins entering their house about an hour ago, returning from their vacation home at Rehoboth Beach.

One talk show host, who has never liked me since I got here ten years ago, pronounces my career now as dead as poor Goodwin. Sam survives as the hero of the hour, although the refrain is he "should rethink who he keeps company with after hours," while Jordan is pictured as an innocent pawn in an unsolved crime.

I flick off the show, snatch up my purse and car keys, when Ming and Jordan appear at the foot of the stairs.

"Morning, sweetie." I kiss Jordan on the forehead. "Hi, Ming."

"You're going in to work?" Jordan asks, voice high with incredulity.

"Only for a little bit. I need to talk to Aaron. Stay here. Do not go out the front door and do not answer the phone unless it is your father, do you hear me? Let the voice mail take all calls." I do not want anyone getting to Jordan without me around. And I do not trust reporters. "I'll be back and you and I are going to meet your father at noon."

"No." She crosses her arms. "I do *not* want to talk to him.

He'll just yell at me because I left the house when I was grounded. He won't understand, Mom."

I hug her. "Jordan, he has to know what occurred." Though I want to be prudent about how much he knows.

She breaks away and I catch her arm.

"Stay here, Jordan," I insist. "Ming, why don't you make some breakfast for the two of you?" When she has gone into the kitchen, I lower my voice. "Jordan, I want you to understand one more thing. You will have to be honest with the detective about everything, including Sherry. I predict he'll come here today to talk more and I want you to be ready. Do you hear me?"

She bites her lip and nods.

"Now tell me everything you know about Sherry Bunting's sales of her pictures and potions."

"Now?" Clearly, she does not care to do this, but I'm done asking. I'm demanding. "Oh, god. Well . . . she has samples up on the Internet. And, um . . . she set up an account online for people who wanted to buy things. Kind of like PayPal, and the money went into her savings account."

"Does she have a record of who she's sold these to?"

"I don't know."

"What are the prices?"

"A hundred apiece for the recipes. Twenty for the pictures."

Interesting. The wages of witchcraft, twenty-first-century style, at first blush seem more lucrative than burning at the stake, Old Salem style. "And did the buyers know her real name?"

"Well . . . her e-mail handle. Her Web site. Yes."

"She has a Web site?" Am I keening? "How could she get that without her parents knowing?"

"She didn't set it up herself. She had . . . um . . . a friend do it."

Terrific. "And do you know who this friend is?"

She hesitates. "Yes."

I wait.

She bites her lip. "Vickie."

"Victoria Enrici? The game organizer?"

Jordan nods.

"Is she nuts?" I wave off any answer. "Okay. Okay. It is what it is. I'm glad you told me, Jordan." I'd call Vickie and learn more. "Go upstairs right now, boot up your computer. I want to see this site before I leave."

By noon, I stand at a rail near the Tidal Basin with my arm around Jordan. While we're watching others paddle around Thomas Jefferson's chalk-white memorial on this pure blue sky day, I'm wondering if that gentleman would have been pleased with what we have wrought here in this town he was one of the first to see emerge from the swamp.

My morning has brought me a mixed bag of results. Vickie Enrici is a no-show, taking voice mail but not calling me back. Meanwhile, Aaron has confirmed that Paul Turner resides quietly at home a few minutes south of here in Alexandria despite his recent release from prison, his problems with his wife—and his attack on Goodwin. Turner—who was happily married and profitably employed for twenty-seven years until the law came to call and put him in the hoosegow for playing fancy with the corporate money—issued a public apology yesterday through his lawyer for his assault on Goodwin Thursday night. Whatever the chances are that he might have gone last night to Deeds's home and killed him is a question that Aaron and I both figure merits Turner a visit from Graham McGinty today.

But Aaron still has no additional info from his neighbor who clerked in the same court as Goodwin. Nor has Aaron learned if any police officer by the name of Brad Wilson was indeed employed by the Montgomery County Police. Just before I'd left to go home and get Jordan to come here, Aaron and I had knocked out a simple press statement that expressed Jordan's and my deep sorrow and heartfelt sympathy to the family at the death of Judge Goodwin Deeds. Further comment I reserved until the close of the District of Columbia Police Department's investigation into the judge's death.

"It's what's done, honey." I tell Jordan about the protocol.

"You didn't say anything about me?" she asks, anxiety lining her brow.

"No, sweetie." I brush her hair back. "Nothing."

Jordan looks absolutely remorseful. She has complained about being out here with me, concerned some reporter is going to attack her.

"Don't worry," I tell her as I search the grounds for Len. "I won't let them near you."

"I've really messed things up," she whispers, her lower lip trembling.

"You will do just fine. Tell the truth and all else follows easily." I wrap my arms around her—and over her head I see her father approach.

Armed with my info from Aaron, I intend to acquire ammo from Len that'll make me dangerous.

Leonard Underwood, at forty-four, takes a woman's breath away. Six-four, raven-haired, blue-eyed, broad-shouldered, Len's a real noir kinda guy. A movie-star cross between petulant Cary Grant in *Notorious* and wise-ass John Garfield in *The Postman Never Rings Twice,* Len's quick, well read, well educated. He quotes Shakespeare and, oo-la-la, Browning, even in bed. Len can be dramatic, intensely yours. Inscrutable like Laurence Olivier in *Rebecca.* Endearing like Jimmy Stewart in *It's a Wonderful Life.* Too bad he could never star in *Father Knows Best.* He doesn't come wired that way. Responsibility is someone else's concept. Some other chump's character trait.

Still, the quality that hits you squarely between the eyes is the charm. Whether it's real or acting, women love the guy. No, really. The looks capture them, and then they get to meet him and you can see their pulse bump up in that hollow at the base of their throats. The eyes impact not only the heart rate but the hormones. Saliva kicks in and suddenly we have, ladies and gentlemen, a woman who has a hard time swallowing for all the drool in her mouth.

No, not pretty. Especially when you are the watching, waiting wife.

So, had I loved him? Yes.

Was I delusional? Yes. My problem with choosing men, I have discovered over the years, is that I can be romanced. Show me a looker with attitude, wit, a hint of being a hard-driving man, and I'm there. Or I used to be. Hey, maybe it's the profession I'm in, that I want to believe that passion and prose equal love and devotion. Only once have I been right falling in love with a man who earned every ounce of respect he got—and he died only two years after I married him.

Less than a year later, I met Len—and rebound or no, I fell into the chapel and into his bed fast. Whatever it was we shared, now the only thing we call ours is our twelve-year-old daughter.

"Jordan." Len walks up to us and ruffles her hair, then gives her a quick squeeze. "You both look well." He peers down over the tops of my sunglasses. "I guess you were up late."

Jordan mashes her mouth in displeasure and turns to watch those on the Basin.

"Let's walk, shall we?" I indicate a direction toward a knoll where cherry trees and rhododendrons offer some shade and privacy.

Jordan jams her hands into her jeans pockets and steps out in front to put distance between us.

"This is a helluva thing to happen again, Carly," Len opens. "Better cover your ass with your buddies in your district."

Mr. Sympathetic. "I'll take care of that tomorrow. For now, I'm mindful of Jordan and what she needs."

He puts his hands in his slacks as we stroll. "What does she need?"

"Information."

He grunts. "Hey, Red, come on. She doesn't need it. You do. What's your pleasure?"

The hair on the back of my neck begins to stand—and I wonder if it's just a bad reaction to Len's old intimate pet name for me—or am I picking up radar that we're being tracked? "My first pleasure is that you don't call me Red."

He cocks a long black brow. "You used to love it."

Long ago, before I started my allergy shots against you. "My second is that you need to tell me about a few people you know well."

That makes him smile, but the smile is that of a crocodile. "Like?"

"Paul Turner."

"Poor Paul."

Not quite. The man is reputed to be worth more than twenty million with the stock options he collected even while he was down on the farm at the Feds' expense. "Have you seen him since he got out?" I ask.

"No. Talked with him, though. Very unhappy man."

He should be. "Did you know that he had to put his wife back in rehab last week?" *Come on, Len, let's get down to business here—and kill the chitchat.*

"Yes, I heard. Barbara has had a very rough time, too."

She signed the fraudulent tax documents for him and her. "She committed a crime, too, Len."

"You have no pity, do you?" he asks like the hard-ass lobbyist he is for the three largest American weapons manufacturers, whom some of my more cynical colleagues dub the Death Star Gang.

"Not for those who do wrong, no. Should I?"

"For a woman who finds herself in the midst of a second murder investigation, yes, you should have some compassion."

Sorry, bucko, that's really bad logic I do not bite on. "All my compassion goes to my daughter today." I am so tempted to add, *If you have some left over for your scheming friend, that's your loss.* But I hold my tongue. Provoking Len is not what I came to do. I need his cooperation. "Tell me about Turner. Do you think he would have the temperament to kill Deeds?"

For a split second, Len halts in his stride. "Why?"

"No need for you to know—"

"What do *you* know?" he insists.

"A lot." Obviously. "I was there. I saw the crime scene. I know how that man died—and it was horrible. Jordan saw it—and I am trying to ensure that she does what she must here and forgets it as quickly as possible. Tell me about Turner's temper."

"Could he kill someone? Sure. I could. You could. Anyone. You just need provocation."

"What provocation does an already convicted man have to kill the judge who presided over his trial?"

Len thinks about that for a few long seconds. "Goodwin married the love of Paul's life."

"Jane dated Paul? Really? Who knew *that*?" I ask.

"Not many."

"If Goodwin and Paul knew each other, why wouldn't Goodwin recuse himself from the trial?"

"Oh, but they never met each other."

"How's that?"

"Jane lived in L.A. for a while and dated Paul, then moved here after she broke up with him. She met Goodwin and they married, so Paul never knew Goodwin. And from what I heard from Paul, he and Jane never crossed paths here in town."

"Do you believe that?" I ask. "Despite the big A-list here, don't you feel as though we all travel in the same circles?"

"Yes, but Paul got here 'long about the time Jane was going through chemo and she cut her social obligations."

Len gazes ahead to where Jordan has sat down in the grass, out of earshot. For my ears only, he asks, "Does she know who killed him?"

I shake my head. "No."

"She's been secretive lately," he murmurs, shocking me with an observation into her character that I did not know he took the time or had the talent to make. "You don't suppose . . ."

"What?"

"That she knows who killed him and she's not saying?"

"No. I don't. She couldn't keep that kind of secret." Loyalty to her friends and protecting Sherry was one thing, but she wouldn't protect just anyone, and certainly not anyone to cover murder.

He smacks his lips. "Kids are funny."

Like you know. "Jordan isn't."

He rolls his eyes at me. "The nail polish. The black clothes. She's doing something funny. When she was at the house two weeks ago for our weekend, she troweled on enough black eye shadow and mascara to look like a streetwalker from Anacostia! We were going out to dinner and she wouldn't budge for me, but Leslie got her to take it off."

"Good. I'm glad. But I will speak to her about that. Tell me things like this sooner, will you, please?" I pick on him, but plan to have a heart-to-heart with Jordan. She had promised me she wouldn't ever use the black shadow again. The fact that she did when she was on her father's parental time meant she used it just to irritate him. That Leslie had enough sway to get Jordan to remove the ugly makeup impresses me because Jordan has a bad habit of ignoring Len's new wives for months after the ceremonies. That she is finally accepting Leslie more means she is getting used to her father's ways. "I will speak to her again about that."

Len glances at his watch. "Anything else? I have a one o'clock tee time up at Congressional."

Neither wind nor sleet nor murder keep this man from his golf—and his work. "Yes, as a matter of fact. I need to talk to Henry Bunting. Quickly. His daughter is in Jordan's gaming group and I want you to pave the way for me."

"Just tell me what it is and I can go to—"

"No. *I* need to do this."

"Henry is not fond of you."

"That's putting it mildly. He doesn't like my politics."

" 'A filly who needs to be broken,' is what he says. Bucking the party's position on the Medicare bill did not endear you to him."

"I'm voting my conscience," I assert.

"Hell, you're taking more risks every day, Red. Your votes on education and Medicare begin to make you look like a damn maverick, that's what. Bunting's not alone when he tells me you don't deserve to be keynote speaker." Len offers this in such a way that he sounds like he's proud of me—and rueful of Henry. For whatever reason that is, I might never know, but today my objective is tangential to whatever Len's got cooking with Henry. "Better be sure you know where your bread is buttered, Carly, or they'll pull the speech—and funding from party coffers along with it."

For now, I shake off that larger danger. "Just get Henry to see me," I instruct Len. "I want a place where neither of us will be noticed. One of your conference rooms at your office. The ones with the private entrances."

"Whoa! Hey. That kind of thing takes a bit of work."

"Whatever it takes, Len. Do it. If Bunting says he does not want to meet with me, tell him I said it is his reputation at stake."

Len purses his lips. "Heavy words, Red."

"Heavy problem, Len. Make certain Henry knows I am doing him a favor he will love me for 'til he dies." Assuming Sam gave McGinty the minidisk last night—and that it'll take McGinty a while to figure out who the girl in the pictures is—I have a window of opportunity to inform Henry. I won't save Sherry from her fate. What I do might even be moot. But I at least need to try to give a few smoke signals to Henry about what's headed his way. "Henry will love you, as well." *How* much more sweet can I make this pie?

Len's blue eyes darken to navy with the gravity of my statement. "Intriguing."

"Make it happen," I declare, then examine Jordan a second and ask him, "Want to come paddling with Jordan and me?"

"No. My game, you know."

I do. But I do try to get him to change his ways when it comes to being Jordan's father. "Right. Thanks for coming. Make sure to have your secretary call Aaron with the place and time of that meeting. Do not call me directly. Allowing this meeting to be traceable defeats its purpose." If McGinty decided to trail me, he'd know only that I had gone to my ex-husband's office building. "And if the police call you on why I was at your office, you could always say you're contributing to my campaign."

"As *if* you'd take our money," Len grouses, complaining about my continual efforts to remain free from his clients, whose interests would tar my impartiality on the Defense Appropriations Subcommittee.

I can't help but grin. "Make this meeting soon, Len. Sooner the better."

"I hear you." He waves good-bye to Jordan and nods to me. What a guy. No kiss, no hug to his only child, but taking the sidewalk like he's won Affectionate Father of the Year.

Crabs are crazy little buggers. I watch thousands of them scurrying all over one another in the well of the fishing boat on Maine Avenue. Carrying their defense with them as armor, they scavenge the ocean, eating all the crap. Then, for their dirty little job of digesting all that dreck, they get to be boiled alive and served up as a delicacy. Sometimes I feel that's what I do as a congresswoman. Scavenging for attention along with 434 others, I languish in the ocean while the bigger ones do as they wish . . . or must. On rare occasions, I climb to the top of the heap and I am seen and recognized. Suddenly one day someone comes along and lifts me out, and I wave my hands in delight at the chance to be heard, acclaimed. I never know, until way too late, if I have swum in the wrong waters, only to get caught and cornered, carted away to be boiled and eaten. By Henry Bunting . . . or Graham McGinty . . . or a host of others.

"Okay, lady, what do you want?"

"Honesty," I blurt, realizing as time goes by I am increasingly dismayed about the Deedses—and the Buntings. Individually and together, each and every one bothers me. Jones, god save his interfering soul, would call this animal instinct my Second Mind. Hell, my first one is having enough problems figuring its way out of the gaming and media mess I'm in.

"Hunh." The scrawny old fisherman with bad teeth before us says, "Just so happens this is the only place in town where I can sell you that, too. But for now, you want crabs"—he gestures from one end of his craft to the other—"or shrimp?"

"Mom? Hey, Mom." Jordan sidles up to me, impatient and irritable. "Just tell the man how many crabs we want."

"A bushel."

He nods. "You got it."

"That many?" Jordan blinks at me. "You're kidding."

"No. What the heck? A bushel."

The old guy starts pulling at the mess of crabs with his long tongs and the crustaceans rise, clasping claws, as if they were holding hands in a big daisy chain.

"Mom." Jordan inches closer and skews up her face. "A whole bushel? I mean, we'll have them for . . . like . . . *ever.*"

"Sure." I am trying to be positive in contrast to Jordan's petulance. "If we have some left, we'll pop them in the fridge and make crab salad and crab cakes. We'll pull the claws to make soup." Meanwhile, that long sit-down in the kitchen will give me time to think and plan to face my colleagues—and my party honchos who are sure to call me, and soon.

"Okay." She puts a hand up. "Just checking. I can live with that, all right."

"We might just finish them off tonight. Ming likes them, too, and you know the rule." I smile at her, and she recites along with me, "Never eat crabs with your enemies."

"Yeah," she says, "I know." And then she gazes across the pier and for the first time today she grins. "Well, I wondered if he was going to come talk to us."

I brace for reporters, cameramen, knowing that the smile on her face belies that possibility. *"Who?"* I glance over my shoulder, but the sun catches me at the wrong angle and blinds me.

"Look over by the stairs. He was down at the paddleboats, too."

I spy the familiar, muscular figure who crawls walls and peers through computer screens. Ah, this means that the trill along my spine a while ago was my normal reaction to a guy who follows me often.

I'm paying for our crabs when I hear his footsteps behind me. "I need to talk to you."

Jones. The bass voice flows over my shoulder like some old Barry White song that promises to keep you occupied and happy all night long. Jones. Jones. *How do we meet in such odd places?*

Though I feel like whirling on him like some ninjette, I turn slowly to examine him. Today he sports more of the black attire I associate with his fashion sense. Black tee (biceps bulging, pecs imposing), khaki slacks (hips hugged—and I bet if you turn him around, buttocks are firmly packed into all the right places). Black sleek aviators, expensive, with an odd silver nose piece that sparkles in the sun, have replaced his wire-rims of Friday night.

"Really?" I squint from the glare and adjust my own sunglasses, then return to receiving change from the fishmonger. "How unusual."

He purses his lips. "I'd like to do it alone." He lifts his specs with the pad of one index finger, zeroes in on Jordan, then lets them drop back to his noble Roman nose. "Now."

Jordan beams. "I want to stay."

"Can't." He shakes his head. "Not for kids."

"Almost a teenager," she objects in lighthearted argument.

"Still not possible."

She grins, and when he knits his brows at her, she bargains with him. "On one condition."

"What?"

"Say please."

He snorts.

"Manners," she instructs him, "are the mark of a gentleman."

I stifle a laugh. Out of the mouths of babes . . .

He huffs. *"Please,"* he concedes, and I bet he's glaring at her.

She chuckles, says, "Sure. Not a problem. So, Mom, I'll catch up with you at the car, right?" And walks down the dock.

He points to my purchase. "Let's put these in your Tahoe."

"I am never one to refuse a man's strong arm. . . ." I step aside. "As long as you are not here to strong-arm *me,* you can heave-ho, buddy."

"Ha, ha," he replies deadpan, then leans over and hoists the bushel onto one broad shoulder. "Let's roll."

"Right." I turn in sync with him and we make our way back along the pier through the throng toward my parking spot. "Okay," I say when no one is within earshot of us. "What's the word?"

"I hear you're asking more questions."

I arch both brows. "Safe assumption."

"You let me handle Turner and Bunting."

I halt. My mouth gapes as wide open as some of the dead fish I saw on those boats. I raise my sunglasses, the better to see him with. "How do you know this?"

"How do I know?" he rasps, nailing me to my spot. "I know *you.* That's all I need to know."

"Nice try. Does. Not. Compute."

"I mean it."

Jamming on my glasses again, I peer at him. For his adamance and insolence to demand and not use any formal address, I haul out my hauteur.

"Ma'am," he says in a huff of conciliation, "you are investi-gating them."

"Ah, well." I let him stew as we both walk straight ahead. Jones, I detect from his squint, is doing surveillance behind those swanky shades. As we climb the steps to the parking lot and the street, I'm trying to figure out who or what he might be scanning for. But I find nothing unusual, damn my hide. So finally I give him the truth. "You hear correctly."

"Cut it out."

"Ba," I scoff. "Just like that."

Unruffled, he repeats, "Just like that."

The hair on my arms stands on end. "Why?"

"You know why."

"Sure I do. I'm on to something."

"Damn straight you are!" he blurts beneath his breath. "Back off."

"Wish I could," I mourn.

"You like this investigation stuff?" he accuses in a hot whisper. *No,* I want to blurt, but choke on the word. *Yes,* I admit, deep down where my guts churn and yearn to get the guys in the black hats.

"And what about Jordan?" he seethes.

"*What* about her?" I whisper between clenched teeth.

"You have to protect her from this."

"And since you won't tell me where to look, Jones, I am doing what I can." I freeze, making him stop to face me, then wiggle my fingers to beckon him to give me the basket. As he begins to drop the flimsy woven wood into my hands, he flinches at the electricity that jumps between us. I, however, am riveted by the contact and cannot move any other muscle except my mouth as I demand, "Give me my crabs."

"You don't need 'em," he grumbles. "You're crabby enough."

"And I have reason to be, don't I?" In the argument, my glasses have been slipping down my nose and I stare over the rims at him.

"Yeah," he concedes, and I almost fall down I'm so astonished at his admission, "you do."

"So give me my crabs and go do your job for your client, whoever the hell that is."

He drops the full weight of the bushel into my care and seethes. "I can't do my job and protect you and Jordan at the same time."

"No one asked you," I grunt, but at his revelation, my scaredy-cat meter jumps a notch, and oh, how I wish I could have his help with no strings attached.

"You need to take my advice," he insists.

"No, you need to take mine. Show your tapes to McGinty."

He shakes his head. "Against regs. That's the property of the company and the client."

"A man is dead, Jones, and you have evidence that could find his killer."

He inhales, scans the horizon. "I am the operative. I don't make the rules."

"Well, then don't ask me to sit around while you play footsie with your boss and your client. I'm not the kind of woman who waits around for men. Especially when I have many reasons—correction, I have one big reason"—I nod in the direction of Jordan—"to pursue my own sources on this issue. So you cannot dissuade me." I try to walk around him, but he steps where I do. I sigh, look away, and turn back to fix him with my eyes. "I believe we have come to an impasse, Jones. And so that leads me to leave you with one thought."

"What?" he asks, and I can tell he's real unhappy he had to.

"Lead, follow, or get out of my way."

He steps aside.

I sashay past him—and conclude from this little tête-à-tête that from now on I'd better be carrying my SIG-Sauer.

"You argued with him?" Jordan asks, sad and almost accusatory as I climb into the Tahoe and slam the door.

"Yes. I certainly did." I jam the key in the ignition and pivot to look backward and pull out.

"But you like him!" She delivers this in a tone that really means *she* likes him. This, I suppose, is a good thing—and I hope it is not too much of a good thing to cause me problems.

"No, not always." I face forward, switch gears, and enter the main traffic.

"But he likes you."

Sure he does. "He likes you, too," I tell her. *Enough to care if we live or die.*

"I was rude to him Friday night," she confesses.

"Oh, I bet he understands you didn't mean it."

"Why do you think that is?" she asks, staring out her window.

I frown. *Because he knows a lot about you and me.* "What's your guess?"

"He really thinks about other people," she offers wistfully.

I know that in Jones's line of work, he damn well better.

"And he remembers"—she turns to me with more serenity than I've seen in her the past few days—"what it's like to be twelve, maybe?"

For the first time all day, I laugh. "Yes, I agree." He is younger than me by ten or more years, so he easily remembers. What I remember from being twelve was terrible. Like how tall and gangly I'd suddenly grown, and the horrible fight my mother and father had the day of my birthday and how my brother Cord and I took my birthday cake out to the bunkhouse and ate it with our cowboys. "It helps to have somebody to talk to, doesn't it?" I ask her, the same way I once had Cord.

"Yeah." She gazes into her lap and blinks back tears. "I miss Zack."

Zachary Dunhill had been her best friend since they were toddlers in Montessori school. When Zack moved with his aunt to Arizona after the death of his father, some of the joy of school evaporated for Jordan. In fact, that's when she took up more with Sherry Bunting.

"Talking on the phone is not as good as him being here." She looks out the window again.

I'm trying to figure out what to say when I hear my own phone jingle. "Get that in my purse, would you, sweetie?" Hoping it's Vickie Enrici, I have this gut feeling that it's McGinty—and my evening will be shot with questioning.

Jordan digs it out, flips it open, hands it to me.

I put it to my ear to hear the one person I have thought of a lot today—and whom I have purposely not called.

"Mother." I gather my forces, because you never want to face Sadie O'Neill without a cavalry to call for reinforcements. "Hi, how are you?"

"Carly, where in tarnation are you?" Sadie's raring to rip into me.

Stay cool, Carly, girl. "We are on our way home from the fish market, Mother. Jordan and I—"

"You didn't call me to tell me what is happening, Carly. I had to learn it on the Sunday news, of all things!"

Sadie can make you feel like you're three in thirty seconds. "Mother, I'm very sorry about that, but I've been rather busy here."

"Too busy to call me?"

I sidestep that show-stopper. "I knew you'd handle my image there, Mother"—and oh, brother, does she love to do it, too—"but I have things I have to take care of here. The most important is Jordan."

"How is she?" I can hear the line crackle with Sadie's concern for her only grandchild all the way from the southwest Texas plains to the shores of the Potomac.

"She's coping well," I tell my mother, and examine my daughter, who wipes a stray tear from her cheek and straightens in her seat. "She had a shock, but she handled it well."

"I imagine so. She's a smart girl—a good girl, like you were. She'll survive. The dead are gonna go outta her life with regularity just like the rest of us. She'll get used to it."

My mother is a Texas gal through to her marrow. Born to a cattleman-cum-lawyer and his rodeo queen wife, Sadie, at sixteen, married a rancher twice her age and twice her size with twice her daddy's wealth. Sadie and Ted O'Neill—though they loved each other like flowers and sunshine and worked together like a pair of oxen to a plow—fought like idiots in the asylum. So when my daddy walked out of the ranch house one day twenty-six years ago, Sadie sat like a ghost for three days, waiting for him to come home. And when he didn't, she rose up, birthed a calf, instructed the hands in the daily doings, hired a house-keeper to cook and clean—and ran the Rocking O with the iron fist her husband had taught her to wield. Today, Sadie O'Neill manages the third largest cattle ranch in the Lone Star State, and keeps one eye on her very fat wallet and the other on her only daughter, who's won the house seat Sadie herself once coveted.

"Are you listening to me," she chides me, "or just humoring me?"

"Ma, I'm driving."

"Well, now, you just hear me out, traffic or not."

I sigh and dig deep for some forbearance. "I'm expecting a call from the detective." *And the game organizer and Aaron—and I don't need this extra hassle.* "Can we talk later?"

"No. We cannot. I do not like that you are falling over bodies, there, Miss Texas." Sadie resurrects my old title every so often to imply that beauty and brains often need to be juggled to be useful to a girl. "So I've made a reservation for tomorrow. I arrive at Dulles at six-forty."

"Mother. I have so much to do I cannot be squiring you around Washington while the police are on me." My mother has friends in this town. Big ones. The two Texas senators, the new secretary of agriculture, and one of my high school friends who works over at State. She occasionally donates money to the national party—and hosts private meetings of policy makers at the Rocking O. Whenever she can pry herself away from the land and cattle she adores—which is rarely, praise the lord—she loves to come here to bother me and parlay with whomever she can buttonhole. Letting her roam alone here without me in attendance would be like letting a cannon loose on the Mall. At any given moment, God only knows who she'd corral or shoot. McGinty. Marie. Sherry. Anyone could be in her sights—and they'd never know what hit them till she'd carved 'em up and served them their own gizzards.

"Now, don't you worry your head," she admonishes me. "I do not want to be wined and dined, little girl. I want to be helpful."

Oh, god. Sadie O'Neill in her helpful mode is the equivalent óf Santa Ana storming the Alamo. If she takes it into her head to harass McGinty the way she does our county sheriff, I'll be coyote bait legally and politically. For eternity.

"No. You just cannot come. Not now, Mother. Really."

"I will cook—"

"I have Ming now."

"Darlin', she's Chinese. What does she know about cooking? Bird's-nest soup and eel."

"Ma! In Texas we fry calves' testicles and barbeque boars' heads."

"And I'm making sure you don't eat your last meal alone and unelected in your little house here down the road. You need help and I am taking a plane to do what I can. Save your breath arguing with me. And do not bother to come and get me at the airport, either. I'll hire a car."

She can afford it. "All right." I give in because it is the only thing to do. I can fight a lot of people, make friends and influence many others, but my mother is one piece of work I can hardly ever move if she declares she will not be. "See you tomorrow night. We'll save you some dinner if you're late getting in."

"Do that, darlin'. I'll bring my chili pot, too, ya hear?"

"Ma. There are all kinds of security regs these days. Maybe you leave the chili pot home, eh?" Besides, one bite of Sadie O'Neill's chili can peel you down so neat, you'll think you've been skinned by a Comanche raiding party.

As I hang up, Jordan is laughing all over herself. A good thing for her state of mind, I think—even if the joke is on me.

"Gramma's coming," she says, and makes googly eyes. "I'm *real* excited."

She does love her grandmother, so I get some play out of this—and groan. "Remember that in coming days. And do not run to me to complain if she puts your knickers in a twist."

seven

Senator Henry Bunting takes one step through the doorway of Len's top-floor K Street private office at eight sharp the next morning—and halts to glare at me. He whirls to examine Len, who holds the door open for him. "Am I going to be disappointed in this meeting?" he asks Len with the arrogance of a man who has been elected by five to eight percentage points every time he's run.

"I doubt it, Senator." Len tips his head in my direction. "I obviously know the congresswoman very well, sir, and she has never disappointed me."

Those are the nicest words Leonard Underwood has said about me in years. Since I haven't yet said my piece—and Henry hasn't offered his gratitude to Len for the favor I'm about to do him—I make a mental note to learn to what precisely I owe Len's sweet talk. But at this moment I focus on making certain Bunting understands my intentions here are honorable ones and worthy of his time.

I push away from the wall where I've been cooling my heels for the past fifteen minutes, watching the bank of plasma-screen televisions that display six all-news channels originating from the East Coast and London. Goodwin's death places only second to the current war news. Unsurprised by that, I note that commentators are now chewing their cud over the astonishing coincidence that

Congresswoman Carly Wagner is once more involved in a homicide. One harpy has dubbed me the Maven of Murder—and I have gnashed my teeth over her, consigning her to my dustbin of tasteless TV tootsies.

Walking forward, I extend a friendly hand to Henry. "Please come in, sir. I asked Len to do me this good deed. I gather he didn't tell you that you would be meeting me." Wondering how the conversation between Len and Henry had run, I trusted Len to know what would sell with this man—and I gather mentioning my name would have sent Henry running for the Blue Ridge Mountains. So be it. "I will be brief and you will be glad we talked."

He swivels his corpulent body toward Len once more. In his deep Kentucky drawl he says, "You come back here in ten minutes. And you tell my driver to pull around front in twelve."

Len nods his dark head, says, "Yes, sir. Will do." Then he looks at me, and gives me a wink that's his familiar old signal for, *Do your stuff, Red.*

As Len closes the door, I turn to clap my hands to shut off the bank of TVs. "Would you like to sit, Henry?"

He eyes the large window.

"This glass is glazed," I assure him. "Len and his partners had it done years ago when they first moved in. Special coating so that no one can see in. Makes these back rooms cozy and confidential as can be." I smile as I move in closer, take a chair in the sitting area, and cross my legs. This morning I have dressed for success. Black suit, knee-length skirt, down-to-a-tasteful-there décolleté, white pearls, black hose that when I sit and cross my legs makes them look miles longer and ever so sleek. I finger the pearl earring at my left lobe and buy myself time for him to absorb that I'm about to deliver verbal goods he's gonna love . . . ultimately.

But ahh, in the meantime, he doth protest a lot. "I do not want anyone to know we've talked."

Okay, so we're starting slowly. "I understand."

"You're being questioned by the police about Goodwin's murder."

"My involvement there is purely accidental," I say, repeating my new mantra.

"Like it was with Alistair Dunhill?" he says snidely.

I'm tamping down my anger. "Yes. Also an accident."

He's still glowering. "The other reasons I do not care for you have nothing to do with murder."

Gotcha. But if you don't get off this kick, there may be another killing right here on this carpet. "Henry, I understand you have never cared for my positions. Like how I vote on the budget."

He advances to place a hand on the back of the leather sofa. "And not on education or Medicare, either."

I purse my lips, uncross my legs, and redo them the other way. He does try my good nature. "We're not going to talk about policy this morning, Henry."

"I will not discuss the murder of Goodwin, either."

I lick my lips. That alarms me. Does it mean that McGinty has discovered what was on that disk? And gone to Henry asking questions? If so, it's better I know now before I see McGinty again. "Why would you think I want to do that?" *Tell me something I don't know, please.*

Henry waves a hand toward the bank of screens. "You're everywhere."

"I'm here this morning to ensure that *you* are not *everywhere,*" I impart in a tone that says, *Do not screw around with me.*

And at that, he comes around the end of the sofa and sits.

Exhaling, unbuttoning his tan suit coat, he huffs, "Okay. I'm here. You have less than eight minutes remaining. Talk."

"What do you and your wife know about Sherry's interest in wiccan culture?"

He blinks. "I'm sorry . . . ?"

I repeat my question.

He squints. "What are you talking about?"

So McGinty has not paid Henry a visit delivering this news. I need to be certain before the good detective calls me in—and by all that's reasonable, that'll probably occur soon. "You don't know that your daughter believes herself to be a witch? A good witch, a wiccan. But nonetheless, a witch."

Henry Bunting seems to crinkle up, like he's been flash-frozen.

I interpret his reaction as *no* and continue. "She believes she can cast spells and make potions, and has been selling disks with copies on the Internet."

"That is utter rubbish." Henry is now beet-red—and for a man of his age—sixty-ish—and his weight—thirty pounds more than it should be—and his temperament—irascible—this is not healthy.

But hey, these are the days of my life—and I detect by the wall clock seven minutes remaining in my hourglass. "I agree—and the way this kind of rubbish will tarnish you will not be pretty. So let me continue while you consider what I'm telling you. You wonder, I am certain, how I know this. My daughter told me. Is she making this up?" I shake my head. "I doubt it. Why, you might ask? Well, because she discovered Judge Deeds's body and she was so upset by it, she blurted this out to me afterward."

Henry's eyes are wandering the perimeter of the room, as if this is a cell he needs to escape.

I understand his reasoning. I'd like to be someplace else myself.

After a long minute or two, his gaze lands on me. "You're serious."

"Very."

His eyes bulge. "I think," he ventures as he digs in his coat pocket and brings out a handkerchief to wipe his brow, "I think I need a drink."

"Coffee?" I point toward the decanter and two china cups and saucers Len's secretary left for me earlier. Damn if I'll play mother and serve him. Not with his attitude.

"Hell, no." He glances toward the credenza that I know—and he clearly concludes—is a liquor cabinet. "Bourbon."

Eight-oh-five on Monday and he needs bourbon. Who can blame him?

He scoots himself out of the leather seat and off he lumbers toward the cabinet. Pulling the doors open with both hands, he grabs a bottle of amber liquid, finds a glass, and pours himself a long, tall draught sure to kill a lesser man. He downs a gulp, then takes another with more measure, and finally comes about to face me. Although still red, at least now he appears less tortured. "How do you know this?"

Concluding that he must not have been listening too well, in the interest of clarity I start again. This time, his Richter scale reading lowers as I speak.

When I finish, he is subdued, almost whispering when he asks, "What proof do you have?"

"Jordan showed me Sherry's Web site yesterday. A one-page preview of all her products for sale, it features photos of Sherry in various attire—"

"Attire?" he asks, hoarse.

"Black capes, purple and green scarves, garlands of greenery in her hair, a few flowers."

"Is she . . . ?"

"Naked? No. No. Not that. She's a wiccan, Henry. She believes she is in alignment with the universe, a Celtic alignment with the stars, the growth of plants and trees and the essence of animals—"

"The hell she does."

I swallow, knowing it's difficult for him to comprehend the oddities of Sherry's activities. Much easier for him to imagine the ramifications of them for his own future. "I don't profess to know the intricacies of what Sherry believes or practices—"

"Practices?" he nigh unto yelps.

"She has a picture of herself holding a magic wand of amethyst and citrine, standing in front of an altar with a crystal ball. She claims she can cast spells on people. She has directions that people can buy, Henry. They purchase online and she sends them disks."

He seeks the sofa blindly. Once seated, he takes another drink. "Like what?" he asks, and again his tone implies I must be raving mad.

"I saw a spell to make a teacher think a student is smarter than he is."

He blows that off. "Silly things."

"She has another for sale that makes someone fall in love with you."

"Absurd."

"Maybe so," I concede, "but that isn't the point, is it?"

He looks deep into his bourbon and quietly says, "No."

The initial shock over, I know proof is now the order of the day. "Let's take a look, shall we?" I rise, go over to the computer deck, and sit down to boot up one of the three computers in the room. "Len assures me that these hard drives are swept for bugs at the end of every day—and that their Internet browser is swept clean of cookies after each person's use, so no one here will be able to trace where we've gone." I click on the Internet and plug in Sherry's Web site URL. Voilà!, appearing before us is Sherry Bunting in all her wiccan glory.

In a hooded floor-length cape with black short-shorts and tube top peeking out, Sherry stares out of the screen, grim as death, black eye shadow ladled on, in a photo that is high-resolution but far from professional. A tall, wraithlike fourteen-year-old, she resembles her striking mother, with heart-shaped face, platinum tresses, and cornflower blue eyes. At the moment she looks like a drugged groupie for a heavy metal band.

"Oh, for chrissakes," her father groans. "What the hell is she thinking?"

That is the substance of a long dialogue that Henry and his wife will have to have with their daughter. But for right now I need to lead him onward through the bad news. And so I click on a tab that takes us to an order form with payment instructions. "Henry, Sherry is selling these photos, and see this here." I point to the list of potions. "She's selling her recipes, too."

He bends closer to the screen. "I'll take that computer away, by god. And she won't get out of the house till she's forty."

I would laugh if it weren't so serious. "Henry, there's more." The worst news.

He whips around to gaze into my eyes. "What else?"

"The night Goodwin died—"

He shrinks away from me like I have the plague. "No, no. You won't include me in murder. I do not want to hear anything about it. I will *not* be involved—"

"But maybe you are," I insist. "I am not certain. But you need to know—"

"What *are* you talking about? I am involved, I'm not. Sherry is, she's not."

"Sam did CPR on Goodwin right after we got there."

Impatient and fuming, he rakes his fingers through his white hair. "I know that from TV news. So?"

"Sam removed a disk from his mouth."

Henry cocks his head.

"The disk was little. Blue. Jordan recognized it when Sam showed us. She gasped, got frightened. It's what made Sam and me ask her more about it. Bottom line, Henry, Jordan thinks the disk was a collection of Sherry's pictures and recipes and Goodwin put it in his mouth to prevent whoever killed him from finding it—or taking it."

"Taking it to . . . blackmail me?"

I shrug. "Perhaps."

"Someone knows Sherry does this"—he waves a hand in front of the computer screen—"this witch's brew?"

"The Internet is open to the world, Henry. Millions of people have access—and many use it for all kinds of nefarious activities. We know that. We can only speculate about how someone might use the knowledge—or who would have purchased disks from Sherry."

He nods. "And do the police have this disk now?" he asks, pursuing his own self-interest.

I lick my lips. "I don't know."

"How's that?" His eyes go round and flat, skeptical of me once more.

"I last saw it Saturday night just before the EMS and the police arrived. Sam had placed it on the couch in the family room of the Deedses' home. I assume he has handed it over to the police. I mean, why wouldn't he? It was evidence—and Sam is an honorable man. Plus, who knows what chemicals or residue there was in Goodwin's mouth from having put the disk in there? If Sam didn't hand it over, the police might come question him again about it. But then, Sam had to have turned it over because they took his clothes for analysis—and ours. It wasn't as if Sam could have slipped it in his pocket and forgotten it. The police would still be in possession. So here's my thinking. . . ."

I gaze at a very agitated Henry, hair ruffled, jaw taut. "I wanted to alert you to what's going on with Sherry. Wanted you to know so that you can take appropriate action with her—and get her squared away. But you need to shut down this site—and close the bank account that receives all this money."

He curses. "Money. A bank account! How could she open one?" When I tell him that Jordan told me Victoria Enrici did it for Sherry, he gets livid. "Hell, Enrici was supposed to be golden. Norreen said so, said she'd been a student of hers at Hampden College, a good kid. Well, Norreen got it wrong again. That relationship'll end quickly." He stares at me. "What else?"

I go on, because I have an even bigger mess to clean up. "I have a favor to ask of you."

His eyes say *no,* but he knows where his bread is now buttered. "Whatever I can do . . ."

"You can call Sam with impunity and I can't. Shouldn't. Make it look like you are discussing business. Ask him to meet you so that you can find out what happened to that disk."

"Why do you want to know?"

I chew on my lower lip. "For now let's call it curiosity." I wasn't going to impugn my own integrity with Henry—now that I had some measure of respect from him—and then blow it by saying I'd said nothing to the police about the disk . . . yet. Plus, he's so unnerved by my news he has not yet asked me what I said about the disk. Call me the lapsed Catholic that I am, but I continue to commit the sin of omission—for both our sakes. "But I need to know something else from you."

He nods. "Anything."

"What's your wife's relationship with Marie Deeds?"

"Norreen likes Marie. Met her . . . not certain where. I haven't paid attention. Why? Norreen pick another bad apple?" He narrows his gaze, strangely critical of his wife in front of me, to whom, until today, he owed nothing. "What's going on there?"

"I have no idea. I just felt that Marie Deeds was very eager to smooth over the Friday night gaming party events by talking with your wife."

He shakes his head. "Marie is an airhead, if you ask me. Not Norreen's usual type."

"If you could ask your wife what she thinks of Marie Deeds, please, and then call my chief of staff and describe what you learned, if anything. Is that a deal?"

"Yes, absolutely," he says, but common sense and instinct for political preservation declare Henry will call me with this info only if it absolves his wife of any wrongdoing. He'll preserve his own honor first—just like the rest of us.

He and I pause for a moment, each checking the other for the new relationship we've just cemented.

But on a low sigh of resignation, he recognizes something else in my eyes and stiffens. "There's more. What is it?"

I move right in, because to wait, to delay, would give him time to recoup and divert his forces. I cannot risk the loss. "Friday night, why did you so readily accept that patrolman into your house when he brought Sherry home from the party?"

"Wilson?"

"Yes, Brad Wilson."

He works his eyebrows. "Long story."

"I need to hear it."

"It's delicate."

"To me, it's vital." *With what I have done for you this morning, I think I have a right to demand this.*

"I know him. Well. About two years ago he helped me with a problem in Louisville."

"How does a Montgomery County, Maryland, policeman help a senator from Kentucky with a problem in Kentucky?" I ask, excitement quivering in my tummy that I have myself one intriguing answer coming.

"He's not with the Montgomery County force."

As if I hadn't predicted it! I lean forward.

"He's employed by a security company. They perform services for clients."

I am out of my chair—and out of my skin with anticipation. "What's the name of the company?"

"Elite Force. Why? Do you need help?"

"No. Yes. Where are they located?"

"Pennsylvania and Twelfth Streets. They are very good. Expensive. Thorough. I recommend them."

"And you just walked right in and hired yourself a security man?"

"I didn't walk in, no. I needed to put some daylight between me and this matter. My chief of staff did the outreach."

I'm salivating with expectation. "You let Brad Wilson in your home Friday night because you knew him."

"He called me from his cell phone and told me who he was. I recognized his voice and I let him in, yes."

"Does your wife know he's from Elite Force?"

"No. She has no idea. She accepted him because I did."

"And Sherry?"

"Same. Thinks he's Montgomery County Police. Plainclothes. He saw Sherry at the game party and got the chief of police to let him bring her home to get her out of the spotlight. I went along with it. Welcomed the favor. Said I'd pay for the service. Wilson refused."

"Why?"

Henry shrugs. "Said he was on another job—and it would be a conflict of interest to accept compensation. He was just doing me a favor as a former client."

A refrain so similar to Jones's. "Endearing past clients to the company for the future."

"A smart move, considering the town we live in," Henry adds.

"No need for a marketing campaign with those kinds of benefits to hiring Elite Force," I state, and go for the other info that may save me lots of time and trouble. "Is Wilson his real name?"

"Oh, of that I have no idea. I think I saw some identification when I hired him years ago. Is that important?"

"To me, not as important as the fact that he works for Elite Force." But then something else bugs me and I put up a finger. "Henry."

"Yes?"

"Why did Wilson let you know who he was?"

"I don't get what you mean."

"You always knew who you were hiring?"

"Of course I did. I don't buy a pig in a poke. Not for the kind of fees Elite Force demands."

"Big money?"

"I shelled out six grand for my little errand, when all was said and done. Took him only three days. I hear these kinds of boys demand double that per diem for protection."

Do tell. "And what do they earn for investigation?" When Alistair was killed and someone hired Jones, they signed him on as my very own secret service with a twist of James Bond.

"That's a right high-ticket price. I'd hate to think what it costs."

"So you met Wilson when you hired him?"

"Oh, yes. I wouldn't have signed the contract if I hadn't had absolute control over who performed the job."

Sounds like visiting the offices of Elite Force will be in my future. "Thank you, Henry." I shake hands with him. "I am very grateful for what you've shared today."

"For telling me all this, I owe you greater thanks, Carly." He smiles briefly before he turns to go.

After he leaves, I sit unmoving for a few minutes.

I pick up the phone, dial 0 for the front desk, get the receptionist, and have her connect me with Elite Force on Pennsylvania. When their receptionist answers, I tell her I want to hire them. She plugs me through to a guy who calls himself a client consultant—and whose abrupt and superior demeanor reminds me of Hollywood's impersonation of German SS officers. I sense his attitude derives from a dislike of southern ladies with a drawl. So I press for an appointment, he asks my name . . . and when he hears it, he puts me on hold.

When he comes back, he connects me through to another man who has a bit more personality but sounds like he smokes more Marlboros than my mother. "Congresswoman Wagner," he begins after he introduces himself with some nondescript name, "we are very happy you have called us. However, I must inform you that we do not work with those who are actively involved in any criminal investigation."

"Why not?"

"Our company policy, ma'am. Perhaps I can recommend you call another service?"

Have a lot of rules and regs, there, do you? "One that does deal with people like me?"

"Yes, ma'am."

"And to what company might you refer me, Mr. . . . forgive me, your name is . . . ?"

"Charles. I would recommend you call VentureX or Howard and Roth. I can give you their numbers, if you like."

"Those are the only two?"

"Yes, ma'am. I am sorry."

So am I. "Okay. One more question, Mr. Charles."

"Yes, ma'am."

"Do all of you in this line of work have Anglo names?"

"Anglo?" he asks.

"Anglo-Saxon. One or two syllables."

"Yes, ma'am."

"And they all seem to be rather unimaginative."

"Yes, ma'am."

"On purpose, I bet."

"Yes, ma'am."

"False names?" I venture.

"Pseudonymns. For confidentiality of employees' real identities," he supplies.

How convenient. "Thank you, Mr. Charles. Have a nice day."

"Yes, ma'am. You, too."

I'm trying, Mr. Charles. But I am shut out. Shut down. Was he telling me the truth? That they didn't take on clients who were involved in a criminal investigation?

I'm riding down in the elevator to the parking level where I left my Tahoe when the hole in Charles's rhetoric hits me.

Okay, so maybe Elite Force doesn't do work for those involved in a criminal investigation. But that doesn't mean they don't let others hire Elite Force operatives to protect them.

I grin. Step off the elevator. But as the doors whoosh closed behind me, I feel a trill go up my spine. The parking level is silent as a tomb, but the overheads are bright enough for a dentist to perform root canals. I squint and pick up my pace toward my car, wondering if Len's firm pays for the lights to encourage speedy departure from their midst. Or if there are cameras hid-

den here. Then I feel another chill. I glance around. See no one.
Hear no one. I'm pleased I put my SIG-Sauer in the glove compartment this morning—and I dearly want to feel it in my hand.
I pick up my pace, dig out my keys. Extend my remote and press
the *Unlock* button.

I climb into my front seat. Close the door. And sit down on
something that gives me a goose.

Reaching under my fanny, I pull out a small, sleek silver square.
And freeze. Smile. Look around the cars in the lot.

I'm pretty certain I know what I have in my hot little hand,
but I can't flip it open, and find only two black bars on one side.
"What the hell?" I give in and just speak into it. "Is this your
newest version of black-ops phone systems?"

Jones's chuckle greets me from wherever he hides. "Yes,
ma'am, changes frequencies at random. Very secure. You need it,
ma'am."

"Why?" I ask, but know I must know something he wants.
"Talking to you gets me nowhere."

"Yesterday you told me to lead, follow, or get out of the way."
I inhale. Hope springs eternal. "And?"

"I'm not doing any of that."

Course not. "That would be too simple." I'm twisting and
turning in my seat, trying to find him within the maze of this
pristinely brilliant lot.

"Exactly. So, since you won't quit investigating—and I can't—
I thought I'd make it easier on all of us."

I note he says *all*, not *you and me*. "So we can work together?"

"Check."

"Jones?" My frustration steams me.

"Ma'am?" He's cool as a Popsicle.

"Want to share yet who went in the Deeds house Saturday
night?" I try for some chill myself.

"No, ma'am. Too dangerous for you to know."

"Is that what your client says?" *Come on, give me something
useful.*

"No. The boss. I do not—"

"Do not know your client," I say in sync with him. "Yeah. I know your spiel." I'm still gazing around the lot for him. "Jones, who *do* you work for?"

"Oh, now, ma'am, you know I can't—"

"Elite Force?"

"One of our competitors?" he chuckles in derision.

"Really? Well, how about your buddy Brad Wilson? He seems to know Elite Force really well."

"And this," Mr. Smooth shoots back without hesitation, "is important because . . . ?"

"I said it is. I need to know, Jones. I'm up to my neck in murder and—" and ultimatums, "and you give me walkie-talkies! I want what you know, Jones. Tell me or just go away!"

I can't find an *Off* button, so I just throw the phone down on the seat next to me.

He's muttering something at me, but I'm too fired up to coddle him.

I hit the gas like the hot-rod Texas driver I am and wind up and out of that blinding lot to head east toward the Capitol. I have a really big itch to introduce myself to the so-called Mr. Charles and his WASPy-named friends at the corporate offices of Elite Force. Too bad that this morning at six I got a summons through Aaron for a nine o'clock command performance before two big honchos in my political party. And for the House Minority Leader William Preston Scott and his deputy, the new minority whip, to call into their weekly Monday morning breakfast meeting little ol' Carly Wagner means only one thing.

I'm on the menu.

It's a good, good thing I keep in shape by walking, because once I park my Tahoe in my spot in the Rayburn garage, I head for my office at a clip fit for a woman who once won barrel races. I drop my briefcase in my office, listen to Aaron recite today's meetings—and zip off for the basement, the tunnels, and the tram. I flash my badge at the Capitol Police guard at the gate, wait until he checks his list and confirms my appointment with Scott and Crandall, then climb into the comfy, creamy little top-less train that chugs over to the old Capitol building every few minutes with visitors.

Breeze in my hair, fear in my heart, I check my watch and bite my lip. I will be, tops, five minutes late—and it is nigh unto trea-son to be late for a meeting in Scott's office—or in any other of his hastily declared venues, like an unmarked car, a cab, or a quiet broom closet.

I climb out of the tram and find the nearest elevator. Up I go to the second floor and navigate the warren that my House mi-nority leader was assigned to over five years ago when we lost sway with the majority of Americans who, surveys said, liked us more for our looks than our tax policies.

Scott's receptionist greets me like a long-lost comrade, but I know her drill. "Wonderful to see you. Been such a long time." She clucks over me like a sage hen because she is paid to step lively and act like the whole world is her pal. And if I could find her clone, I'd hire her, too. Since I fired my receptionist, who was tangled up in the last murder I stumbled across, I haven't found anyone who quite fills my job description.

What the hell? I go with the flow. "Thanks, Susan. I am happy to be here."

"I'm sure they'll be just a few minutes more. They've been at it since seven."

Good to know. Or not. If what they've been at is my slot as keynote speaker, I don't care if they ever emerge.

But my luck is not holding.

The doors open. Big, wide, solid, handsome wooden doors carved in . . . oh, 1810, maybe, and out comes the leader of my party.

He is just as big. Tall, short crew cut in white, a former Ma-rine who has won the Marine Corps Marathon here in this town far too many times—and who goes for daily "walks" that make others who try to keep up with him cry. Yes, William Preston Scott emerges in all his big, wide, magnanimous glory, and stands over me with a grin.

We are not confused.

I know the signs of persuasion when I see them on his face. This seventy-two-year-old man, who has walked these hallowed halls since the year I was born, hails from a southern good-old-boy state—and I can bet my share of the Rocking O Ranch that here he intends to rope me into some corral I cannot abide. I can see it in his lime green eyes. Feel it in his gorilla handshake. Understand it in the way he dwarfs me, all six-foot-four, 230-odd pounds of him to my five-foot-ten. I note how he kisses both my cheeks, French style, and far too friendly for the topics at hand. I admire his cobalt blue shirt and one of his signature bow ties—today in cotton-candy pink with white polka dots. Speculating if he dressed just to appeal to my strong sense of color, I grimly decide he's slated for a talk show later. But I give him a toothy smile, dripping sugar worthy of my cheerleading days as a born-to-charm Texas State Strutter.

He croons, "You come right in, Carly," and ushers me forward with a hand to my shoulder blade.

His office is just like him. Huge and encompassing, books chock-full on the shelves and newspapers and files spilling over a reading table. Only his desk, also big and wide at eight-by-six feet, is clean. All of this implies, of course, that the man knows far more about far more people than my comparable pea-sized status could ever catalogue, while his action list—his desk—is swept neat and ready for battle.

So is his deputy.

Kirk Crandall is Alistair Dunhill's newly elected successor. A buff salt-and-pepper-haired fortysomething who reminds me of Michael Douglas in his salad days, Kirk hails from California, and his dimpled, camera-ready good looks are many women's wet dream. Kirk has won our party's Young Leader Award for the past two years, so his ability to engineer his minority whip election means he has a leg up for whatever he wants next. And word is he wants my keynote slot. But he's gonna have to wrestle me for it.

"Good morning, Kirk." I shake hands and flash them a diplomat's grin. "I am glad you both invited me here this morning." I want to make my points first—so they realize encountering dead bodies never was nor will be my main ambition.

"Good." Scott indicates that I take a chair near a table in the corner of his office. "Coffee? Have you had breakfast? We can have some eggs and bacon made up . . . ?"

"No, thank you, I've eaten. I will take coffee, though." At the least, I do want to appear congenial.

"Cream, right?" Scott asks, and sits so that the two of them flank me in what any military man knows is a pincer. Meanwhile, he plays host and pours for me.

"Thank you, yes." I reach over and take my saucer and cup.

"We are, quite frankly," Scott begins, "very concerned over this newest set of circumstances."

"I am, too." I take a sip of my coffee, then sit straighter in my chair and launch my offensive. "The D.C. Police detective on the case is much slower to investigate this than the one who was responsible for looking into Alistair's death."

"That," says Kirk, "was a Capitol policeman?"

"Yes." The Capitol force's jurisdiction includes this building, plus the congressional office buildings and grounds of the Mall, and so they have few crimes and even fewer homicides to cover. "The relatively lighter caseload alone allowed that detective to investigate Alistair's death more quickly." I inhale. "Whatever the reason now, we seem to be pretty much at a standstill. And of course, because of legal restrictions, I cannot tell you much about Goodwin's murder." *And it tingles my toes that I don't have to share the details.*

"We understand," Scott commiserates. "What do you think the process will be?"

"Well, I know that police and forensics can move more quickly in the homicide of a high-profile official, but I have little knowledge of how long anything like DNA tests really take unless they tell me. And they haven't."

"Hmm." Kirk thinks a minute, deepening his dimples. "Do they have any suspects?"

Fishing anyway, are we? "Not that I am aware."

He leans forward. "Do you think Turner is a suspect?"

Intriguing to me that he asks that. I do know that Paul Turner originally hailed from a technology firm in Silicon Valley, so might Kirk Crandall and Turner have mutual friends . . . or mutual interests?

"I think so. Oh, not because of anything the detective said to me, but logic alone would say that Turner figures prominently because he attacked Goodwin the other night."

Kirk quickly adds, "Paul had his reasons, all personal, of course. But his company does suffer without his leadership. This year they've had chunks of sensitive data stolen twice. The latest theft is time-sensitive."

Now I lean forward, my antennae keenly attuned to the unusual. "I gather you're implying the missing info is national security data?"

Scott grumbles a bit. "Let's just say we need to hear from the FBI that the laptop is recovered . . . and soon."

"Turner committed a crime," I state. "He cannot blame Goodwin for sentencing him to do time that then takes him away from the company whose good name he tarnished with his own actions," I assert.

"True," Kirk says, "but Paul once dated Jane, long before she met Goodwin. He carries a grudge because he never stopped mourning her loss."

"I see now why Barbara Turner has mental health issues," I conclude. "A wife who is always unfavorably compared to another suffers." *No wonder she attacked her husband. I would.*

Kirk agrees. "The fatal blow was the trial where Turner got

convicted for misusing funds for lobbying. Goodwin threw the maximum punishment at him—so you have a man who hates the ground Goodwin walks on."

"And would kill him for his loss?" I ask because I have to know.

Kirk plays with his cufflink in thought. "Maybe."

My instinct says no—and my rational mind struggles to figure out why.

I stare out the large window that faces west toward the Mall. From this vantage, I see only the tip of my confusion.

If Turner is the murderer—and personal revenge was his motive—would it be logical that he would tear the room apart? Would he do it to find a disk? Not the disk with Sherry on it. Why would he care about a child doing hocus-pocus? He wouldn't. And Goodwin would have no need to put Sherry's disk in his mouth. Alternatively, if Turner is the killer—and a missing laptop with information was what he wished to reclaim—why would he ever think Goodwin would have it? Goodwin was a judge, a federal judge, with a pristine reputation and no reason to possess stolen goods. Turner might be depressed. Crazy. Desperate. Jealous of the man who won the hand of the love of his life. But if he did kill Goodwin, he would have had to do so quickly and then be lucky enough to have someone else enter, muck up the crime scene by tearing the house apart. The coincidence of that is nigh on improbable.

The person who did destroy the Deedses' computer room was looking for data, all right. That's why he or she destroyed the place. Maybe the perpetrator was looking for the disk with Sherry Bunting on it. Maybe not. But for certain, Goodwin was the Good Judge to his dying breath when he put Sherry's disk in his mouth to hide a child's actions from the intruder.

And the only person in this world who can refute my logic is the one who videotaped those who left Goodwin Deeds's house before seven-thirty. Jones.

I blink at William Preston Scott and Kirk Crandall. They

both are regarding me like I'm about to give birth. "Sorry. A momentary . . ." I wiggle my fingers near my forehead.

"So what are you thinking, Carly?" Scott probes.

"You had some insight . . . ?" Kirk pries.

I shake my head, close my eyes.

My party leaders are disappointed.

"Horrible business." Scott takes a detour and puts on a dour demeanor. "Come, now, let's move to another topic. What about your daughter? How is she? Discovering Goodwin must have been a shock."

"Yes," I say, recovering my aplomb. "A big one." This morning she wouldn't get out of bed—and while I was glad that school is already out and she needn't deal with facing her friends, nonetheless I worry about her change in behavior.

"Do you want to take her to see a professional?" Kirk asks.

I am appalled. In the O'Neill family, we solve our own problems. "I do not think so, no, not unless or until I see a really good reason. She's a very wonderful child, bright and happy, and I'm certain she will cope just fine. With a little time and patience."

Kirk scowls. "But this is murder—"

"This is violent death. Yes. I just want to get through this period of investigation. The grilling, the going over and over the events can be grueling. She did well with the detective the other night and we'll have another interview with him. We'll see how she does with this . . . and if I need help with her, I will see she gets it." *Until then, stay out of my private business, boys.*

"We're concerned for you as well, Carly," Scott says in solemn tones.

I believe him. Up to a point. "I'm sure you are. I'll do fine on this. I'm suffering from sleep deprivation and a distaste for the arduous process of investigation. And the media may serve me up for lunch right now, but you know and so does Sam that neither of us is responsible for Goodwin Deeds's murder. We tried to help revive him. Especially Sam, who was terrific, I want you to know."

Kirk says, "I spoke with his chief of staff this morning."

Kirk doesn't say who called whom, but who cares? I need to know what was said. "And?" This is a message from Sam, I feel it coming.

"Sam regrets he can't talk to you."

That makes two of us—and a very concerned Henry Bunting for number three. "No contact means no collusion among key witnesses." I put my cup and saucer down on the table and smile with no mirth. "I've understood that about law enforcement for decades—ever since my father disappeared when I was sixteen and the local sheriff and the Texas Rangers came to call." I run a hand down my skirt. "I am not as flustered by a police investigation as many would be—and you can take that to the bank." Because we are not really talking about me this morning so much as the national party—and its ability to earn more donations for the good fight—and the good win come this November.

"We're very troubled about your image." Kirk, sharp lieutenant that he is, delivers the one-liner I knew was front-loaded into this conversation.

"So am I, but as I said, I'll do just fine."

Kirk arches a brow. "Maybe in your district."

"Where I have won handily the past five times—and where my pollsters tell me I now run twenty percentage points ahead of my opponent." I level my gaze at Kirk and then Scott. Then I haul out my big ammo. "National polling tells me I am still the most admired female representative, largely because of my stance on education and Medicare." *Argue with that, if you can.*

"We're hearing from Louise Rawlings, too, and her adviser, Chad Elliott."

This makes me fold my hands in thought. Senator Louise Rawlings, the senior senator from Texas, was the first politician in this town to take me under her wing, call me her trusted colleague, and treat me like her fair-haired girl. I call her my mentor and my friend. Since last January, Lou has won most of our party's presidential primaries and, save for a hundred-odd votes, now has our party's nomination for president in her pocket. Her campaign strategist, Chad Elliott—known to insiders as the Wizard—had revamped her campaign from assets to Web site, and helped her become the first woman most likely to be elected to 1600 Pennsylvania. But he doesn't like me. Called me a wild card. And wanted Lou to cut me loose. Even before Sam, Jordan, and I had found Goodwin murdered.

I consider my nails. I need a manicure. Hell, I need to sleep and see what Estée Lauder and her pals can do for my dark circles and bags. But the only thing going on in my head is the clang of a death knell. "Tell me Chad's opinion of my position."

"The only way to clear your name again—and come out clean as a whistle . . ."

I lift my head and arch both brows in question.

Kirk glances at our noble leader for clearance and then lowers the boom. "He laughingly suggested this morning that you should find out who killed Goodwin, just like you figured out who killed Alistair."

Chad Elliott never "laughingly suggests" anything . . . without clipping on a price tag for failure. He's great at strategy. Not so great at psyching me out. "Don't you think that's presumptuous?" *Chad, Chad. What do you eat for breakfast? Fantasy Pops?*

"No. He says he's got a set of stats that say—"

I stand. Go to the bottom line of their argument. "Gentlemen." I use the term with more respect than I feel. "Chad Elliott spouts more numbers than a banker over his balance sheets. But he's got a mite to learn about people—and me. You cut me loose now from the keynote speech and you lose popularity with working women, young voters, and senior citizens. I bet they see me as a strong woman who's had the misfortune to find two prominent men murdered. Desert me, and they will revile you and see you as my persecutors." *Oh, lady, where did you get that hat you are talking through?*

But hey, it *feels* right, so I charge onward. "I'm assisting the police with what I saw and what I know, but as for who killed

Goodwin and for what reason, I'm as much in the dark as you are. And to ask me to perform a task that is not my responsibility or my expertise to save my slot at the convention is an attempt to intimidate me. Furthermore, it absolutely blows my mind. And I venture to say Chad Elliott needs his examined." *So to relieve you of the burden of insulting him with my words, and* . . . "To make sure he hears my point, I'll deliver my message to him myself."

I walk away from both men, who are aggrieved from the looks of it but jumping out of their chairs to be courteous and get the door. But my momma taught me by precept and example how a girl shows her guts and grabs her glory. So at that big wide door, which I now may exit for the very last time, considering my big wide mouth with big wide foot inserted, I pivot and give them my winning Miss Texas runway assurance. "Thank you both for your time this morning. I appreciate your interest and your help."

And do not look for mine for a while.

I have other fish to fry. Like one Mr. Chad Elliott . . . and one Mr. Enigmatic Jones.

eight

Discovering the interior decorating talents of homicide departments of local police forces has become my new pastime. And let me tell you, if the Capitol Police believed that bile green was the new rave color, then the D.C. Police's choice of gray comes in a dismal second.

Their coffee is worse. I'm on my second cup for lack of something better to do when Detective McGinty sweeps out of his office to tower over me.

"Thanks for coming," he begins, and continues with a bit about how he's trying to conserve time, hopes I don't mind coming in, yada yada, all the polite stuff that lawmen tell you before they come at you with razor-sharp questions and machine gun repetition.

"We're still processing the scene, and our medical examiner is about to finish with the autopsy." He's imparting this as he shows me into the drab environs of his cubicle with its matching gray walls and beat-up steel furniture. He himself is gray with fatigue—and rumpled. "How's your coffee?" He indicates a chair for me. "Want more?"

"No, thanks. It's truly terrible." I grimace.

He crooks his mouth in a lopsided laugh. "We make it that way so folks keep coming back."

"I hope to break the mold." I try to look congenial and sit on the skimpily padded chair he has in front of his desk.

"Yeah, well . . ." *We'll see,* is what I figure he's thinking as he plunks himself into his own chair and swivels toward the large window with a view of the parking lot. The Violent Crimes Branch is the centralized homicide unit for the entire Metro Police force—and their offices off Pennsylvania Avenue sit in the back of a shopping mall in deep southeast. "Have trouble finding us?" He nods outside.

Odd question. Why would he care? Or is he trying to make nice before he filets me? "I had my chief of staff drive me here. It saves time, gives him a few minutes with me alone to go over issues. I'll call him on my cell and he'll pick me up when we're done." Aaron had been happy about my decision—and I was delighted when he said he would borrow the car of one of my legislative aides. Taking mine from the garage would mean Aaron would wonder what the heck the little silver square was that I'd left on the passenger seat. Besides, Jones could stew about why I wasn't answering. Serves him right for his on-again, off-again way of sharing info.

"I want to interview your daughter again. This afternoon, say two o'clock."

"That sounds fine. I will call the house and let them know you and I are coming. You do mean that you are coming to the house to do this?"

"Yes, bringing two agents from the Bureau with me, too."

Ah. Perhaps the Blues Brothers who came in late to the crime scene Saturday night? "Not a problem," I tell him, but it ratchets up my anxiety for Jordan.

"Death of a federal judge, so they need to be on this case."

"I understand." I try to look relaxed, but my palms are starting to itch.

"They're helping with forensics, looking at Deeds's convictions," he says, more informative and personable than he needs to be. That alone puts me on guard for what's coming. "I'm at the house, looking over the crime scene again." He opens his drawer and takes out two Hershey bars with almonds. The guy likes nuts. "Want one?"

He must think he needs sugar to make him sweeter. "No, thanks. My downfall is salt."

He grins, and I tell you, the effect feels like sunshine from one of those tanning machines. Bright, hot, and not altogether natural. Not to me. I'm wary of friendly lawmen from back in the day when a passel of them questioned me for over a year about my daddy's disappearance. They all had miles of smiles—and all in the service of seeing what they could pin on me—or my brother—or my mother. Back then, I never bought any friendship a police-type was selling without a hearty dose of reality pills. Not now, either.

Meanwhile, McGinty is getting his sugar high as he sits back, relaxes, and starts at me gently. "I need to hear from you again what happened Saturday night."

"Okay." I always appear cooperative. "From what point?"

"Jordan comes in your house and hollers for help."

Take it from the top, Carly. "Senator Lyman and I are on my sofa in my family room off the kitchen. The doors bang open, Jordan charges in, and she stands there—"

"You and the senator are talking?"

Am I blushing? "No." I let him have the truth. "Kissing. Necking." *Getting ready to get busy.*

"Why is he there?"

"I invited him to dinner."

"I hear you. Go on." Graham McGinty stifles a smile, but waves a hand at me.

I inhale, look out the window. "Jordan runs in and she's upset. Yelling. Crying. Shocked. And Sam and I jump up and we run out the back door."

"Who's first?"

"Sam. I'm running, and Jordan's behind me. We get into the

kitchen and rush to the computer room—and there's Goodwin, eyes wide. He was gone then. I knew he was."

"Why?"

"The way he looked. Vacant. Limp. His hand hanging down . . ."

"The one that was cut open?"

"Yes."

"Why do you think that was?"

"Originally, I had no clue. But Jordan said that he had an implant to open his computer and garage door. He was a techie type. Liked gadgets, I gather."

"Do you?"

"What? Like gadgets?" All I can see is that silver square from Jones. But this guy couldn't know about that. "I like things if they're easy to use. If not, I have no time to learn. My life is already too filled with taking care of people and staff and colleagues and . . . well, you get the picture."

"I do." He propels himself forward to look at a pad of paper he's got on his desk. From this angle, with the sun beating down on it, I can't read what he's got there. Notes? Questions? What good is my nefarious talent to read upside down if glare bleeds out the text? "How would you describe the room where Judge Deeds died?"

"A mess."

"Someone searching for something?"

"Yes, indeed. Wildly searching."

"What's your impression of how the judge must've died?"

"Detective, I'm no expert," I assert, fearing he's going to go into some song and dance about my previous experience with a homicide case.

But he just waves his hand again. "Yeah, but if you had to make a stab at what went on in that room, what would you say?"

"The killer came in, found Goodwin in his chair, asked him for whatever he was looking for, and Goodwin said no." I check McGinty's satisfaction level and he's nodding. I go on. "Since

Goodwin couldn't get out of his chair, he was stuck, a victim of his own body. And the murderer knew he had the advantage."

"So, what do you think the intruder is looking for?"

"Oh, lord." I shrug, unwilling to make any statement.

"Not to open Goodwin's garage door?"

"Maybe. If there is something in the garage he wants to steal," I conjecture. "Sounds more likely that he wants to open Goodwin's computer."

"I agree. So then, the question becomes what does a judge have that someone wants to steal from his computer?"

Pictures of a senator's daughter and her wiccan recipes? I sit very still and look perplexed.

He chews on his lower lip a bit. "Opinions? Sentencing guidelines?"

I freeze, unnerved, not knowing where he's going with this. "I doubt that. Why would he have professional files on his home computer? He wouldn't want to compromise his work that way. Not Goodwin, the Good Judge."

"Yeah," McGinty says, nice and slow. "That was my thought, too. But then, people aren't totally pure. Maybe he wasn't. What do you think? Ever see any behavior by the judge that you thought was . . . out of line with his public persona?"

I tip my head and recall his handling of the twins Saturday morning. "He might have been inclined to be soft with his children. But that was an impression I had only recently and I have no understanding of why that might be."

"Okay." McGinty picks up a pencil, twirls it in consideration. "Let's go back to the room. What you think may have happened there."

"Well, it's sort of a game room. What were there—four PCs in there? Plus, the twins love to play video games, so they have Xboxes and a Wii in there. You don't get to Goodwin's position and bring home files to where you are mixing business and family life like that."

"You don't?" he challenges me.

"No. Of course not."

"Why 'of course not'?" He leans forward, pursuing me.

"It's not practical. Not at the judge's level. I mean, he has staff, doesn't he? And so why take official documents home?"

"He could."

"Right. But he had such a solid reputation for always doing the right thing, in court and out, I find it hard to believe he would store valuable documents on his home computer." *Where they would be available to his children to read. Or their friends. Like Sherry . . . or Jordan. Oh, brother, that would not be good. But it is possible.* Blinking, I shift topics. "Plus, his PCs were all networked. Linked up together so that they could all four play some games as a family."

"Interesting. So that's a reason not to bring home office files, right?" McGinty is just looking for affirmation here and I give it to him in spades.

"I would assume it's not ethical—maybe not even legal—to remove them from the courthouse."

"And you? What about you? Do you take work home?"

"Reading, mostly. Not sensitive documents," I tell him.

"Why not?" he asks with hard interest, and I register how he's steering this interrogation—and make note to examine his logic later.

"Insecure handling. I mean, what if I were in an accident and unable to trace who might take items from my car? Plus, computers are not my favorite item to work with—at home or at the office. I have staff to write my documents—and I mark them up and edit them and they do the rest. I don't need to do my own record keeping, banking. I have a CPA who does that. Plus, I just don't have time to learn all that mumbo-jumbo."

"But your daughter likes computers and video gaming?"

"Yes, she does. They're the technology of her generation. Ubiquitous."

"How many computers do you have at home?"

"Two. One for her, one for me." *Why?* I want to ask, but save my breath.

"Networked?"

"No. Jordan's is upstairs. Mine is down on the first floor in my home office."

"No gaming computer for Jordan?" he asks.

"No. If she wants to play on something other than her PC, she does it with friends at their homes. The Deedses'. Or the Buntings'."

"Henry Bunting. The senator?"

I nod. Wait. He's going to launch into Sherry's escapades now. . . .

"All this gaming equipment is very pricey," he fires back. "I understand an Xbox or a PlayStation runs upwards of four hundred dollars."

"True. Not everyone has that kind of money," I agree.

"So . . . do you think the intruder was looking to steal the Xboxes and games?"

"Maybe the gaming hardware," I respond. "Games tend to be more affordable. Twenty, thirty dollars, so that thousands can buy them. But robbery isn't easy. I would think there's an easier way to make a heist than target a house in Georgetown."

"It happens," he says, dismissive of my logic.

"Maybe on the east side of town," I say.

He scratches his temple. "And that leaves the motive that the perp was really looking for something, data maybe, you think?"

I concede, "Could be."

"One problem."

Oh, boy. "What?"

"On the hard drive of the computer where Goodwin sat . . ."

"Yes?"

"There is no data."

"Really?" *Am I relieved or is there some other fact yet to come that cancels that out?* "How can that be?"

"My forensics experts in computers tell me it was swept clean

Saturday evening. The last time for the delete action was seven thirty-nine."

"Goodwin deleted everything from his own hard drive?" Four minutes after the last visitor left the house, according to what Jones told me his camera recorded. "Why would he do that?"

"Don't know. That's why I thought I'd ask you."

I pull back. "Why would I know what's on Goodwin's computer?"

He narrows his eyes at me like a cat before the kill. "Your daughter is very good friends with his children."

"Yes." I wait for the rest.

"Are his children into something illegal?"

I blink, shocked at the question. "I have no idea." *Don't you, Carly?*

"Your daughter has never told you of anything the twins did that might cause the judge to be angry with them?"

"No. What I saw . . ." I drift off, realizing I'm chatting like a talking doll when I should be *quiet, Carly, quiet.*

"What did you see?"

"Last Saturday morning, I was at the Deedses', talking with them about the gaming party the children had been to the night before." I see interest sparkle in McGinty's black eyes—and I argue with myself about giving away the candy store on that one. I hate my continued silence and my acceptance of the favorite treatment Jordan received. I hate my own reticence to reveal it. Yet I urge myself to stick to the topic of the twins. "I detected tension there among the family. The children with the father." I'm recalling how Marie looked at Goodwin. "Marie called the twins 'your children' . . . and then corrected herself to say 'our children.' "

"This is the second wife, right? So, in your opinion, were they happy?"

From Aaron's sources, from Jones's, from my own gut reaction to Goodwin's weight gain and Marie's obsequious demeanor,

I say, "I have no firsthand knowledge. I never saw them fight. Never heard Jordan say they did. You should ask the twins."

He glides right over that to ask, "What do you think of the twins?"

"I liked them both as children. But not lately. I put it down to them becoming teenagers. I didn't really think about them a lot, to tell you the truth. I mean, after all, they're not my children."

"But they are your daughter's friends," McGinty comes back at me, gangbusters. "So do they have problems? Do you like the girl? What about the boy?"

He's giving me the bum's rush and I'm not pleased. "I'm not the best person to ask, clearly." *But I should be paying more attention, shouldn't I, to Jordan's friends. To Jordan herself. And the black nail polish she wears . . . and the eye shadow she takes to her father's to irritate him.*

"I want to ask your daughter about them," he tells me flatly.

"Yes, do." *And this time, by god, I'll make sure she's going to fess up about Sherry. Loyalty, friendship be damned.* "Is that all, Detective? I need to go."

"Yes. Thanks. See you later." But as I get to the door, he calls to me. "Better yet, ma'am, tell you what. It'll save me a lot of time if you just meet me at the Deedses' house. Can you do that, please?"

Oh, I can. But if I dislike dealing with lawmen and I hate going over details of a murder, I loathe revisiting the scenes of crimes. "You want me to bring Jordan there?"

"If you would, yes, please, ma'am." He's watching my reaction. From TV, I know that Marie and the children came home Sunday morning, but I have no idea where they are now. And I can only hope I might see one of them at home this afternoon so that I can ask them a few questions.

True, I'm not crazy about Jordan or me going there and reliving the event. But McGinty wants something out of our appearance there—and my greatest fear is that he thinks there's something more we haven't yet told him, besides the bit about what's on that infernal disk of Sherry Bunting's.

I fly out of there like the hounds of hell are after me.

"Did Bunting's chief of staff call you back?" I ask Aaron without greeting when I climb into the Toyota that belongs to one of our LAs. Bunting hadn't called me, so I was compelled to send Aaron on his trail.

"Yes, he says Bunting told him to tell you that the item you're looking for is in the right hands." Aaron zooms out of the parking lot and heads west back toward the Capitol and Rayburn. "Does that make sense to you?"

"It does." And if McGinty has the disk from Sam, why didn't he ask me about it? Why not hammer me for details? All the more reason for Jordan to spill the beans this afternoon. "Did he say anything about Bunting's wife?"

Aaron shoots me a questioning look. "No. What about her?"

"Her relationship with Marie Deeds."

"Why is that important?"

"Nothing specific." I ruffle both hands through my curls to wake me up a bit. "Little things mean a lot sometimes. Maybe not this."

I watch him pull into traffic and head back toward Rayburn. "And what about Victoria Enrici?" I had asked Aaron to look up the gaming organizer while I was in police headquarters. If Enrici will not come to me, I am now about to visit her like the dark angel. I need to see the cut of her once more in light of what I know about her actions with Sherry Bunting. I trusted her when I first met her, and, of course, she came on good recommendations from Marie Deeds and Norreen Bunting. Now I'm skeptical. "Did you get her address?"

"In Greenbelt."

I check my watch. "We have just enough time to get up there

and back before McGinty descends on Q Street. Let's roll." God, I'm beginning to sound like Jones.

Thirty minutes later, when Victoria Enrici opens the door, I'm sincerely wishing I had Jones's presence. Vickie is one of those women who does not emote for other women. They are ever and always one thing: the Competition. And today, I present her with a suited, polished opposite to her frizzy-haired, no-makeup, scruffy jeans and shirt.

She greets me at the door of her one-story brick bungalow with shock, her bulging eyes, which always put me in mind of anime characters, even wider with suspicion.

"Hello, Vickie."

"Hi. Hi, wow, hi, Congresswoman Wagner, how are you?" She's totally startled to have me on her doorstep, floundering for words, pulling at her cropped T-shirt to try to conceal a tattoo on her ribs.

"Good, thank you. And this is my chief of staff, Aaron Blumfeld. May we come in and talk to you for a few minutes, please?"

"Sure," she says, "not a problem," yet she sounds like it is. "Jim," she calls over her shoulder, then flings wide the door and falls back a few steps, talking about not being prepared for company. Put money on that. The house is a wreck. Clothes strewn on the floor. Laundry basket overturned, with toys spilling out. A huge plasma TV against the wall sports the daytime soaps, but no sound. A complex stereo system sits on the other wall, with stacks of CDs. In the kitchen, I can see the latest appliances, stainless steel stove, Sub-Zero refrigerator. Granite countertops.

Vickie's partner, gaming organizer Jim Wyatt, steps forward, a grin on his face, hand out. "Hi, come on in. Good to see you." Tall, thin, and pale blond, he seemed quiet, reticent, to me on the one previous occasion that I met them. Today, much about him is different. He normally says little, smiles less. Today, he's affable. He usually dresses in tailored slacks and nondescript white shirts. Today he's in jeans with bare chest, with a hefty display of silver hardware hanging from both nipples and one ear. None of it compares in shock value, however, to the other decoration that surprises me: tattoos on both biceps that resemble eagles in mid-attack. Claws bared, beaks open.

Vickie introduces him to Aaron. "My friend, Jim Wyatt." And they shake hands.

"Nice to see you, ma'am." Wyatt smiles at me. "Come in. Please. Vickie's had the flu and we haven't picked up much the past few days. Coffee? We have a fresh pot."

"No, thank you," Aaron speaks for us. "We're in a time crunch."

I had filled Aaron in on the way up here why I needed to talk with Vickie, so we were now working this pair like a team.

"Okay, great." Wyatt walks over to the sofa and in one stroke brushes clothes and litter to the side, in the same grand motion I recalled Sam had swept aside disks that had skittered across the floor of the Deedses' computer room under one console. *And they had been blue. Blue. Just like the one Jordan wanted to retrieve for Sherry.*

"Ma'am?" Aaron brings me back from my reverie.

"Yes. Sorry." I take a seat on the couch. "You've done some refurbishing of the kitchen, I see."

"Little by little, we're redoing the house. It was built in the twenties," Wyatt says, sounding like a real estate agent who wants to sell me. "It's what we can afford."

What do you both do, aside from gaming, that you can afford expensive entertainment and hi-tech appliances? "I think it's important to work within your budget. But let me tell you why my chief and I are here. I'm concerned about what occurred the other night at the gaming party."

I watch Vickie open her mouth to speak and her boyfriend puts up a hand to ward her off. "The sale of marijuana is nothing we knew about," Wyatt affirms. "We told the officers that. Vic and I run clean games. The police arrested the kids who were carrying—and that's that."

"How many were there?" I decide to take this detour to my goal.

Wyatt lifts his shoulders. "Not sure. You'd need to ask the police."

"Have you ever had troubles before this with the ones who were arrested?"

"No, ma'am. None." He smiles.

I don't. "The Montgomery County Police sent in quite a few officers and they authorized my daughter to be taken out of the room, along with three of her friends."

"Yes, ma'am. They thought it best for everyone not to have any flash out of this. I did, too."

"Why?"

"Well, we do these parties regularly. If we get negative publicity, we're done. Just like anyone else."

His implication is clear to me. "I do not like favoritism, Mr. Wyatt. Do not approve of it."

"Really?" he exclaims, folds his arms. "Makes you unique."

Doesn't it. "There are other problems . . ." I begin.

He's still nonchalant when he says, "You mean Judge Deeds's murder. I heard. Sad."

I nod. "Very."

"You found him, too." He tries to look sympathetic, but I hear in his words interest in the details.

"My daughter did. She walked into the house within minutes of his murder."

"Tough on her." He uncrosses his arms, clasps his hands together, and his eyes narrow on us. "How's she doing?"

"Okay. A little shook up." *Silent, brooding. And I worry about her.*

"Vic and I like Jordan. Don't we, hon? Hope she gets better." He's getting impatient.

I drag this on. "I know she will."

He spreads his hands wide. "Anything else?"

"Yes. Do you have a list of all your scheduled gaming events?"

"MMOL or MMOLRPG?"

Aaron says, "Both," and I'm glad he does because I am stymied by the jargon.

Wyatt rises and says, "Yes, just a minute. I'll get a copy for you."

He walks down a hall and opens a door at the end of it. Inside is neat and clean as a pin, with hundreds of disks stacked up in racks atop two computers, at least. That's within my line of vision—and I wonder what else is in that room.

He returns, stands in front of me, and hands me a stapled set of papers. The top one has a replica of his tattoo. "Jordan could have gotten this online at our site."

"She's being restricted, Mr. Wyatt. Thanks for these." I take them and fold them to insert into my purse. "She can't get on-line because she cannot use her computer. She's grounded, too. Won't be to a party for a long while."

"Sorry to hear that. Aren't we, Vic?" He glances at Vickie, who sits like a statue. "We like Jordan a lot."

He's said that once. Repetition implies nerves. "Do you like the twins, as well?" I ask.

"Nice kids, yes. Sherry Bunting, too."

Given the opportunity, I walk into that topic. "What do you think of Sherry?"

Wyatt's face does a few contortions that imply he does not care for Sherry much.

Vickie speaks up. "Sherry is fun. A little wild. She'll grow out of it. We all do."

Do we? "What do you mean, wild?"

"She's experimenting with a few identities. Has no idea which one to pick." Vickie smiles. "I like her."

That rings true. And tempted as I am to tear into Vickie about how she helped Sherry with her Web site and bank account, I figure that is more Henry's responsibility than mine. Still, I can't help but add a jab. "I'm not certain I like her being friends with Jordan."

"That's a shame," Vickie offers. "Sherry has a few . . . ideas that are . . . well, odd. But she isn't a kook. She's straight. Nice kid. Really."

Why do I get the impression that Vickie approves of Sherry being straight? "That's good to know, Vickie. Thanks."

We chitter at each other for a few more sentences, making nice—and then Aaron and I make our excuses and our exits.

In the car, Aaron says, "I don't know how to read her." When I agree, Aaron adds, "And I don't trust him."

"Neither do I. Let's learn what we can about Mr. Wyatt. If he lives here. If he works another job, and about Vickie Enrici, too." Vickie had come well recommended by Marie Deeds—and Norreen Bunting, too. But now I'm questioning their wisdom big time.

The interview with McGinty begins like a charm. Call me shocked.

One Blues Brother—John Sullivan, by name—prefers the role of supervisor and lets McGinty take the lead. I'm used to people observing me—as a barrel racing champ, a jazz singer, a beauty queen, and a politician—so Sullivan does not ruffle my feathers with his silent technique.

Initially, he makes Jordan wary. But she settles in, concentrating only on McGinty as he begins his questioning.

Not totally assured that Jordan would do the right thing and tell him about what was on the disk, I want this interview finished soon. So I am perturbed when he begins with an old topic—the discussion of her relationship with Nicholas and Nicole Deeds—and her views of them and their stepmother. "Did the twins like Marie Deeds?"

"Are they here?" Jordan asks, and her gaze goes toward the stairs. "Nicky and Nick—and their stepmother?"

"No," Sullivan replies. "They went to a hotel on M Street. Don't want to be here while we are."

McGinty adds, "Makes our lives simpler, too. We can look at the crime scene in detail. Have you in, too."

Jordan nods, accepting this, relieved by her friends' absence.

And then she inhales and rises to the occasion with a maturity that makes me proud. She tells McGinty that the twins disliked their stepmother. When McGinty asks why, she reveals that "Mrs. Deeds doesn't like Nicholas. She thinks he's nerdy. A vegan and a piano player. And into gaming and math. She wants him to be a jock—and Nick hates that stuff."

"And what about Nicole Deeds? What does she think of her stepmother?"

"Nicki's not real pleased with her. I mean, she's for her brother. All the way. If I had a brother, I'd be on his side." Jordan glances over at me—and I smile at her.

"But does Nicholas protect Nicole?"

"Well . . . sure!" Jordan says, and then wrinkles her brow. "Why?"

"Just wondering."

Alarms go off in my head—and in Jordan's, too, because she glances at me. McGinty and his ilk never *wonder* about just any old thing.

But he's moving into the computer room and walking around. None of the four personal computers remain, nor the Xboxes or PlayStations. All of the disks that had been strewn all over the floor are gone. So are the chairs. Only the massive wraparound desks remain.

"Come with me, Jordan." He beckons her to follow him—and we all four move into the computer room. He points back toward the kitchen door. "Describe what you saw and did when you came in," he instructs her. They walk through the horror, the fright, her disbelief, her flight back home to summon Sam and me. She recounts how she felt sick to her stomach when Sam swept the judge's mouth out, and when she heard me say the judge was gone—and how she felt terrified to dial 911—and finally, how she lost it when she saw Sam Lyman announce the judge dead and display the disk that was in the judge's mouth.

"I think it's a disk—a flash drive that has my friend Sherry's pictures and things on it," she says in a quieter tone.

McGinty crosses his arms and stares at Jordan. "Why do you think that?"

"It's blue."

"Lots of disks are blue."

McGinty's statement has me tipping my head. Sherry's disk is blue. The disks that Sam swept aside to help Goodwin were blue. A few different sizes, but all robin's-egg blue. *How important is a color?*

"I know," she admits, eyes going to her shoes. "But I just thought . . . you know?"

"Well, you know what?" he says so kindly you'd think he was a saint.

Jordan shakes her head and stares.

"The disk that was in the judge's mouth has nothing on it."

Jordan and I stare at him.

"You're kidding?" Jordan asks. "You're *not* kidding."

"It was wiped clean. We're trying to bring up what was on there, but it had so much fragmented data on it that it's touch-and-go to recover everything. Plus, some of the files on there were encrypted—and that part we'll never get into. Not unless we're able to decode the encryption that it was written to."

I stand very still. Wiped clean. *Just like Goodwin's hard drive. He did this? He must have.*

Jordan is gleeful. "Is that right? Wow! That's *great.* I mean . . . I mean for Sherry."

"Maybe so," McGinty says, and looks at Sullivan, who gives him the chin-up okay sign. McGinty turns to me. "Agent Sullivan and I would like to talk with you a minute, ma'am."

"Yes, certainly. Can Jordan go home?"

"Yes, thank you, Jordan. You've done the right thing today." He puts his big meaty hand out to shake hers. She grasps it and then, with a huge smile on her face, she practically runs out the back door.

"I'm glad she told me," McGinty offers. "Finally." He walks around the perimeter of the room. "You realize I would have had to come down hard on her if she hadn't." When I nod, he adds, "Does Senator Bunting know about this activity of his daughter's? Yes? Well, good."

I'm waiting for him to ask me if I told Henry—and that would surely incriminate me, wouldn't it? I try to look sorrowful, but all I'm able to do is accuse myself of that old adage, the ends justify the means. And I tell myself I need to have a heart-to-heart with myself soon on this matter, while McGinty says, "Kids will be kids, huh? We don't need sidebars like that screwing up a murder case, do we?"

I shake my head.

Sullivan, curly black-haired double of John Belushi that he is, comes to stand next to McGinty. The two of them look like halfbacks for a mean Irish football team. Sullivan crosses his arms and glares at me hard. "You know anything else we should know about this case, ma'am?"

What can I tell him? Suspicions, half-facts, Jones's observations that I cannot prove? "If I learn anything, I'll be sure to tell you what I can."

He comes closer—and looms over me. In his all-fired authority, he is ferocious. The panther to McGinty's bear. "You do that, ma'am, or you, McGinty, and I are going to have a serious talk, because your congressional immunity extends only as far as my good graces allow. And don't you dare forget it."

Back at my office, I am a mental basket case. Try as I might to work, I absorb nothing, and by eight I've got a skinny tuna sandwich for dinner, plus a headache.

Finally, I throw in the towel and tell Aaron I'm going for a walk.

The night is gentle. The sky just dying to red in the west as I make my way out of the Rayburn Building and across Independence toward the Mall. I hear music and I am drawn.

Every summer night, one military band or another puts on

their summer duds, picks up their tubas and trombones, and to-night we have a medley that drifts on the breeze. I know it well. I used to sing it. From Rodgers and Hammerstein's *South Pacific.*

Maybe a hundred or more people have brought blankets and chairs from their homes to sit out for a few hours and enjoy the grass and the sky, the majesty of the American capital, and American music. As I approach the West Steps, I note tonight we have the Navy Band. And suddenly, in lockstep beside me, I have company.

I glance up at the sculpted planes of Jones's face. Looking as haggard as I feel, he merely nods in greeting, but trains his eyes on the band. His hair is trimmed closer to his head. His mustache has disappeared, revealing the spare lines of his Roman profile. With hands jammed in the pockets of crisply tailored charcoal slacks and a sky blue button-down rolled to his forearms, he's in the guise of a staffer, after hours. One of the crowd, he's in blending mode. He's not talking—and I'm not feeling too gabby myself.

That's okay, because the music is just what the doctor ordered. "Some Enchanted Evening" wafts over us, with me singing the lyrics in my head, transforming them to apply to the stranger who stands mutely beside me and who constantly comes to me, not across a crowded room, but over my garden wall. For certain, I wish my problems were as simple as Nellie Forbush's and I could just wash this man right outta my hair.

"Where did you go today?" he asks when one song segues to another.

"Lots of places," I tell him.

"You didn't call me."

He is accusing me of not staying in touch? "Pardon me? I have work to do."

"And a murder to investigate?" He pins me with wide-eyed blame. "I gave you the phone as a tool to keep for safety. So you could call me if you needed me."

"Yeah, well, you know what?" I lower my voice because one

couple is gazing daggers at us. "I'm a big girl and I can go around town without your little toy phone."

"I am telling you, keep it with you. Use it."

"I had no occasion to . . ." I halt in my thinking. "Why do I need to keep it with me?" I sidle closer. "Why?" I have a sneaking suspicion that the phone may do more than convey voices.

"Where did you go?" he demands through clenched teeth.

I remember where I started this morning. Eons ago. "Len's office."

He rolls his eyes. "I know *that*."

"My office."

"That, too. Then you left it in your office."

I note that is a statement, not a question. "My car," I give him, testing the waters of my logic. "I had an appointment in the Capitol with William Preston Scott and Alistair's successor, Kirk Crandall."

"Okay."

"And then I went to talk with McGinty over off Pennsylvania in southeast."

"His office. How'd you get there?" When I tell him Aaron drove one of our LAs' cars, Jones looks pained. "And how was that?"

I'm getting a bit chilly, knowing he's tracking a murderer, too. "Good." I cross my arms.

"And then?"

Geez, he gives new meaning to relentless! "Greenbelt."

He faces forward, but I see his eyes spark. "Why? For what?"

"To see the game organizers."

"Enrici and her boyfriend, Wyatt?"

"Yes."

He gets real quiet. "And how was that for you?"

"Oh, okay." I'm being cagey, coy, cool, though I can't say why other than to nettle him. And I watch his reaction.

It is not nice to make Mr. Jones angry. He breathes deeply, his words sharp and hot. "Did you like them?"

I tread carefully in this new and dangerous terrain burnt by his fury. Working on staying calm in the face of it, I pull out my base reaction to the pair. "No."

"Why not?"

"Nothing I can name. You?" I ask, hoping for a crumb of evidence he'll share.

"No. Are you tracing their backgrounds?"

"Yes." *Are you?* I want to prod, but know I'll get no answer.

A ghost of a smile curves his lips. "Good. Let me know if you find anything I should know, too." When I don't readily agree, he whirls on me. "Hear me?"

"Right. The same should go for you."

His eyes lock on mine as he ruminates on that one. But he turns away, his massive shoulders rising and falling as he exhales. "Good. Go home. Take it easy."

For a few minutes after he leaves, I stand there. Alone with the night and the music.

But at times like these, when a girl has a sore heart—and sore feet—the next-best thing she can do is go home to Mother.

nine

So that night you sleep, your head hitting the pillow and your brain telling you there is some good news. Your daughter is out of danger. Your name and your mug are out of the headlines. The murder of your neighbor is safely in the D.C. Police's corner. Your duty to your colleague whose rep was in peril is all nice and tidily done up with a bow. Even your mother has arrived on the last flight from Dallas with her rational demeanor firmly in place for her Washington visit.

Okay, so a few things are not peaches and cream. You still have to give one of your party's strategists a piece of your mind. You don't have a good feeling about the two game organizers—and you're considering ending Jordan's attendance at gaming parties. No, your romantic interest hasn't danced back into your life, but you figure he's AWOL because it's protocol during a crime investigation for you two not to discuss the gory details. Okay, so you don't have any cooperation from your shadow, but you're used to that. And then you wake up the next morning to a racket raising the rafters. "What in the world?"

You grab your robe and spring out of your bed to see what is the matter. Out into the hall, to the top of the stairs, you run down to your kitchen. And there before you . . . You screech to a stop, stunned at the sight.

One chimpanzee hooting from atop the refrigerator. The

automatic vacuum that he turns on every chance he gets nudging your bare feet. Pancake batter dribbling down his hairy chest— and splattered on the walls. One mature Texas female fuming at him, arm raised, finger pointing. One young Chinese woman chattering in Mandarin to herself, to him, to my mother. One twelve-year-old standing beneath the chimp, counseling him to *chill, Abe,* pancake batter decorating her, too, as she stifles a grin at the sight of me, clears her throat, and all of a sudden finds not too much funny.

"All right. All *right*! Hold it!" I raise my hand.

Everyone freezes and turns to me.

Instant and total silence.

"Thank you." I inhale, pray for world peace, and take a gander at the clock. "It is not even seven o'clock and people can hear your wake-up call in Idaho. What," I demand, "is going on here?"

"I made pancake for breakfast," Ming huffs.

"I thought she should certainly add blueberries," adds my mother.

"Abe wanted a taste," says Jordan.

And Abe pounds the refrigerator top and says, "Che, che, che." His version of, *Why not? I'm entitled.*

I keep my hand raised as I move with mute determination to the coffeepot. The tiny vacuum follows me, pushing at my heels. I pour myself a cup, take a gulp not quite big enough to satisfy my need—and then I face the chaos. "But we don't have blue-berries, do we?" I ask, groggy from my rude awakening from my first full night's sleep in three. "And if we did, Abe can't have them. He gets sick on berries."

"But Mom, he thinks he likes them." Jordan walks forward with a roll of paper towels and begins to clean batter off the re-frigerator.

Abe seconds that idea, waving the spoon aloft like a trophy— and dripping more batter down the fridge.

I bend over, turn off the circular robotic vacuum, point a

finger at Abe and motion for him to come down. "Right now, Abe. Down here."

He hangs his head and scoots over to where he can jump to the counter and then the floor. He looks up at me—and his sad demeanor reminds me of pictures I've seen of Abe Lincoln after Antietam. Confused that he's lost. Determined to win next time.

"Give me a cucumber," I tell Ming, and she goes to the pile of them she peels each morning for him. I hand over a few sticks. "Thank you, Abe. Now, please, leave the Roomba alone and forget the pancakes. You go over there to your cage, sit, and eat this and be quiet for a while."

He blinks at me, reluctant. Jordan takes the spoon from his fingers and murmurs something in his ear.

"If you are bribing him, Jordan," I start, "with promises of food he should not have, I tell you I can't afford the vet bills."

She straightens up and both she and Abe look like they have just robbed a bank. "No, Mom, I didn't. Wouldn't. He and I are going to play ball in the yard this morning. And I said we'd watch *Cinderella* again. That'll calm him down."

Abe loves Disney movies. "And play that Cole Porter CD he likes. That always does the trick."

He looks happier now, munching on his cucumber.

Jordan adds, "And maybe he could go for a walk with Gramma and me down to Wisconsin and get some ice cream?"

"Yes, take him by the harness, and for heaven's sakes"—I glance at my mother on this one—"no ice cream for him!"

At the mention of ice cream, Abe goes bananas.

Ming mutters to herself in Mandarin, which means she's probably cursing in Chinese, and to us she asks in resigned tones, "Still want pancake?"

Jordan says yes and Abe mimics her.

"I will put on," Ming says. "You curl, yes?"

My mother joins me at the coffeepot and winks at me. "Better yet, I will cook, Ming. Just leave it for now." This is the closest

Ming will get to an apology from Sadie for any contretemps this morning.

"Good." Ming puts down her spoon. "I have class. First one for summer. Must go fast."

I smile at her. "Go ahead, Ming. Jordan and my mother can clean up here."

Sadie takes her cup, sips, watches Ming remove her apron and march out. "You treat that girl too well and she will not have any respect for you."

"You treat that girl too poorly and she won't have any for you, either. Bear in mind, too, that I like her—and that I need her." I take my coffee and go sit in my family room chair, close my eyes, and try to prepare myself for the day. I hear my mother come to sit opposite me and wait for me to engage her.

When I open my eyes, Sadie O'Neill is smiling at me. Given her marching orders, she always comes back around. My mother will take every ounce of power you leave available—and try for more that you may unintentionally leave untended for a spell. But set her to rights, and both of you are golden. "You had a good night's sleep," she drawls in that scratchy, husky contralto that some say rivals Kathleen Turner—or Bob Dylan. "And god knows, you needed it."

I hadn't seen my mother for but five minutes last night. Once I had reached my house, I had felt like it had fallen on me. I'd begged off any niceties beyond hugs and glad you are here safe and sound, and taken my sorry self to bed.

I haven't seen my mother for more than two months. The last few times I've gone home to Texas, I'd been working my fanny off, what with a conference on border immigration, plus meets and greets around my district. None of those events had come close to the Rocking O—and my schedule, tightly serviced by my staff driving SUVs or flying one rickety Piper Cub, wasn't improved by my district managers' tendency to overbook. But sitting here for a few minutes of relief, I get a chance to look at my mother. And for a woman of sixty-five, she is still a beauty.

With hair that used to be wine-red like mine and now bears a few broad streaks of white, she looks like a green-eyed Irish witch. At an age when most women have lost any shape, she wears jeans like a second skin and starched plaid shirts that tell you right away she is all Texas, fit, female, and feisty. At five-foot-four, she has a cowgirl's slim-hipped figure, with mile-long legs and a pair of tits that stand full and almost as high as ever. She keeps that way because she runs a four-hundred-thousand-acre cattle ranch in the southwest plains of Texas by riding the range, able as any hand she's ever hired. Sure, she's got a tan that, if she hadn't been careful with all that sun, could've made her into a right tight piece of rawhide. Instead, with gobs of sunscreen and a collection of finely fitted Stetsons and Resistols, she's got a complexion soft as cream and a body that, if she so decided, she could use to attract a man and keep him well pleased. But to my knowledge, she hasn't had a man in her bed since my daddy walked out twenty-six years ago. To some women, that lapse might mean they were boring or bored. My mother was never either.

"Can I fill up your cup?" Without waiting for an answer, she rises, knowing me so well, and I'm *relieved* to hand it over. I examine her, my perfectly groomed parent at seven in the A.M. She's showered, hair blown out into the natural curls, makeup on, ready. She's come to Washington, which she avoids like a rash, to support me and help me with Jordan.

But if I know my ma, she has other cards up her sleeve as well. She works quietly, and I smile, knowing she's percolating a conversation stronger than the coffee. She pours herself a mug— black, no sugar to sweeten her up—and starts to tell me about our ranch. I own half, ever since my brother Cord drifted off years ago into drugs. She says my mare, Star, misses me. The hands are asking when I'm coming home to visit. She contemplates culling the cattle late August or September. "Unless the rains come, the drought will force us to sell off maybe ten to twenty percent of our cows. Hay is twice the normal price. The creeks are bone-dry. I hate to do it. But that's the money talking."

I nod. Wait. That was her windup. She's going in to her pitch.

"I'm having quite a few problems, Carly, with the hundreds of illegal immigrants running up from the border through our land. Traffic is getting heavier since New Year's," she tells me, her low voice dipping downward with sorrow. "Butch and the boys'll go out to herd strays and instead they find four or five hiding in the old barn down by Verde Creek." Butch is my mother's ranch foreman, a forty-five or -six-year-old who hails from Colorado, but she doesn't hold that against him. He's good. Efficient. Hardworking. And I bet my birthday money that my mother has noticed he's not hard on the eyes, either. "These folks are downright pitiful, Carly. No shoes, in rags, hungry, and determined they're never goin' home."

"Ma, that's the way it's always been. Sad." And lately, add a growing concern for national security when no one knows who many of them are—and what they intend once they're here.

"But now there are more of them."

"Can't blame them, coming for a better life," I add. "And at five dollars an hour, picking strawberries and lettuce or clearing someone's cedar sounds like heaven to a person who cannot earn a peso at home in Mexico."

"But they're getting bolder," she tells me, the lines of her face stern with the power that has made her a force in Texas ranching in the southwest for four decades. "They slaughter a cow when it appeals to them—and grill the meat, leaving what they don't eat and can't carry for the buzzards." She stares at me. I know this look. It is mine when I'm angry and frustrated. "Last week, a group butchered a steer, grilled him up, and the sparks started a brush fire that took out forty acres before it hit the creek bed and had nowhere to go." She rolls her tongue around her mouth and gives me another level glance. "I can't have it, Carly. They're costing me money. I can stand to lose a head of cattle here and there, hell, that's nothing. But sure as I'm sitting here, I can't have them accidentally burning up my grassland, on top of me losing cattle to the drought. A woman's gotta eat. And I have eight cowboys to support—as well as two new tractors to buy. A new bunkhouse to build."

I nod, consider my coffee. "I hear you, Ma." I'm also concerned with the legal and political issues of migrant workers up out of Mexico, trotting over land I own with my mother. "Tell me what's happened to that militia group that sat north of the border last month. Have they disbanded? Completely?"

"Butch says every once a week or so a few set up their RVs on the shoulder of the county road north of the Border Patrol's checkpoint, but they don't put a toe on our property."

I swallow my coffee, smiling at her instinct to protect her land. "They're just taking out insurance you don't put buckshot in their backsides."

Ma lifts a brow. "Serves 'em right if they get a load of my justice. I told 'em I'd get the sheriff after them if they so much as looked cross-eyed at my land for searching or camping. Vigilantes. That's what they are."

I'm grinning into my empty coffee cup. Sadie does not take kindly to anyone who does not know she owns everything thereabouts—and trespassing is cause for shooting first and talking later. Except she has never authorized harming the immigrants who cross on her land heading north. Instead, she often lays out food in lean-tos made of brush. To all on foot, she turns a blind eye.

Fueled by her knowledge that wounding or killing an illegal could cause her bad press—and therefore, me as well, she kept quiet about those who traipsed across her land. Privately she complains to the sheriff. Publicly she talks in generalities. Socially with other ranchers, she supports any local efforts to close the border. But she never discusses particulars of how many or how often she and her wranglers find immigrants . . . and urge them back across the line.

Because our ranch runs parallel to roughly one hundred miles of the Tex-Mex border, my mother laments to me often about the rising tide of men, women, and children who come to America every year. They come without money, shoes. Some of them give everything they own to truckers and runners—"coyotes," we call them—who promise to hide them in airless, sweltering trucks or steel containers. Sometimes they die inside, abandoned, clawing at each other in the one-hundred-degree hell that they paid for with their last precious peso. Sometimes they are abused, raped, sodomized by others who receive them in this underground railroad that promises jobs and a better life at the end of the rainbow.

The border issue, I know from previous laments I've heard from her and others along my eight-hundred-mile border district, is an ongoing saga that just gets louder and longer these past five years. So Sadie spends maybe five minutes on her immigrant problem—and then heads into the issue that is even more dear to her heart.

"Where are we with the investigation of Judge Deeds's death?"

Smiling at her use of "we," I bring her up to date, leaving out the particulars about Jordan and Sherry—and all the facts about Mr. Jones and his merry band of anonymous buddies.

"Now, then"—she sits forward—"you can't mean to tell me that you didn't think of the ramifications of all these dead men?"

I stare at her. This was her unreasonable side that always chapped my hide. "Hell, no, Ma. You think I'm worried about me when I see a man dumped in my own office chair—or another one slumped over his keyboard? Whenever you've found a dead man—even an illegal—dead on our land, did you stop to think what it would cost you to report him? Bury him? No." I cross my legs, peeved. "That question is far from worthy of you."

"Where's your sense of self-preservation?" She hits me where I'm vulnerable.

"Guess it got up and went." I take another swig of my coffee and swallow it back hard, like a gambler with no face cards. My mother lives by one rule first and foremost: self-preservation. I occasionally move it to one of my back burners, and for that, with Sadie O'Neill, I pay prices.

"For that"—she nods at me with her signature emerald-eyed fire—"you now have a mess of trouble in your reelection."

Yeah, I'm shocked. I have no clue what she's getting at, but I'm not going to ask for clarification, because I know that the sprightly little lady who is the largest landowner in my congressional district is about to lay it out for me.

"Your honorable opponent"—she clears her throat at her reference to the man who has run against me for all of my six races—"is talking up your tendency to find dead men as a ruse for you to grab media attention."

"That," I snap, "is absurd."

She puts up a hand to me. "Now, you just hold on there." She settles herself in her chair and delivers the coup de grace. "He says if you are running around doing police work, you haven't got time to be working for us."

"Dustin Hyde has always been more full of crap than a Christmas turkey," I retort.

"You and I know that, but the point is—"

"They will want an accounting of what I have done for them lately."

"So right."

"And they will have it."

"You have that planned?" she asks with brows arched high in expectation.

"At the end of the month for four days. We're doing a quick swing west of Alpine with Esme flying her Piper Cub." Esme Navarro is my office manager in my Uvalde office, a smart beauty who can fly in more ways than one.

My mother shakes her head in woe. "She holds that old bird together with Scotch tape—and someday, the two of you are gonna go down in it and die."

This was an ancient complaint of my mother's that had some merit, but I wasn't in the mood to fight it today. "However, it is cheap and fast—and with more than 45,000 square miles in my district, you know I need to use it." I rise. "And now, excuse me, because I have to go see what the rest of the world is doing while we're flinging pancake batter and I'm finding murderers."

I grab a yogurt from the refrigerator and am halfway out the door when Sadie says, "Now, darlin', you just hold on a minute."

She approaches with a wide smile on her face, our tiff done for. "Dinner will be fish. Salad. French bread."

She likes to order the menu when she's here—and it's always fresh fish, which she can't get, landlocked as she is.

"Salmon, please," I say, always conceding what points I can easily and leave the fighting for other battles with her that I really need to win.

"Grilled. I like it grilled," she croons, happy as a clam.

"Works for me. Please have Ming use the inside grill. I'd cook it outside, but I'm not sure what time I'll be home—and you should all eat without me if I'm not here by eight. 'Bye." I lean over to peck her on the cheek.

"First thing this morning, I'll get you an appointment for a haircut." Sadie switches now to her imperious manner that says *no arguments.* "I saw your calendar in your office, there"—she nods toward the hall—"when I got up this morning." She rises at five, come hell, high water, or drought. "I noticed you are going to that Metro Hospital Dinner Dance Thursday night and you need to get yourself gussied up."

"Ma." I run a hand through my hair, testing her theory of haircuts. "I am not going to any dance while I have this much work to do." *I am so far behind with this murder investigation, and oh, where are you, Dustin Hyde, that you cannot overhear my thoughts?*

"It'll do you good," she announces as if I were five and she were still the boss. "I've heard you talk about this before. The event everyone kills to go to."

I level my gaze at her. I know this tactic. "You want to go."

"You have two tickets, don't you?" Anticipation melts years from her face. Next to ranching, my mother's second most favorite pastime is partying. Political partying. "Besides, when was the last time you went dancing, darlin'? And you do love it so."

It's not like I have a man for a date. I look at the ceiling and chuckle.

"See? You feel better just thinking about going." She beams, so pleased with her sales job. "I'll have Lucille put you in for a pedicure and a facial, too. You need the pamperin', sugar pie. Do not deny it." She walks into my office, puts a red nail on my calendar book spread open on my desk. "Eight-thirty Thursday?"

"Earlier, if you can get it. I have to be on the floor for a vote that afternoon."

"And then I will follow you, if Ming is here for Jordan. I do need it—and I just adore Lucille. I'd wrap her up and take her home with me if I could." She gazes at me with feigned innocence, because she has no other type. "You wouldn't want those tickets to go to waste," she adds, pushing her agenda at me one more time. "Now, that wouldn't be right, would it?"

"No, ma'am, it surely would be a sin." I grin and point toward the hall. "And now I have to go. But before I do, let's get the house rules straight here. No interfering with Ming. You let her clean, cook, and shop, and you enjoy Jordan. Take her to the zoo, the movies, ice cream. She's bored to tears without gaming—and I won't let her do it again until I figure out . . ."—at my hesitation to reveal all my thoughts, my mother cocks her head—"what is going on with her friends."

"Fine. We'll occupy ourselves, dear. You just go." She makes a shooing motion. "Go, go."

I get into my office a little after eight-thirty and, like yesterday, I leave Jones's little phone in my Tahoe. He hasn't tried to call me this morning—and I have nothing to say to him. Nor do I plan on going anywhere but to my desk and the mountains of paperwork and reading I must do to catch up. And that'll be just fine. It's not like Jones is so devoted to communicating with me.

I open the door to the office, and right away I see Aaron inside his glass-enclosed space and he's got two men in there with him. One looks like my legislative aide, Antonio Salazar, who is responsible for researching all issues relating to my seat on the Appropriations Committee. The other man I don't quite place . . . and then I do and freeze. Mickey G.

I lift my chin in silent greeting to Aaron and enter my own office, then close the door. Whatever they're discussing, I figure I'm next to hear it—but I want to be focused for the arrival of the correspondent for the *San Antonio Express-News.* Mickey Gonzales has not been very kind to me. And I am not inclined to do much but return the favor. If I have frozen him out since I suspected he committed a faux pas during Alistair Dunhill's investigation, tough. He deserved it.

I drop my briefcase, settle myself into my chair, unlock my top desk drawer, and take out my red pen. On my desk, as there is every morning, lies a printout from my press aide of the major headlines from yesterday's papers, including all the majors in Texas cities. A few headlines from this morning's TV news shows are also listed—and one has me rising out of my chair, barreling toward the door—and finding Aaron in a heartbeat.

He excuses himself in a rush—and comes to me. "I know what you're going to say," he announces as he waits for me to enter my office again. He closes the door behind us.

I am breathing fire. "What the hell *is* this?" I shake the papers at him, trying not to shoot the messenger.

"I couldn't believe it myself," he murmurs. "She's got a lot of *cojones* to do that to Jordan."

"Get her over here," I order him. *"No."* I won't give my ex-husband's new wife the opportunity to say she had a private interview with Carly Wagner, not after she has surreptitiously interviewed Jordan and gotten herself headlines out of it. "On second thought"—I have a finger in the air—"get her producer on the line—and we'll make it a conference call."

"Ma'am." He's looking mighty pained, running a hand over his bald pate. "There's something else you need to know about before you go off and get Leslie Underwood fired."

"Really? What?" I am seething. "For taking advantage of her personal relationship with Jordan, I'm going to adjust her clock to reality time!" I wonder, too, if McGinty has any tasty treats he gives to the media who mess with witnesses. Underage witnesses. I smile like a Cheshire cat, no punishment too severe for Leslie with the Little Brain.

Aaron smacks his lips. "Mickey Gonzales has a story he wants to check out with you."

"No." The last time Mickey G. checked out a story, evidence says he entered my home without an invitation. If I didn't have an excuse to install home security alarms because of Mr. Jones's unexpected arrivals, I had a really great reason to keep the likes of Mickey G. out of my home. And out of my life.

"Yes," Aaron insists. "This time he's helping."

"Why?" I put my hands on my hips.

"Because he's trying to verify a story he's picking up and he came to us to see if we have any drift on it."

Color me unconvinced. "He can check his facts lots of ways. What does he need us for?"

"For one thing, he's trying to give you a heads-up on an issue—and for a close second, he's trying to get back in your good graces."

I snort. "That'll take an act of God." I simmer down, cross my arms. "But he chooses today to do that? After this fiasco with Leslie? He'll have to leap tall buildings in a single bound."

"He just might. Listen to him, ma'am."

"Now?" Aaron and I usually go over our schedules first thing when I get in each morning.

"Now."

Letting Mickey G. into my office gives me the creepy-crawlies. I have likened him often to a scorpion, poison stinger and all. This morning he is certainly trying to change his image. Respectful and pleasant, he takes a seat opposite my desk, Aaron to his left.

"I don't want to take up a lot of your time this morning, ma'am. I know the other issues you have on your plate with the media."

I wait, fighting to keep an open mind with him.

He rushes on. "I am checking out a story about missing information from a company in your district."

I cross my arms. "What kind of missing information?"

"Identity. Social Security numbers. Pay records. Synerdynamics of San Antonio has an employee who has disappeared, taking a laptop and disks loaded with sensitive data."

I fold my hands atop my desk. Synerdynamics is a subsidiary of Paul Turner's corporation. Is this the theft Scott and Crandall hinted at yesterday morning? "Synerdynamics runs computer training programs for the Army's personnel branch."

"Yes, ma'am."

"How long has this employee with the laptop been missing?" I ask, careful to remain cool. After all, lots of laptops have been stolen from various federal departments over the past few years. This could be related—or not—to my leadership's missing item.

"I have sources who say ten days."

Long enough for Jones to be hired to track the computer, the info, the culprit. Long enough for the FBI—and Homeland Security, in general—to have their panties in a bunch over the loss. Long enough for knowledge of the theft to leak out to the company's board of directors—and Paul Turner—and a few worried folks in San Antonio.

So for relevance, Mickey has acquired my interest. And my primary concerns are his professional—and his personal—motivations. "Why are you coming to me, Mr. Gonzales?"

"I wondered if you had heard anything. If you would want to share with me?"

One eyebrow arches at him. "If I did, would I call you?"

"I hope you would. The missing info is vital to people who live and work in your district."

"If this were so, you realize that the questions you ask should be directed to Synerdynamics, the Department of the Army, and the FBI?"

"I have. They are closed down tighter than a fly on horse manure."

I smile. That is the first humor I have ever heard from Mickey G.'s lips. "And so should they be. I mean, in an active investigation, they would be very sure of what they reveal to protect their sources, the possibility of catching those at fault."

"Yes, ma'am. But citizens deserve to know if they are at risk. And I thought you would want to know about this. Just in case."

"Just in case . . . it starts to leak, no one has told me and I need to be out in front of it?" I venture.

"Yes, ma'am." He smiles, and now I can see in his eyes he really is bringing me this as a peace offering. Even if the story could become a feather in his cap.

I rise. Extend my hand. "Thank you, Mr. Gonzales. I appreciate your thoughtfulness."

After he leaves, Aaron comes back into the room and takes a seat. "He played nice. I'm pleased he gave us a heads-up on this. The other ID info that has gone missing in the past few years has given the folks at the Pentagon nightmares."

I glance out the window. Connecting the dots in this puzzle requires vital input from Mr. Jones, who as usual may not be talking, and Turner, who seems beyond my reach, what with McGinty and Sullivan probably breathing down his neck. "It'll give me a few as well."

Aaron gives me time to collect my thoughts and so, when I turn back, he's got his gaze on me. "Want to share why that is?"

"No, thanks. Perhaps after I learn more . . ." I incline my head toward his office and the powwow he'd just had with Mickey G. and one of our two LAs for defense issues, Antonio Salazar. "Was Tony any help in that interview?"

"I just turned him loose on that. Told him to go see what the committee staff might know, then go over to a few buddies of his in the secretary of defense's Public Affairs Office across the river."

"Tony has turned out to be a great hire." Straight back from Iraq, this young man hails from Alpine, in my district. A weapons expert who has comrades-in-arms now ensconced in the Pentagon, Tony has a knowledge of techno-weapons and a sense of diplomacy about him that I fully appreciate—and so do quite a few of the white-shirts in Defense and their counterparts among the military. "Let's see what he can learn. What else have you got for me?"

Aaron looks like the cat that ate the canary. "First things first. On Marie and Goodwin Deeds? Marie wants a divorce. Or wanted one. The Good Judge was crushed. But the twins evidently were delighted."

Does Jordan have any knowledge of this? "And this comes from . . . ?"

"My neighbor who works in the district court." He crosses his legs, smoothes his trousers. "Scuttlebutt is that she wanted out, but first she wanted money from the family trough."

"And?"

"The judge was not inclined to part with any of it."

Ah. "No-fault divorces killed alimony deader than a doornail." I consider if Marie had enough motive, passion, and physical strength to wrap a cord around her husband's neck and squeeze the air out of him. *But then, why destroy the place?* Unless it was a ruse? Why slice up his hand? A ruse again? That's a bit elaborate, if you ask me. And why would Goodwin put Sherry's disk in his mouth to hide it from his wife?

I run two hands through my hair. There were other blue disks scattered around in that room. *Was that disk in Goodwin's mouth Sherry's—or someone else's?*

I get up from my chair. Gaze out my window to South Capitol Street below. People drift by, intent on their next appointments, their companions, or their BlackBerries. I haven't followed any of the details of the case and what Marie and the twins say occurred Saturday night. And I must correct that, if I'm to make any sense of this latest. "See if you can find out if Marie and Goodwin had a prenup." I run a hand over my mouth. "If there is—was—what happens in the event of his death?"

"That's going to be a hard one. Insurance companies aren't inclined to divulge death claim benefits."

I agree. "But they most certainly would send an investigator out on Goodwin's suspicious death. See what you can find. What about Vickie Enrici and Jim Wyatt?"

"Enrici works as a clerk at a boutique in Bethesda. It's a new job for her. Two months ago, she was terminated from her employer of six years. The Department of the Army. Fort Meade. Personnel records, housing, and medical."

I turn to face him. Our eyes speak of our fear of the coincidence of the missing info that Mickey G. referred to. "Is that so?" I mouth the words, but my mind churns on the knowledge that Meade houses the National Security Agency. Do any of these bread crumbs lead from Enrici and Wyatt to Synerdynamics and the Army, laptops, and disks—and the death of Goodwin Deeds? And what does Jones know? Why did he really go to the gaming party Friday night? Does he know anything about Enrici that I should? Like why she got the boot?

I turn to Aaron. "Any idea why Enrici was terminated?"

"No, but I'm trying to learn. Meanwhile, we have it on good authority that James Wyatt works as a computer programmer for Marsand Hotels. The night shift. Eleven to seven. Laurel headquarters."

"Any criminal records?"

"Not even a parking ticket. Clean. Both of them—or at least,

Enrici was till she got axed. Both straight-A students from B–CC High School, class of '98. Computer tech grads from University of Maryland, College Park. Class of '02. Living together for the past five years. At that address."

"Wait, Enrici went to Maryland?" I ask him and he nods. "Are you sure?" The Gaming Group put out literature touting their careful hiring process and the respectability of their organizers. For parents like me, Henry, and Goodwin, this was necessary assurance. But I wouldn't have learned about this group if Norreen hadn't referred them to Marie—and Marie to me.

"Yes," Aaron declares. "I got a rundown from the Gaming Group, who cleared them to run the in-person gaming parties. Why?"

"Henry told me Norreen had her as a student in one of her classes." But to my knowledge Norreen had taught college political science at a small school in Kentucky—never at the University of Maryland, up in the nearby D.C. suburbs.

"He might be mistaken," Aaron offered. "But knowing his penchant for detail . . ."

"He might not," I finish the thought.

We look at each other a long minute when Aaron says, "I'll see what I can learn about Norreen Bunting."

And if she had never taught classes at College Park, what part of Vickie Enrici's declared background was a lie?

"Until then"—Aaron comes around the desk—"let's look at your schedule, shall we?"

I go for the problem I can solve immediately. "First, get me Leslie and her producer on the phone."

Within minutes, Aaron has them both on a conference connection with me in my inner office. Mark Dreyfus is Channel 8's news producer for the morning, Aaron introduces him, and then he tells me that Leslie's joining us on her cell.

When Aaron clicks off, I make certain I have them at hello. "You can imagine, Leslie, why I need you to hear this conversation. Mr. Dreyfus"—I then ignore her—"Leslie Underwood took advantage of my daughter and used her personal relationship to advance her own career."

"Carly—"

"At some point in the last few days, Leslie talked with my daughter under the guise of friendship and the role of being married to her father. This is not only low and underhanded, a sneaky way to treat anyone, it is downright unconscionable behavior with a minor. And I intend to not only take it up with the detective on this case, but also my lawyer."

"Ma'am," begins Dreyfus, but I have little time for any pussyfooting, "we had no idea that Leslie would do this."

"You don't review your reporters' stories, Mr. Dreyfus? What kind of news station are you running over there?" When he tries to answer, I decide I have little time for negligence. "I want your assurance, Mr. Dreyfus, that you will pull any reruns, clips, or references to this interview from your airways. Immediately."

"Yes, not a problem."

"Carly, I want to—"

"Mr. Dreyfus, I am fairly cognizant of FCC regulations about interviewing minors, and those actively involved in criminal investigations." When I was a radio talk show host in San Antonio, I stood clear of potboilers like this. "You don't have to break the law to make a name for yourself, Mr. Dreyfus—and I want your assurances that if you decide to keep Mrs. Underwood on your payroll—"

"Carly! You can't do that to me!"

"Quiet, Leslie," Dreyfus barks.

"I want your assurances, sir, that in the future, if she has one with you, you will closely edit her content."

By the time we hang up, Dreyfus is mopping the floor with Leslie.

Dusting my hands of her, I know Len'll back me. For all his faults, Len knows the law. And ninety-nine percent of the time, he abides by it. We'll see if he also knows what he needs to do to protect his only child.

Shooting daylight into ol' Leslie's career does not pain me one mite. Yes, it might put holes in her marriage. Maybe even in her budding relationship with Jordan. I can deal with Jordan—no problemo. But Leslie had become a bandita. And if you live by the gun, you get to die by it, too.

That night at ten, I crawl into my Tahoe and head home.

My day's tally included going down to the floor to vote on a bill to develop a new federal highway system, doing some catch-up research for Defense Appropriations hearings tomorrow, and later meeting with two delegations from my district, both of whom wanted only to shake my hand and wish me well with my "current troubles."

But now I'm riding in my car. I turn on the radio—and find nothing on that thrills me. Deciding I need to sing to decompress, I plug in a CD of Ella's, and the first selection is a swell rendition of "You Do Something to Me." I'm singing along, having as fine a time as a lady with my problems can—when Jones's little phone barks with his greeting.

"Hello, there," I address him—and turn down my audio, "and how goes the security biz these days? Got anything new to report?" *Please say yes.*

"Yes. But where've you been that you haven't talked to me again today?" he gruffs.

"Missed me, huh?" Two can play at coy, but it gets so old. "No more games, Jones." I pause to navigate the corner of M Street up onto Wisconsin, north to Q Street, and home. "Have you given any info to McGinty yet about the two people who entered the Deedses' house Saturday night?"

"Haven't gotten clearance through my client yet."

Yet? "So you asked?" When I get no response, I go for broke. Show my hand. All face cards. "Let's try this, then! Might your client be Homeland Security or the FBI? Or how about the Department of the Army? Fort Meade? National Security Agency? What?"

He goes right into his old refrain, called "I have no id—"

"No idea who the client is. Your lips are sealed with Crazy Glue. I hear you, Jones. So here's another sixty-four-thousand-dollar question." I brake in front of my house and hit the garage door opener.

Suddenly the geography gives me a whole new outlook. "Jones."

"*What?*" He's angry, a good sign, I think.

But I'm gazing down the street, looking at the row houses, my home attached to my next-door neighbor's, and his attached to the Deedses'. No lawns in between. Only the street, parallel to the houses. "Saturday night . . ."

"Yeah?"

"Did you see Jordan enter the Deedses' house?"

"No. Why would I?"

I am slow to voice my fears that Jordan has left out another vital piece of information about her actions the night Goodwin died. "Because Jordan told McGinty she left by our front door. Which I thought was logical, because I didn't see her leave through the family room." Where I was busy. And since she entered the Deedses' by the back door . . . and came back home through the garden gate that is normally locked . . . how in hell did she get out?

"Well, she didn't come out your front door—and didn't go in theirs."

"Right." I lick my lips. "If she did, you would have her on the videotape. So she left some other way." *And I am ashamed to say I do not know how that is. Or why she would lie . . . again.*

"Ask her."

"Oh, believe me . . ." I toss the phone down. Pull into the garage. Turn off the ignition. Jump out and shut my car door. Close the garage door. Open the connecting kitchen door.

Deposit my briefcase in my office. Kick off my shoes and head up the darkened stairs.

The house is quiet. Everyone asleep.

I rise to the third floor. Angry. Hurt. Fearful that my darling daughter has once more lied to me and I'm not sure she has a justification for it this time. Not even as good as loyalty to a friend.

I don't knock. I turn the knob. Open the door. Walk to her bedside.

And blink in the moonlight.

Jordan lies there. And cupped to her like a spoon is Zachary Dunhill.

Both fast asleep. Looking like teenage cherubs.

And making me mad as the devil!

ten

"Wake up!" I nudge her shoulder, then his. Fighting to be gentle, I don't want to scare them to death—just give them a taste of my Texas thunder. "Come on, Jordan. Zack. I have to know what's going on here."

They sit up, startled as only kids are in the middle of the night, dead to the world when they sleep. Zack is the first to take one gander at me and stiffen with the fear of god in him. Jordan rubs her eyes and pushes back against her headboard.

"I need an explanation." I take a seat in her chair, cross my legs, and wait.

"Um, Mom, it isn't—" She puts out a hand toward Zack. "Not—we weren't . . . well, you know."

Do I? Oooou, I hate the very suggestion that I might have had that suspicion. "Explain it to me."

Zack clears his throat. "No, ma'am. We didn't. I wouldn't—"

"I get it," I tell him, though I am not certain I really do . . . yet. "*How* did you get here? *What* are you doing here? *When* did you come?"

"Well, ma'am, the truth is, I came to be with Jordan. To be her support in this. Just like she was for me when Dad died." He's confident, innocent, his black hair and dark eyes alight— so reminiscent of his handsome father. His voice is deep, too. Deeper than it was when he left here two months ago. He looks . . . older. Lankier. More of a teenager than a child. He's got on a T-shirt and, from what I can tell, a pair of jeans. So sleeping with his clothes on is a small consolation, maybe even an indication that they weren't being more than friends. "I got here . . ." He gazes at Jordan and this devotion alone tells me that I was wrong: We are dealing with more than friendship. "Tonight."

Jordan sniffs now, more awake. "He hitched and came on the bus."

"Hitched rides and rode the bus?" Call me foggy, but that is hard to process. "From Phoenix?"

"I got on first thing Sunday morning when I knew she was in trouble."

I focus on my daughter. "You called him and told him about . . . ?"

"Yes." She pulls up her legs to sit Indian style. "I had to. I mean, I . . . I *needed* him!" She lifts her chin—and I recognize the look. It's mine. And I call it *Do not mess with me.*

I hone in on Zack. "Does your aunt know you're here?"

He waits—and I know the answer.

Jesus Christ! I run both hands through my hair and then scrub my face. "She must be out of her mind with worry! Come on. Up. Out." I stand.

He looks wide-eyed, reluctant. Afraid.

I pick up the extension on Jordan's desk. "I'll dial and tell her you're safe and sound. Then you can talk to her. What time is it there? Seven?"

He nods. Hangs his head. "She'll want to punish me."

"I think she should. What's the number?"

"You cannot make him do this!" Jordan rises up on her knees and speaks to me in a tone I have never heard her use before.

I stare at her and she slowly descends to the mattress. "You certainly understand that his aunt is wild with worry and despair that he's been missing for . . . *three days*? Jordan. *Please!* Zack, you have to realize that the FBI is probably looking for you, as well as the local police." *Great. And that means I probably can soon add them to my list of personal acquaintances with law enforcement. Won't McGinty be happy to know that!*

More than a half hour later—with my mother and Ming awakened by the din and serving as a bleary-eyed audience—we have calmed his very frantic Aunt Sarah Mae in Phoenix. Interestingly enough, Zack has pleaded his case in such a way that I conclude he has a great future as either a lawyer or an actor. His aunt, grateful beyond all that's holy that he's safe and sound, has said if he wants to visit—and it's okay with me—he can stay for a while.

Am I going to turn him out? Send him back? Well, no. Not right away. And not while it is clear I need to see the interaction between him and Jordan to fully understand their relationship. Why? Hell, I don't want to be surprised like this again—and I bet Sarah Mae doesn't, either.

For now I'm considering hanging a sign out front and calling my home a hotel. Jordan is tickled silly, smiling and hanging on Zack's arm, recognizing she had better back the hearse up to this argument because I've won.

But when I insist he move into the only other available sleeping space—the pull-out couch in my first-floor office—she lays into me. "Why can't he sleep here? He and I weren't doing anything. We don't do that. So what's the big deal? My bed is *huge*."

I let her rant on, my arms akimbo, stunned to my bones at her audacity. When she quiets down, I don't say a word, but go about my business of getting Zack bedding from the hall closet—and handing it to Ming to assemble.

At the top of the stairs, as my mother waves a dismissive hand and returns to her room, I tell Zack, "I would like you to come downstairs in exactly five minutes. Bring your bag. You do have clothes and things, don't you?"

"Yes, ma'am," he grins at me, grateful as a young man who has just escaped the noose. "I brought a few . . . things."

I knit my brows. "Why the hesitation?"

"I brought my invention," he announces, so proud that if his T-shirt had buttons, they'd pop. "Want to see?"

What else am I to do, curious up to my eyeballs, except say yes? "Why not?"

And what he shows me has me dropping my jaw—and him grinning, and Jordan clapping and crowing. And me blinking in admiration.

"Don't you just love him?" Jordan enthuses.

I do. I do.

I am gazing at a little man. Two-foot-two. Eyes of blue. Coochie-coochie-coochie-coo. A man of steel. And whirligigs and whizzing sounds.

Zack points a remote control at the robot, so that suddenly the little man is heading for the stairs. "His name is BEN."

I gaze at Zack—who I always knew was brilliant, articulate, shy—and who now also merits the word *inventive*. "Ben."

"An acronym," this young man says with authority beyond his years. "For Being Efficient Naturally."

Aha. "And the reason for this acronym is . . . ?"

Zack looks wistful. "He picks things up. Watch." He pushes a few more buttons and BEN retrieves Jordan's jeans from a messy pile, then wheels about toward her bed.

Jordan adds, "And he can turn things on."

"Fascinating," I commend him, and ask for more explanation.

"He's a prototype I worked on last year in Saturday robotics class."

"Robotics class? Where?" I ask, unaware of such a program.

"In Gaithersburg. NIH sponsors some and NASA sponsors one. Do you like him? He's really user-friendly. Got five pro-grammable functions. See? All you do is adjust the remote. . . ."

Zack pushes a few controls in a series of moves that remind me of Jordan or her friends madly playing video games. To Zack's moves, BEN changes course, one hand going up and down and the wrist rotating, which—to my understanding of genetics is the movement that changed us from animals to humans.

"Does he have an opposable thumb?" I wonder about the ability that would make BEN nigh unto indispensable. I bend down to gaze at his tentacles that might be, with more work, hands.

"I've got to perfect that," Zack says. "I mean, because he can pick up some things, and when I get him up to speed, he could be good for old people to use around the house. Empty the trash. Count pills they have to take. Some bots even give meds—"

I'm stuck on the concept of cleaning, watching this little dude hustle around the perimeter of the walls. "He reminds me of the Roomba that Ming loves." The automated vacuum hugged walls to stay oriented and orderly.

"BEN is better. I mean, he still needs improvement," Zack says, "but I want to show him around, you know? Here in D.C. There are lots of tech companies here that sponsored that Saturday robotics class I took, friends of my dad's who make these things for the Army and NASA. So, see, I figure I can sell him for lots of money, get the patent, and then I can live anywhere I want." He pauses, looking gloomy, and I ponder if that means he'd like to come back to Washington and be near Jordan. Doubtless, his aunt would have a few words to say about that— and she hates D.C. "I *hate* Arizona," he murmurs. "It's so hot all the time, every day. And, god, is it bright! I feel like I'm living inside an electric light bulb!"

I smile—and so does he. The only one still frowning is Jordan—and I am too exhausted to figure out why. I rise. "Okay. More about this tomorrow. Let's get some sleep, shall we?" I start down the stairs. "Good night, Jordan. Zack, you have five minutes to bedtime."

And in ten, I hit the sack myself. Just before I drift off, I recall I didn't ask Jordan about her exit from the house Saturday night.

But I'm loving the feel of my mattress too much to get up and do anything about it. Scarlett—I assure myself and roll over—was right. Tomorrow is another day.

*I'm in the desert, and geez, is it hot and bright. I'm squinting when Jordan, Zack, and BEN appear at the top of a gigantic rock. I think the rock's in Big Bend, but I've never seen this particular formation before. The two children are walking toward an abyss and BEN's trundling along behind them in his chug-chug little way. I'm waving and jumping up and down, trying to figure out how to get their attention to stop them from falling in—*and someone I can't see pushes me on my shoulder and croons, "Carly, wake up. Come on, we have to talk."

"No," I object. "Not talking to you."

"Yeah, really, ma'am, we have to. Come on," the voice insists, and nudges. I nudge back—and then I bolt up and scramble back, and I just can't seem to utter a freakin' sound. "Hey, now, it's okay, it's just me," soothes Jones as I start to open my mouth and scream.

"Holy sh—!" I'm mumbling with Jones's hand clamping over my mouth. *"Wha' a' u' do'g?"*

Sitting in front of me, he circles an arm around my shoulder and draws me near. His body is warm.

Mine is hot with fear. *"Take'ur han——"*

"Shhh. Pipe down." He drops his hand, grips my arms. "I had to talk to you. You left my damn phone in the Tahoe, didn't you? So what am I supposed to do?"

"So you break——" I start out, but then lower my voice from a roar to a whisper. "So you break into my *house*? What the hell is the matter with you?"

"I told you your house alarm system is defective. But that's tomorrow's problem."

I open my mouth to object, but he barrels on.

"We have to talk." He's rubbing my arms up and down. "It's all good now. Just calm down."

"All good?" I look around my bedroom, bewildered by this visitor in the still of the night. "You are sitting in my bedroom and I'm—" I glance down at my nightgown. White embroidered cotton. Thin cotton. Little straps. I groan.

He grins. "Nice. I like this look better than the pink flannel I saw in April."

I scootch back against the headboard and cross my arms. And the pose is not just for effect, either. "*What* do you want? Spit it out and get out of here."

"Yeah. I know. You need your beauty rest. You sure as hell aren't getting much lately."

With the draperies closed in the gray light of my bedroom, he is all spartan shadows and sounds. And the smell of him assails me. Man in black M5, smelling of testosterone and male sweat. Sexy and hot in the middle of the night—and *what in hell am I thinking?*

I grab a fistful of my sheets and pull them up to my neck. "Speak to me and do it quickly, Jones. It is . . ."—I gander at the white digital numbers on my bedside clock—"*midnight,* for pity sakes, and that means it is time for all good boys to change back into pumpkins."

"Where did you go today?"

I snort. "This is getting tedious, you know."

"I have to know," he growls. "You are not helping—"

"Like you are," I complain.

"You did not take my phone with you. *Again.*"

"That's a crime?" I'd jump up and down if he didn't have my legs pinned by one strong arm across them.

"You bet." He gets a real hard neon glare going at me, and I feel like I've been lasered by Superman. "I'm not leaving till you tell me where you went today."

Men who have more brawn than logic I comply with . . . for starters. "Rayburn—and the Capitol to vote."

He's looking like a mean machine. "Nowhere else? In no one else's car?"

"I had too much work," I offer in strong objection.

"All right. From now on, do not," he emphasizes, "go anywhere without the phone. Hear me?"

I nod. Protection was job one for him. And clearly, with all the possible nefarious doings—and the list of his possible clients—I am in need of protection. Again. "I'll take it with me."

He squints at me to see if I'm feeding him prime bull.

"I promise."

He seems to allow himself to breathe again—and then he gets a new freak on and says, "Did you ask Jordan about how she got into Deeds's house Saturday?"

I hate being called to task. "No. But I got inside and discovered"—I lower my whisper another decibel—"I have another problem."

"Zack Dunhill." He nods, shifting to the side of the bed, and running a hand through his hair. "Yeah. I saw him come down the street—then duck around to the alley—a couple doors up at the end of the row." He nods toward Wisconsin.

"You did?"

"I think I know now as a result how Jordan must've gotten out, too, without you knowing on Saturday."

"Well," I say when he doesn't continue, "don't keep me in suspense here. . . ."

"She must use another blind spot in the garden wall. Not the one I use, but her own." He smiles in admiration.

I frown. "Where?"

"The neighbors next door. They're not home, are they?"

I shake my head. "No. They're in London. They go often for weeks at a time. He's with BBC America."

"They haven't had their maple tree trimmed in a long time— and the newest branches reach far enough over to Jordan's bedroom balcony that she can use them to climb down into your own garden—or into theirs, if she wants."

I see. "And tonight, Zack used the tree . . . ?"

"To climb into the house." Jones gives me a lopsided grin. "Smart kids."

"Too smart." And in the case of my own daughter, too smart for her own good. I scowl. "What else?"

He shrugs. "That's it."

I narrow my gaze at him. "You break into my house, wake me up, and scare me half to death—to yell at me for not using your phone, then tell me a tidbit I'm going to learn tomorrow morning?"

The winds pick up and the trees rustle in silhouette on my shade. Moonlight splinters across the bed. In those scarce illuminations, I see him train those X-ray eyes on me, and in that bass voice that can hollow my bones, he says, "I wanted to make certain you knew what the answer was."

I examine him, his implications piling up like dominoes in a long snaky line to a conclusion I'm not fond of. And from the looks of his sad and sorrowful face, neither is he. "Do you have reason to believe Jordan might not tell me the truth?"

For far too long, he thinks before he answers. "I'm not sure."

"But you thought it important enough for me to know."

He nods.

"Why?" I whisper.

He glances away, then back, his eyes now hard as glass. "According to the statements by Marie Deeds and the twins, the timing of when they left the house—and when Goodwin's two visitors arrived—and then Jordan, I think it likely that Jordan saw more about who came and went from the back door than she may be telling . . . anyone."

Including me.

"And you?" I ask him a long minute later, when I have my senses back to some vestige of reason. "When will you begin to ask yourself how long you can live with yourself without telling the whole truth—and nothing but the truth—about what you know to McGinty?"

"You want me to have a crisis of conscience." He sounds in-trigued, amused, trapped.

I lift both brows. "If the shoe fits."

"You rattled off quite a list of potential clients out there in the street." He pegs me with those electric eyes. "If I ask you to elaborate, will you?"

Oh, can you see me lick my lips in anticipation of my coup de gras? "Come back to me after your client approves we share secrets." I bat my big baby browns at him. "Then we'll trade horses."

eleven

The next morning before seven, I down two cups of coffee to get me revved. I hadn't slept much after Jones left. My worries only multiplied. Jordan. Shelley. Zack. Pictures, missing laptops and ID info. Leslie. Balconies and maple trees. A killer on the loose forever if Jones's client never gives the green light to divulge who entered the Deedses' Saturday night.

Finally at five I gave up and climbed out of bed, started to go into my little office, then backed out the door because I'd forgotten Zack was here. At the kitchen counter, I tore off a piece of paper from the grocery pad and began my list of what I know, what I can prove I know—and what I can't. Now, hours later, that last is the longest.

Distressed, I fill my cup again and go awaken Jordan, telling her to join me in the kitchen. When she comes down the stairs, I send Ming and my mother off so we have some privacy. I sit Jordan down at the kitchen breakfast bar and begin another heart-to-heart. I open with the issue of her discussion with Leslie, lay out why she must not talk to anyone about this case, and watch her squirm in her chair.

"Leslie should never have taken the liberty, Jordan. What you saw that night, what you remember, is strictly for Detective McGinty or Agent Sullivan to hear."

Jordan rubs her eyes, still waking up. "Leslie didn't say anything on TV that I didn't tell her. She promised she would say what I told her. I watched her—and she did. She just said that I was surprised when I found the judge. And sad, too. That I was the first one to find him. That's the truth—and it's what's in the papers—and what the police said to the reporters, too."

"The person who killed the judge is still out there, Jordan, and you have no idea what he knows," I say, and register the twitch of her hands and shoulders. "Let the police issue the statements. You say nothing. Not to the people out front—and not to anyone who calls." A few reporters and two camera crews came and went out front of our house, but none dared come on the property. And in the *Post* this morning, a small story appeared on page three about the press release from Leslie's management—and my reaction.

"Leslie wanted to help me." Jordan's quick to defend her—and that tells me Jordan cares for Leslie—and her affection riles me. Makes me feel betrayed on behalf of Jordan. "She didn't mean anything by it."

"Perhaps not." Perhaps she did. We'll never know. Unless she herself decides to tell us. Or Len. And Len might reveal her motives. But they mean nothing to me. "It was still wrong for her to do this. She took advantage of your relationship. If you were another child, unrelated in any way, do you think she would have tried that exclusive interview?" *God, I do hope not!* "You are a minor. You have certain protections from the law—and the media should honor those, as well. Leslie has responsibilities to her profession and to her network to produce viable news. Otherwise," I point out, "she's breaking the law and codes of ethics." To get ahead, to make headlines, what would she have done in the future?

"Okay. I hear you." Jordan fingers a napkin on the counter. "I just wanted Leslie to know that I ran in and ran right out of the house that night—and that's what she said in her piece."

"Okay, so noted." I move from one topic to another, giving her no time to circle her wagons and deflect me. "Tell me how and why Zack is here."

She glances up; our eyes lock. "I called him Sunday. He came to be with me."

"Why did he sneak out here?"

"Because his aunt wouldn't have let him." She chokes up and the tears start to come. "And I needed him."

"I wouldn't let you go across the country at your age for a friend who was involved in a murder case. Why do you need him here, Jordan?"

She remains silent.

"What is it you're afraid of, Jordan?"

She looks to her right, back up at me. "I don't understand."

"Sure you do." I give no quarter. There is more to her behavior and this deception of Zack's arrival than simple need for companionship. "You didn't tell me how you got out of the house Saturday night."

"How did you learn that?" she asks, her doe eyes huge.

"Does it matter? Now I know you use the maple tree to climb down from your balcony. How long have you been doing that?"

She sags, shakes her head. "Just a while ago. The tree got so big and that limb crossed over farther. It was nifty . . . I thought."

"And you told Zack to come in that way?"

"Right."

"Because he couldn't come in the front door without me knowing. Okay . . . I get it. But then, how long did you think you could keep him here without me learning?"

"I just thought I could bring things up from the kitchen, you know. . . . And once he got to show BEN to some NIH people, he'd have money and live here all the time."

"Jordan, he is thirteen years old. Who lives alone at that age?"

"Yeah, well. Some kids should." She looks fierce on that.

I shake my head, incredulous. "What does *that* mean?"

"Some parents don't want kids."

I have a sinking feeling she means her father. "Some parents need to learn how to—"

"Yeah, well. Some can't! Look at Nick and Nicole. They

loved their dad—and hate her. And now they're stuck with her for the rest of their lives."

"Jordan, that is very sad and—"

"Wrong, too! She doesn't love them. She didn't love their dad, either. She loved his money and his job and she took every chance she got to punish Nick and Nicole for little stuff."

But she stood up for them Saturday morning. Why? "Not for the gaming party, she didn't."

"Yeah, well, call me shocked." She's sarcastic now. "She took her nice pills, I guess."

More than that. "She defended them."

"Weird," Jordan says, like it's final.

How weird? "Have you talked with them since they got back from the beach?"

"Yeah, today," she says sulkily. "On the phone. She won't let them come over."

"They have a funeral to plan, honey. They're all in a terrible time there and—"

"Nick wants to run away," she sputters. "I don't blame him."

Wow. More than one child itching to get out from under a parent. "When your father dies," I tell her because I know first-hand what it's like to have him go, "you have no anchor. It surprising and painful."

"Is it?" she challenges me. "I think I already know because I don't have one."

"Jordan! That's a terrible thing to say." Shock has me putting one hand on my hip.

"Yeah? Why? You don't think he's any good, either, so why are you sticking up for him, huh?"

"That's . . ." *Don't lie to your daughter, Carly.* "That's something your father needs to learn. And he can, Jordan. He's not totally insensitive." I remember when he did have affection and consideration for me and Jordan. *When did it die? And why?* My god. I only noticed the lack. Never looked for a cause. Now we have—Len and I—this result of it to deal with. A daughter who thinks she has no father worth the name.

"Can I go now?" she says, interrupting my regrets.

I stare down into my coffee a moment. "One more thing. Don't hold back information any more on this case. You saved the information about Sherry's disk when you should have told McGinty about it Saturday night."

She firms her jaw. "He didn't know I did that."

"Oh, but you are wrong."

She stills.

I pursue my point. "Do I lie to you?"

She begins to scowl, considering her answer. "No. . . ."

"No, *but what*?" I press.

"You didn't tell him." It's an accusation.

I nod. "True. That was your story to tell. Not mine."

"But you were protecting me," she says, justifying my behavior.

"Yes," I admit, and none too happy about it, either. "I was."

"So you left it out of what you told the detective," she repeats.

"I did. But you should have told him, Jordan."

"I was protecting my friend!" she complains. "What's wrong with that?"

"When you are involved in a criminal case, you have a responsibility to tell everything you know to the police."

"Really." She folds her arms and glares at me.

"Yes." I am adamant.

"So . . . then"—she considers a second—"it's not okay for me to not tell them about Sherry . . . but it is okay for you to not tell them about it—to protect me—until you warn Senator Bunting about Sherry."

Jordan must have spoken with Sherry on the phone, too, to learn of my meeting with Henry. "I was doing him a favor," I reply.

"Yeah, well, I was doing Sherry a favor," she fires back.

"One is not the same as the other."

"Why not?" she insists.

Call it my Good Samaritan tendency. Yes, I wanted to lessen the damage to Bunting. Yes, I wanted to make certain Sherry's Web site was taken down before the police got to it and put things in the media. "I didn't want an innocent child to pay prices for her folly when she didn't have to." I say it, but then I note how much the words she might use would be the same.

Jordan is seething. "You didn't want to tell Senator Bunting so that he'd *owe you a favor?*" she yells.

Whoa. That was one wild conjecture. But I could see how she might conclude that. This was a town oriented toward favors. Even she had been the recipient Friday night of Jones's favor to me. "No. That was never my goal."

She squints at me. And finding her answer, she falls back in her chair. Tears flood her eyes and dribble down her cheeks now.

I walk around the counter and wrap my arms around her.

She pulls away. "Don't."

"Jordan." I smooth her hair and plant a kiss on the top of her head, pulling her close and letting her come around in her own time. "I understand why you did this."

She sobs now. And I let her.

When the phone rings, the voice mail takes it, and it's McGinty.

"Stay here," I tell Jordan, and go to the hall to pick it up. When I finish talking to him, I return to the kitchen and she's composed again. "He and Sullivan are coming in an hour to talk to us. Go get showered and dressed."

Wiping tears from her cheeks, she scoots off her chair and darts for the hall and the stairs to her room. I turn to watch her go.

Standing in the hall are Ming, my mother, Zack, BEN, and Abe. None of them is smiling—and none is too happy with me.

Well, shoot, that makes seven of us.

McGinty looks spiffier than he has the past few times we've been together. Perhaps the case is finally making sense to him or he's just getting more sleep. Whatever the cause, he appears relaxed in a pale blue shirt and navy jacket. His alter ego, Sullivan, has the same taste in clothes he had when first I spied him Saturday night—white shirt, dark tie, dark suit. His attitude matches.

I invite them into our living room and McGinty takes the huge Chippendale to one side of the fireplace. Sullivan stands behind him, refusing a chair. Jordan, cowed from our confrontation, comes down the stairs, dressed in jeans and a T-shirt. Taking the Chippendale opposite him, she sits on the edge. Her hands between her knees, she's jumpy as a frog in a frying pan.

"I have just a few questions this morning," McGinty begins, and pulls from his jacket pocket a skinny notebook. Flipping it open, he gazes at me. "Wanted to tell you, I have the results of the autopsy."

Why do I need to know this? "And?"

"Judge Deeds died from multiple causes. The mouse cord was one. Wrapped around his neck, it cut off some of his air. Too bad we have no prints or trace epithelial on the cord. Perp wore gloves. He was prepared for this. Second cause of death: Judge Deeds's attempt to keep the disk in his mouth didn't help. He tried to keep it there and held his breath. This wasn't helped by the fact that he was so overweight. His throat had quite a bit of fatty tissue in it—and impeded his air flow. Plus, he had high blood pressure—and the fright of an intruder pumped him up high and hard. The assailant also did try to strangle him manually. Asphyxiation and heart failure combined killed him."

Jordan's eyes go round with interest . . . *and is it also fright?* "Wow."

McGinty's black Irish devil comes out as he turns his hard gaze on me. "So that means I have a problem."

Carly, you are not gonna like this. "What?"

"We found patterns of bruises on his neck," McGinty tells me. I nod.

"The mouse cord—and impressions of the strangler's hands."

"And fingerprints?" I ask.

"No." He stares at me.

"That's a shame," I respond.

"I doubt I'll need them," he offers me, and, none too happy to do it, if I am to judge by his dour expression.

"Why not?" I ask with some trepidation.

"Because measuring the bruising means I get a hand impression. A perspective. Strangled from behind. I also get a hand size." He raises his palm and turns to Jordan. "The measurements indicate the hands that wrapped around his throat were not large. Perhaps not an adult's."

I sit straight as a board. "What are you implying?"

He gazes at me with compassion, but turns none of it on Jordan. "I'm going to ask you to permit us to take a cast of your hands, Jordan."

"No!" she shoots back. "I didn't kill the judge."

Her words sound like gospel truth to me, but I grab a breath, hyperventilating at the thought that she's now considered a suspect.

"How do I know that unless I have a cast? Compare the sizes?" he pressures her.

I'm reluctant to interrupt him, but know he has to follow the lead of logic.

"I didn't kill him!" Hands clenched, she's breathing fast herself.

"How do I know?" he demands.

She considers the rug.

"Jordan, look at me. We know that the last files on the computer where Judge Deeds sat were deleted at seven thirty-nine. We know you made an emergency call at eight-fourteen." He's reading from his little book, checking her reactions as he reads.

I'm praying, *Oh, Jones, will you please pull this out of the fire for Jordan?* Only Jones has the videotapes of the two people who entered the house. I can't tell McGinty because I have no proof, no occasion to know this. Hell, I was kissing Sam Lyman while

Goodwin was gasping for air. Without Jones—and his client—I'm just a nutty mother trying to save her child.

McGinty continues, "We also know that it must've taken you three to four minutes to exit the house here, make the trip there, walk inside, discover the body, another three to four to run back here and get your mother and Senator Lyman. Jordan?"

"Okay. Yeah. Maybe."

"Maybe?" he asks. "That's not a lot of time for someone to go in, attack the judge, kill him, and leave. So if you didn't kill the judge, did you see anyone else in the house when you went in?"

I sit back, openmouthed that he'd even ask such a thing, shocked that Jordan might hide such a thing. *Would she? Had Len been right to question if she knew who killed Goodwin?* Horrified, I turn to her.

"Jordan," McGinty pursues her, "I am asking you, did it seem like anybody might be in the house when you went in?"

"No!" she shoots back. "I mean, I didn't look around, you know! I saw the judge and I freaked." She shudders.

"Was there anything unusual you saw when you went in that you didn't see when you returned with your mother and Senator Lyman?"

I never thought of that, either. But then, I haven't thought she was withholding any facts. Ever.

"No. I didn't think of anything like that."

"Okay," he responds. "Understandable. But was there anything else that happened that night we should know about?"

They stare into each other's eyes and I see Jordan's face register acceptance.

"Yes," she tells him softly. "I . . . I climbed down the tree from my balcony that night to go to the Deedses'," she admits, her chin quivering with fear. "I was grounded and wasn't supposed to go out." She swallows hard. "On my balcony, I can see people over the top of our garden wall and the neighbors' next door."

I sit glued to my chair, aghast, waiting for her next revelation.

McGinty prods, "And what did you see?"

"Someone . . . someone in a dark sweatshirt or a shirt, I don't know. It was getting dark out, too, you know? He looked skinny. Like a boy. A man, maybe?"

"Did you recognize him?" McGinty asks.

She sets her jaw, remains silent.

"Jordan, *did you recognize him?*" he pressures her.

She shrugs. Shakes her head. Winces. "He was tall, skinny with blond hair. Nicholas, maybe."

"Why Nicholas?"

"Because he has lots of fights with his stepmother and he always has to run away to feel better."

"I see. But when you got to the Deedses', the only person there was the judge."

She bites her lower lip. "Yes."

"And no one else was inside?"

"No, no one." She gets a wild look to her. "Or I didn't think so, you know. I didn't look around! I just went home. He looked so horrible—"

"Okay. So then tell me something else, Jordan."

"Yes. What?"

"When you learned that the twins and Mrs. Deeds had gone to the beach—and that the plan was that Judge Deeds would join them later—did you still think the person you saw running from the house was Nicholas?"

She swallows so hard we can hear it. "Yes," she whispers. "I didn't know when they left. Just that they did."

"Have you talked with Nicholas since then?" he asks.

"No. His sister."

"I see. And did you tell her what you saw?" he leans forward.

Jordan stares at the floor. "Yes."

He smacks his lips. "What did she say?"

"That Nick had to go back in the house just before they left that night for the beach."

Oh, my god, I'm thinking, *she was protecting him.*

"Through the back door?" McGinty prods.

"I don't know. I didn't ask. I didn't want to know. I just thought he had to go back in the house to get something, maybe? I mean, their carriage house back there is where they keep their SUV."

"All right." McGinty jots that down, checks my expression, and goes on. "In your opinion, would Nicolas hurt his father?"

Jordan stares at him.

"Jordan." He gives her no room to prevaricate. "Would he?"

"Maybe," she whispers.

"Why?"

She squeezes her eyes shut. "He was really unhappy with his dad and his stepmother." She goes quiet for a while while McGinty waits. "She picked on him, you know? Nicole, too, but not as much. She made their dad really unhappy, too."

From this, I gather that Nicholas, Nicole, or Marie could be suspects, and perhaps in that order of probability, too. I feel sick to my stomach. Neither Jordan nor I move.

After a long minute, McGinty inhales, stops writing in his little book, repockets it, and stands. "You have been very helpful, Jordan. Ma'am." He nods. "I'll let you know if I need more." McGinty gives her a compassionate look. "Thank you."

We walk to the front door with him and after I close it, Jordan asks me if she can go upstairs for a while. "Sure, honey, if you—"

"Mom, just . . ." She puts up a hand. "I'm okay. I just wanna be alone for a while."

Needing space and time to recoup is a process I fully understand. "Yes. Anything you need today, you let me know. I'm going in. Hearings at ten-thirty."

She rubs her arms and tries to smile a little. "Sure. Not a problem."

From the corner of my eye, I see other figures appear. BEN whizzes forward. Abe comes to take Jordan's hand. Zack rubs his eyes and jokes, "You did well, J-girl." And my mother says, "I think we're ready for pancakes, don't you?"

Ming chirps, "Yes. But we have no blueberries. Must make no berries."

Sadie says, "Right. And I'll curl 'em. Got a class today, Ming?"

"No, missus. Here all day. Cleaning today. You must go away." She makes a shooing motion with her hands. "I clean. Yes, Taitai, they go? I clean?"

I widen my eyes at the rest of them. "You heard Ming. You all have to find something to do today."

Jordan likes that idea—and grins at Zack and Sadie. "Maybe we can all go to the bookstore and later we'll get ice cream on Wisconsin?" Abe jumps up and down, chocolate ice cream with sprinkles his fave.

"You stay here, Abe. Help Ming," I tell him. "We could use a good housecleaning." Of sorrows, regrets—and good intentions gone awry.

twelve

Greeting a delegation from one of San Antonio's chambers of commerce this morning, I'm eager to usher them in and just as eager to escort them out. In less than half an hour, I'm due downstairs for Defense Appropriations Subcommittee hearings on new technologies—and one of those slated for testimony is an old friend of mine who used to be stationed at Fort Sam Houston. A retired Army one-star—now the undersecretary of defense for acquisitions, technology and logistics— Edward Aguirre eats, lives, and sleeps computers, cybertech, and weaponry of the future. Better yet, because I seek new technology industries in my district, Ed has supported me since I first ran for Congress. Across party lines, too.

"I would like to have a few minutes alone with Secretary Aguirre," I tell Tony Salazar as we walk down the hall toward the elevators. "Either before or afterward."

"Yes, ma'am," Tony responds. "I'll see it happens."

"I want to know what the Army is doing about information security, especially . . ."—I turn to capture Tony's dark eyes— "in light of recent breaches." He knows I mean the missing laptop.

"The chair may have a few questions on that," Tony ventures, "don't you think?"

"Since it's still not public knowledge that the item is missing"—

I lower my voice as a group of staffers pass us—"the chair may not know about this particular item."

The chair of this powerful subcommittee, Sebastian Marconi, was a media-hungry, headline-grabbing hound dog. If he knew about the missing laptop from Synerdynamics, he would be sure to broadcast it like a braying ass, embarrassment to his cronies in the administration be damned. So far, on this issue, he'd been mum as a mummy. That meant he knew nothing—and I alone was the proud possessor of knowledge I wish I never had.

We arrive on the first floor of Rayburn, headed for the hearings room—and as we round the corner, Ed Aguirre is just clearing the magnetrons and the Capitol Police guards. He's got a few aides around him, some in civvies, some in brass, but when he spies me, he smiles, wide as he can, and hails me. "Ms. Wagner."

I halt and grin. "Hello, Mr. Secretary." I use his title for public affect—just as he's used mine—although we have known each other for a decade as Carly and Ed.

"Just the person I wanted to see this morning," Ed says as he directs the two of us to pause off to the side. Our mutual aides close in, a cordon sanitaire for the private discussion he's signaled he desires. "Looking good." He offers his hand to shake mine, and then continues to hold it. "Though you sure as hell could use some sleep."

"I have problems, right here in River City." *And why do you want to talk?*

"I heard. Police handling this well, are they?" He's digging for details.

I tip my head. "As well as possible."

"Last time, you did the spadework." His gray eyes twinkle sadly.

"Only because I had access to information that might not have come to light otherwise." *And just how much do I have now that's worth more than two bits?*

Tony clears his throat. "Pardon me." Mixing among Aguirre's staff, he leans over toward us. "They've just rung the five-minute bell."

"Sir, ma'am," one of Ed's men puts in, "we'd better get in there."

Ed lifts his chin. "We will talk here a minute." Shorter than I, he's looking up into my eyes. "We understand you know about some missing property."

I arch a brow. "Word travels fast."

"It's our business to know."

"What I'm concerned about is how and why that kind of property gets lost in the first place," I whisper, seeking a real answer as opposed to any comeuppance it may sound like. "In this day and age, don't we have systems in place that prevent theft?"

"We have policies in place to track who has access and why, when. But in this particular locale, we had not yet put"—he is almost whispering—"an encryption system into place. So they could take the hardware and as a bonus get the files."

"Meanwhile," I murmur, "I have constituents whose identities are at risk."

"We're working on recovery. We have investigators tracking."

"In San Antonio?"

"And here," he admits.

Stunned, I blurt, "Here in town?" Would it be too coincidental to hope that a missing laptop fifteen hundred miles away would be tracked by a security type named Jones here? "Why?"

Ed smiles slowly. "Some roads lead to Rome. This one certainly seems to."

What are you telling me, Ed, old pal? "Is that right? A network of criminals?"

He tips his head. "Headquartered here. We're working with only the best to dig them out. Shall we go in now?"

I nod and begin to walk with him, as I tear my thoughts from Elite Force and Jones to the matter at hand. "How will you fix this problem so that it doesn't happen again?"

"We have a new encryption system we're installing as we speak. Solid. State-of-art. Data is automatically encrypted, locked down, in complex algorithms, the second a flash drive is removed from a hard drive. At the same time, too, the hard drive is locked."

"How do you work with the system or the data if you can't transport it?"

"Oh, but you can. Our method is to have the right set of passwords plus the right software version for the day to open it."

"Foolproof?" I hope.

"We've perfected it on transporting medical records with our injured GIs from Iraq. Every solider gets his personal flash drive attached to his wrist or his bed frame. This works, Carly. Well," he assures me, and we make our way to the hearing room.

For a few minutes, my heart is lighter. I take my seat on the dais in the hearing room, greet Marconi and the minority ranking member of the committee—and promptly sink into a funk. Sure, our conversation soothes my dismay over the missing ID info for my constituents. But it also raises my suspicions that Ed may be Jones's employer—and that Ed has come to me to talk as a peace offering for not being able to let Jones share other information with me. It does nothing for me except make me madder than a saddled bull.

And by the time Marconi, my colleagues, and I have asked our questions of Ed, I am raring to get out of here . . . and go see who else I can sink my teeth into—and win.

First up is the man to whom I've been hankering to give a piece of my mind since Monday morning. As Tony and I leave the hearing room, I tell him to make a call down to Rawlings for President Headquarters over on Seventeenth Street and ask if Chad Elliott is in. When he is, I instruct Tony to make an appointment for me—and "tell Mr. Elliott I'm bringing lunch."

Thirty-five minutes later, I set a brown paper bag down on Chad Elliott's polished desk in his huge suite overlooking the street. "I brought minestrone from Reggiano's and their whole-wheat focaccia." Both were the little man's favorites from the restaurant two doors up, where they put a permanent hold on a table for him seven days a week. A butterball of five-one, Elliott is a complete circle. As high as he is wide, everything about him is round. Eyes, nose, face, head, body. On TV he looks like a harmless and humorous cartoon character from Comedy Central. As soon as he opens his mouth, that changes. A fast talker and a smooth operator, he has statistics in his head from the Nixon-Kennedy confrontation forward—and few can substantiate or discredit any strategic policy to compare with his lightning stroke. Few try. Including my mentor and friend, now his boss, the senior senator from Texas—and soon to be the nominee for our party for president—Louise Rawlings.

"I'm happy to see you, Carly." He glides forward, both hands out to me. "Come, come sit." He smiles, but I know the animal beneath. Like Abe, Chad always has an agenda. His own. And it is always primal. Inscrutable. "Thank you for lunch!" He walks over and opens the bags, wafting up with one hand the aromas and closing his eyes. "You know the way to a man's heart."

"A woman has to eat, too, Chad." I settle into his sumptuous artsy digs. For a man who is round and fully packed, his love of art deco seems incongruent to me. His taste for hard Italian red and black leather and lacquer still somehow speaks of the wizard, if not the vampire, he is. And these pricey frills come to him for his magic as a fund-raiser for the party, which is grateful he has put Lou within striking distance of 1600 Pennsylvania. "But then, in addition to the soup and bread, I've also brought you a generous serving of crow."

"Did you, darling?" he dares to sound paternal with most women, except Lou. If he ever did it in front of her, I know she'd mop the floor with him and throw him out with the garbage. "You are so kind."

"It was that or hemlock."

He throws his head back to laugh. "Enough of that silliness." He waves it off in such a way that reminds me of Aaron's gestures when he's ticked. Aaron, you see, is gay. And not in any closet. Suspicions are that Chad is, too. But any similarities between the two men—and their likability—end there. Aaron is a consummate gentleman, a diplomat, and cool as a cucumber. Chad is a consummate politician, a conniver, and mauls anyone who defies him. "You know I love you," he croons as he hands me a Styrofoam cup and plastic spoon. "Just not all the time."

I pop the top of my soup and inhale. My eyes drift closed. God, I'm starving. Murder doesn't make a nourishing diet.

"You're losing weight," he says as he swallows, then breaks off a bit of bread to drop into his mouth. "For a woman your age, that's good theoretically, but frankly, you look like shit. No good for the cameras." He grins his little nebbish smile. "This murder is killing you. Get some rest. Christ, have some fun! I hear you're on tap for the Metro Hospital Dinner Dance tomorrow night. I'm going, too."

If I let you live that long. "I think by then I'll have reason to celebrate." I eat some bread, content as a clam to stir him up.

"Really?" He's chomping away on his vegetables, unconcerned. "How so?"

"I have a few ideas on who killed the judge." *Okay, so that's pure manure.* I smile around my morsel of focaccia.

He drops his spoon into his cup. Wipes his mouth with his napkin. "No. How could you?"

"Same way you're getting a woman nominated for president for the first time."

His round eyes go beady. "How's that?"

"With special insight into the situation."

His shoulders flex. He thinks a long minute. "Like what?"

"Can't tell you." I take another sip of soup, cross my legs, let him get a good long gander at my gumption, hollow as it is. "Against the law for me to share info except with the police and the FBI." I smirk.

He pushes his food away. Stands. Rolls up his sleeves to his elbows. Runs a hand through his thinning hair as he faces the street—and pivots back to face me. "Talk to me about what you've got."

"No, Chad. I can't do that. I came here only to inform you

that you can't issue ultimatums to me like you do through Scott and Crandall—and then think I'm going to walk away with my tail between my legs."

"You listen to *me*," he seethes. "I'm running a solid game here. We can win if we have unity in the party. I don't need an amateur Hardy girl running around solving murders. Leave that to the folks who do that for *a living*! I need you out there getting the women to vote for their own—not intimidating them! And I need that other Carly Wagner." He stretches out his hands marquee-style. "Looker, magnet for men!"

Color me chuckling. "I sell my brains—not my looks!"

"I don't care!" he yells at me. "I need compliance!"

"For that"—I've got a good belly laugh going now—"you picked the wrong girl."

He snickers at himself a second but falls serious. "Yeah, well, if we win in November, you'll play with us."

"Only if I decide I want to, Chad. Meanwhile, I'm beginning to think I like what I do, how I do it." *Who am I kidding?* I could go it alone for a while, but if he got Lou into the White House, he could control forces I didn't have. More, he could influence how campaign money in my district that, at the moment, I supervised more than any others was spent. There were advantages to *not* belonging to the party in 1600 Pennsylvania.

"Don't be too hasty, Carly." Wary, he examines me. "We haven't grabbed the brass ring yet. I suppose you haven't seen Lou in the past few days, have you?"

"No. Too busy. Why?" I chew on my bread—and why he's changed direction.

"Problems. I got problems. You're only number three on my hit parade. You saw Scott and Crandall Monday. Did they tell you what's happening with Halstead?"

Halstead? Gunther Halstead, currently governor of Nevada, was the second most popular candidate to run in our party's presidential primaries and caucuses this year. Ten days ago, he won the primary in Mississippi—which meant Halstead now had the votes to threaten Lou, if he wanted to challenge her in Chicago. Scuttlebutt said Lou wanted to end Halstead's charge to dethrone her by putting him on her ticket as her vice president.

"What about him?" I grab my napkin and crush it, then put it aside.

"Halstead was our best hope for this ticket. I told Lou this when we started two years ago—and I still think so. But hell, why he didn't tell me about his history before beats me. By now you've got to know that kind of thing always comes out. *Always*."

Whatever *history* Gunther Halstead now faces must be big, because Chad didn't foam at the mouth over any old thing. And whatever the problem, Chad thinks I fully understand what it is. Complimentary as it is to be thought omniscient, I have to ask him, "What are you talking about?"

"You don't know? All right, well . . . he's gotten threats. An underground political group none of us has ever heard of. They want him to quit the race. He's gotten two demands from this group since Sunday. They've stepped up the timing. Want him out by Sunday noon. He phoned me an hour ago. He wants to resign—and I don't blame him, but if he goes now, they win—and we're screwed for any other high-profile ticket. He has to issue a press release. Don't let them get the upper hand."

"Chad, what are we talking about here, that he's in trouble?"

"Since his tours of duty in Nam in '68 and '70, he's had bouts of depression. Four years ago, he slit his wrists. Until a year ago, he took antidepressants."

Gunther Halstead has a history of depression? For a politician, hey, I understand the possibility! Never was any job more prone to frustration where so few give their lives for so many for so much grief—and at such a huge cost to family and self. "Meanwhile," I say, "ten million Americans take some medication to control their emotions."

"And another ten drown their sorrows in booze," he adds.

"But to be a heartbeat from the president," I say to Chad, "we can't have a vice president on drugs."

"You know we can't. Insulin. Avodart. Lunesta. Viagra and three shots of Johnnie Walker, straight, no chaser," he says, listing substances the current vice president enjoys daily, "are all A-okay. But when it comes to happy pills—if you do the drug, you sweep it under the rug."

"And how in the world did this information ever get out?" I ask Chad, knowing that Halstead had been Army infantry in Nam—and wondering what kind of coincidence it might be that this blackmail occurs so simultaneously with the Army data heist.

"Good question. Halstead says he was always treated in Nevada by his personal physician, whom he trusts like God, a rehab center up in Frederick, Maryland, and by a doctor over in Silver Spring. Shrink named Trainor."

So then, what are the chances that this is unrelated to the missing laptop from the Army in my district? "I'm sure Secret Service is checking him out." Secret Service was responsible for protection of all candidates and their families—and all threats against them.

"Course they are," he declares. "The Bureau's pitching in, too. Looking at the Nevada and Maryland possibilities. But Trainor died last year."

"So then . . . that's a dead end, unless he gave away the records," I conclude.

"Somebody's got loose lips. And meanwhile, I'm doing damage control."

"Or cooking a new ticket. You do have problems." Feeling as frustrated as he, I struggle up from my seat and my head spins, dizzy once more. God, what I wouldn't give for full night's sleep. "I'll leave you to them."

He puts his hands on his hips. "We need every hand on deck to pull this one out, Carly. Halstead was appealing to the great majority of the opposition. Complemented Lou. If we can't find a replacement to match Halstead, we'll have a hell of a time winning this election. And we lose our best chance of putting a female in the Oval Office for another eight years. So you see, you either give up on the sleuthing, far away from Louise—or I'll make certain you wear your new moniker like a shroud."

A maverick, cut off from my mentor and my party central. Swell. So I have to ask him, "My moniker?"

"What did that newswoman call you Monday morning?" His eyes go diamond-hard and just as unsympathetic.

Gnashing my teeth, I put up a warning hand—and in disgust, head for the door.

Maven of Murder. Oh, Chad Elliott, them's fightin' words.

Minutes later, I pull out of the parking lot and head for home, driving in true Texas spirit. Fast and hot. True, it's one in the afternoon, and the traffic backed up on Seventeenth Street looks like a Sunday jam at a border checkpoint across the Rio Grande. But I'm brain-dead, angry—and, from all reports, coyote-ugly. I'm still dizzy and cultivating a headache big as all outdoors. So now I vow to do something I never do. Take a nap.

My regular cell phone rings. I dig it out of my briefcase and answer.

It's Aaron with news via Tony Salazar on the Army's missing laptop. "Army security found it in a field outside Frederick, Maryland," he announces, but the tone of his voice indicates the news is not all good. "Hard drive was wiped clean."

So Ed Aguirre had been right about the laptop coming to Washington. But why? "Well, why not? Isn't every hard drive clean these days?"

"What?" Aaron asks, totally confused, since he knows nothing about Goodwin's actions before he died.

"Nothing. Where are you? In the office?" Aware that Jones's little phone on the passenger seat can pick up whatever I say, I instruct Aaron to call me in about fifteen minutes on my cell. By then I should be safely inside my house—and able to talk freely without Jones hearing I want Aaron to track what happened to Dr. Trainor's office records. Now that the laptop is found—and cleaned—I wonder if all I'm doing is chasing nits. Certainly nothing connects. But dismissing my folly, I go with my gut, and Aaron and I hang up.

Soon I'm rounding Q Street. Hitting the garage door opener, I pause in the street and notice a white van parked in my neighbors' space between our house and the Deedses'. Computer technicians. CAPTURING WORMS AND BUGS! is emblazoned on the side—and at this angle, the logo looks like a kind of bird. My brows knit. Why would McGinty and Sullivan need computer gurus for the Deeds's hardware if they had taken them all in custody for forensics techies?

Not my problem, I assure myself as I climb out of my Tahoe, shut the car door with my fanny, and watch the garage door descend. When I open the connecting door to the kitchen, I smile. The overpowering aroma of PineSol hits me. Ming's favorite, the cleaner was one she'd use on us and Abe if she could. From up stairs, I detect the sound of a vacuum cleaner—and that would make me smile, too, were it not for the clattering and chittering I hear from far down the hall near my bedroom. Dumping my briefcase on the kitchen island, I kick off my shoes and head toward the din.

As I zero in on my bedroom suite, I catch a glimpse of Abe and BEN running amok around my bed. Passing my office, I note activity in there, too, but don't stop to examine it.

I get to my bedroom doorway and halt. Before me is a chase worthy of Charlie Chaplin and his silent screen pals. The Roomba, whose mission in life is to march to someone else's drummer, is scooting along one of the walls, doing its duty, minding its business and vacuuming the pale white carpet. Sitting before it like cheerleaders in a stadium are BEN, silent and motionless, and Abe, talking up a blue streak and clapping his hands.

"*What*"—am I raising my voice here?—"are you guys doing?"

Abe spins on his rump and grins at me, telling me monkey talk that pleases the hell out of him.

"Look, Abe," I begin, and then stop as he takes BEN, makes him face him, and then uses the remote to push a few buttons. BEN begins to walk toward the Roomba double-time. When he hits the wall, Abe screams in delight and the Roomba keeps on rumba-ing. "Give me that thing." I take the remote from Abe. "Go to your cage." This is the equivalent of *go to your room* and Abe, ordinarily compliant with this tone of mine, starts jumping up and down. "I do not care." I point toward the kitchen. "Go."

Meanwhile, BEN is trying to walk but is pressed up flat against the wall—and the Roomba just keeps on keepin' on. At this rate, I could have the cleanest carpets in D.C.

I groan and look at a reluctant Abe. "I'm right behind you. Start walking."

He complies and when we get to my office, he keeps going . . . but I stop.

Inside are two men in white coveralls, their backs to me with their motto emblazoned there and telling me they are sweeping for things I don't have.

"Excuse me," I say, and they startle and turn.

Young, perhaps in their twenties, thin and rather nerdy-looking in their glasses and their gauntness, they stop tearing apart the innards of my computer. "Hello."

"Who are you?" I ask, stepping forward so that they cannot exit the door without squeezing around me.

"Eagle Eyes," announces one with brash assurance, while his buddy hangs back, eyes shifting to his pal.

"And what are you doing here?"

He reaches into his pocket—with rubber-gloved hands, I note—and gives me a business card with eagle logo, Web site, and e-mail address, but no phone number or address. "We're doing a sweep for you." He smiles in a vaguely friendly way that tries for professional.

"Who hired you?"

He shrugs. "I don't have that here," he tells me quickly.

I'm wondering, *Was it McGinty and Sullivan?* Wouldn't they need a court order? And to acquire it, have to show just cause? How about Jones? What would he be looking for? What would anyone be looking for on my computer?

The hair on the back of my neck starts to stand up—and I put my hand out. "Stop whatever you're doing. Get me your supervisor on the phone."

The spokesman announces, "We don't have phones."

"The hell you don't," I tell him as I hear a crash and bang back in my bedroom. I try to ignore it, but a louder crash means something large is now much smaller. "Do not move," I order them, and then rush toward my bedroom. There, Abe is back at it, bouncing up and down on my bed like the monkey he is. He evidently jumped on the bed—and broke the slats so that the entire thing is askew. He's got the remote to BEN in hand and has pressed—evidently—too many buttons because the poor bot is whirling and whizzing like it's got Saint Vitus' dance. The Roomba, thank you very much, is still chugging along. "Abe! For god's sake, stop this! Go to your cage! Now!" And as I turn, I see the two guys in white hightail it around the corner of my hallway, headed for the front door.

I run for the kitchen to grab my gun—but jerk open the island drawer where I keep it only to recall that, *damn!,* it's in the glove compartment of my Tahoe! I whirl and run like hell.

But I'm not only barefoot but too far behind, so that as I get to my wide-open front door, the white van is squealing away from the curb.

I curse.

Anger has me charging back inside—and I reach for my house phone and call the office. Aaron answers and says, "I was about to call you."

"Right, but my priorities have changed. Get me a reputable computer technician team for the house—and have them here within the hour," I instruct him.

"What's going on?" he asks, concerned.

"Someone has tried to mess with my computer. Whether they wanted to see what was on it or ensure they had access for the future, I have no clue. Get me someone—and just make certain they're trustworthy and discreet."

"Wait, before you go," Aaron hollers, "I have news."

"What?"

"Enrici."

Riled by the computer techs, I pause to catch a breath. "And?"

"I am looking at the Bethesda–Chevy Chase High School yearbook for 1998—and Victoria Enrici is in here, all right."

"There's a *but* in there somewhere."

"Since then, something made her brown eyes blue. And her brown hair blond."

"Hair dye and contacts?" I offer.

"Not unless she also had plastic surgery that broadened her forehead and made her long face and pointed chin round and pudgy."

"A different woman?"

"Entirely!"

"Are you checking Maryland records and Norreen's college . . . what was it?"

"Hampden College. Yes, checking both for our chameleon here."

Victoria Enrici was not who she claimed to be? And Norreen inadvertently told her husband she taught Enrici. Stunned at this turn, I say good-bye, more uneasy than before.

Two hours later, at the departure of the computer tech experts Aaron has gotten over here, I have another answer that makes me angry, to boot.

The three communications analysts whom Aaron hired have swept my computer, Jordan's, and the Internet cable lines, plus the phones. When they're done, they tell me Jordan's computer does not seem to have been tampered with—and Ming confirms that when she let the Eagle Eyes boys in, they remained down-stairs. Then Aaron's three analysts show me two items that make me see red. One is the hard drive that the two intruders were in the process of removing from my computer. The second is a tiny circular device that they found attached to the underside of my phone in the hall.

"It's an audio transmitter," one informs me. "Used to listen in on conversations throughout the house. This one activates at any sound and transmits to a receiver. Funny thing about this one, though." He examines it with a reverence that makes me shiver. "It's cutting-edge." He looks at me and fear crawls over me like a bad rash. "I've only seen one of these, about six, eight months ago."

"Where was that?" I am dying to know, hating to learn.

"We swept the home of a senator here in town. He was being blackmailed. He needed it for surveillance, he said, and we should put it back because he knew it was there. Turned out the audio transmitter belonged to a private security firm."

Well, isn't it a small world. "Which one?"

"Howard?" He screws up his face, thinking hard. "Maybe . . . Howard and . . . something."

"Howard and Roth?"

"Right!" He snaps his fingers.

And who'd come into the house recently who would place such an interesting device? Who had opportunity? Who had the gadgetry? Who had motive?

Only one man, who walked around my home Friday night looking like he was locking up. Making us secure. Or so he claimed.

After I let the guys out of the house, I take the tiny transmit-ter with me into my office, close the door, and sit down at my desk. Setting it on my desktop before me, I feel a rush coming on of some Texas hellfire. And I speak into the device.

"Jones, I do hope you're there to hear this firsthand. On tape, I reckon, it won't be as ripe. I discovered—as you can tell by the

sound of me addressing you on your own little microphone—
that you've got some explaining to do. Yes, sir, it does look like
you've been bugging me, Jones—and in more ways than one. So
now, you realize, not only do I need to know what you know
about who visited Judge Deeds Saturday night, I need to know
why you put this microphone in my house—and why you intruded in my private life like I was some common criminal."

thirteen

At eight the next morning, I still haven't heard from Jones. Telling myself there's no love lost, I figure he's got to have listened to my message by now. Riled that he wouldn't call me—or even do me the dubious honor of breaking into the house again to try to apologize—I head out the door for the salon appointment my mother made for me.

From the sleepless night I had drawing diagrams, listing what I knew about the murder of Judge Goodwin Deeds and when I knew it, I also figure I have a better chance of shoveling sunshine than I do of finding the murderer and making good on my challenge to Chad Elliott. Hell, I drew so many big fat red zeros over my doodles that I figure I not only need a manicure, pedicure, and haircut, I also need a face-lift—and a lobotomy. Once Chad gets finished with me, I soon may also need a career change.

Swell.

I climb up into my Tahoe, slam the door, and close my eyes. I can see my squiggles written on my eyelids, for god's sake. I know three people came to the Deeds home Saturday night. Two came in the front door and—if Jones is to be believed—left by the front door. A third person, seen by my daughter, left by the back door. He or she was tall, thin, and blond—fitting the description of half the population of Georgetown. We know, too, that my daughter entered the back door and found the body.

We know the Judge died with a disk in his mouth, at his computer, with his hand cut open. And I don't know why. I do know he was having problems with Paul Turner. But Goodwin was also in conflict with his children. He was having troubles with his wife, whom he was divorcing. Did any of these people have motivation to kill the judge? Perhaps the one with the most desire to hurt him was Marie, but that conclusion cannot be proven. Furthermore, if there was any tie between the gaming party and Deeds's death, I found no hint. The only thin thread from one fact to another was Vickie Enrici's recent employment and termination by the Army—and an Army laptop, vaguely connected to a company owned by Turner, that had gone missing in San Antonio—but had turned up blank. Not even Vickie Enrici's questionable identity and Henry Bunting's claim that his wife taught her, shady facts though they were, connected or made sense.

That included the unexplained reason why Jones had intruded on my privacy and sunk an audio transmitter in my hallway phone. All the time he'd been playing Mr. Protector, he'd known what was going on in my house. And then for him to give me one of his gizmo phones so that he looked even more sanctimonious just fried me to a crisp.

The one intriguing possibility that grew more credible each time I thought about it was that when Jones brought Jordan home Friday night—and when he insisted that all four children return to their homes—he had a reason greater than doing me or any of us a favor. He did it because he suspected someone in this group of something. And he even put a big bad bug in my home to try gathering proof of it.

So much for favors.

Reaching over to my passenger seat, I pick up his transmitter and phone and roll down my window. I'm ready to heave them both out when I get a conscience, of all things. Don't want just any ol' person in possession of one of Mr. Wonderful's hi-tech, hi-dollar gadgets, now, do we? Who knows who might pick them up and figure out how to use them for more nefarious deeds than those by our Mr. Jones?

Ah, hell. I throw 'em back to the seat. Just what I need this morning is to be stymied by another set of slice-'em-and-dice-'em nuances to Jones's ethics.

I have enough trouble keeping my own on target, doing what I do, trying to be all I can be. Hell, what ever happened to vote your conscience—and working for the good of your constituents? Period?

Instead, I've got to think about Chad and his needs, Lou's, Gunther Halstead's, of all people—and my own campaign coffers. I might as well resign now if I'm going to have a crisis of conscience.

Which reminds me of the one I asked of Jones.

I snort.

Fat lot of good that did me.

I turn a corner.

"Good morning, ma'am," the phone speaks to me in the dulcet tones of Jones.

"Is it?" I ask the disembodied man.

"I need to talk to you."

"Unless you'd like your nails and toes done—and you get a sex change—you can't."

"I'm right behind you."

I look into my rearview mirror and hugging my tail is a shiny black Hummer, roof rack and some dish device on top that I bet is a satellite receiver.

"Turn at the next light and go up Canal Road."

"No." I pull up at the stoplight, headed straight south for the salon I go to in one of the new shiny buildings along the banks of the Potomac.

"Come on, ma'am. I'm really sorry."

"Novel." No one in Washington in a long, long time has said the word *sorry*.

"I want to apologize in person."

I scoff. "Want to kiss and make it all better?"

"Sure," he says in a voice that suggests midnight, not nine in the morning.

Shocked, I find my own vocal cords once more and reply, "Well, sorry you may be, but you and I are no longer buddies."

"Yes, we are. We'll always be."

"Whatever goodwill you had cookin', son, is gone."

"Look at me."

I lift my eyes. And swear to god, in his swanky armed vehicle with his flashy aviators on his noble head, he is sight-for-sore-eyes handsome.

"I had to plant that mike. I want to tell you why. Please drive up to Great Falls and pull in the lot."

I sit, stubborn, unmoving.

"I traced those guys who broke into your house yesterday."

That gets my attention. "Who were they?"

"A couple of punks from Frederick."

Frederick means eagles and techies, gamers and children—and a lot of dots that at the moment I'm not able to connect.

Then the light changes and I zoom ahead. At Wisconsin, the traffic opens up like a speedway. I dart straight down to the waterfront and veer into the entrance to the spa's parking lot. In the lot, I swerve up and around and around to the appropriate level, park, lock my car, and as I jump out, I grab Jones's gizmos. The building's construction makes me smile because it is open-sided, and the view of the Potomac this morning offers a lady on a mission a swell opportunity. I see the black Hummer swing around one more time, but me? I'm jogging toward the cement balustrade of the building, and as I hear the Hummer's brakes squeal and jam to a stop, I turn, wave cheerily at the man yelling at me as he parks his damned car. Then, in one fine arc, I hurl his stuff into the drink.

"Your goodies sleep with the fishes, Jones," I tell him as he climbs out of his Hummer and runs toward me. No, he can't hear me—but then, he doesn't need to. He's watching me, needle-eyes on me to read my lips. So I take the few steps to the entrance to the secure and very ritzy spa where men may not ever go—and plug the door code into the keypad. The door swings open—and I step inside as it closes. "Just like our relationship."

By early evening, I sit before my bathroom mirror and admire my fab haircut and wiggle my red-lacquered nails. I sure look glam, but I do feel glum. I've just finished putting on more makeup than a rock star because I'm off to this Metro Hospital Dinner Dance—and I'm trying to get revved to have some fun. Yes, it's one of the biggest do's of the Washington social season—but it'll be no picnic for me. No, sir, I'm working this gig. Why? Because at my request, Aaron and my legislative aide Tony Salazar did a bang-up job of sleuthing this afternoon.

Aaron asked around at my request and learned that the noted but deceased Dr. Robert Trainor folded his practice into Metro Hospital and Health Care Group two years ago, just before he died. All his patient records now reside in the group's headquarters in northwest D.C. The same place Marie Deeds works—and has charge of patient records and accounting. If any link exists between Marie and Trainor and the blackmail attempt on Gunther Halstead, I'm all fired up to learn it. After all, who's sitting at the same table with Metro's director tonight but me?

And from what Marie Deeds always told me about the illustrious Dr. Graves, he is a ladies' man. And one who is interested in meeting me.

All the more reason to dress to the nines—and lure the gentleman as best I can. So I'm tickled pink that I had presence of mind not to blurt out anything when I had Jones's phone or his audio bug in my possession. Jones would have been on me, and on the case, like white on rice—and why would I welcome his help anyway?

It's not like he's been so forthcoming with me.

Still, I feel like I've lost someone I might have valued. Given time and . . . circumstance.

I sigh. Aside from that tasty bit from Aaron, it's been a sad day. At my order to get everyone in the house out of town ASAP, Aaron finally booked everyone—except Abe and BEN—on a flight out of National tomorrow morning to San Antonio, destined for the Rocking O with Sadie. But no one's happy. Jordan fought with me when she learned she was going, demanding to stay to support the twins at their father's funeral. Only the fact that Zack is going to the ranch, too, mollified her. Ming, who has classes and who would have to have been hog-tied to get her on a plane with my mother, left an hour ago to go to Reiko's to stay. Sadie, too, at first argued with me like a bobcat. She wouldn't budge going home so soon until I ushered her into my bedroom, closed the door, and told her about the Eagle Eyes dudes, what I know about Goodwin's murder—and how I fear further invasions because of what I know . . . and what I don't. A Texas rancher who understands protecting her own, Sadie immediately asked me where my SIG-Sauer was—and warned me to keep it with me wherever I can. During our conversation, I watched her flexing her fingers, itching to plug anyone who'd come near her family.

"Let me stay with you, Carly. I can call Butch, have him pick up the kids at the airport in San Antonio—and they'll be safe as being with an angel. Besides, you give me any gun, sugar pie; I do not need my brace of Colts to shoot the fat out of a hot dog."

I'd smiled, thanked her, and told her I wanted her with the young people. And she accepted my need for her to go.

So now here I am, trying to look like a lady who's happy to be going to a dance where she not only has her mother as her date—but who has to charm the director of this hospital and HMO group to reveal info about his staff and his operations.

"Knock, knock!" I hear her at my bedroom door.

"Come in," I call to her, and go to my closet to find my shoes.

"Carly O'Neill," she breathes as she appears in my doorway. "You are a picture."

I seek out my gold sling-back stilettos. "Ma. I look like I'm on death's door!"

"Now, that is not true, Madam Congresswoman. You're a little peaked, but you have some character to you. Who wants to be a twenty-year-old doll? You are the real McCoy. With breasts and legs and a brain. A working woman." She makes a spinning motion with her hand.

I twirl in my closet, arms out for her to see my attire. "If I can stay awake tonight to bring that title home, Ma, I will try."

"Love the dress." She arches both brows. "Who's it for?"

"Me!" I brush the material over my hips, where it cascades into a waterfall of royal purple silk to a tea-length handkerchief hemline. The halter top fits me like skin—and I have the cleavage, the arms, and the waist to do the dress proud. "I can really cut a rug in this if I find a man without two left feet."

She smacks her lips. "In that, my girl, they'll ask you to do more than dance."

I grin. "Like I know anyone I'd accept!"

"Still"—she drops her voice a serious octave—"you need a man, Carly."

"For what?" *Kissing? I tried that this past week, and it died along with Goodwin.* I hunt for my gold purse among others on my closet shelves.

"One thing, primarily," she informs me.

I peer out at her a second. "Yeah, well, for that they make vibrators."

"Do you own one?" she asks, flat as a pancake.

"No." *Should I buy one? Nah. Fake is as fake does.*

"Hence, my point. One day, you will need a man. For more than one thing. Perspective. A shoulder to cry on. In private, of course," she replies.

"Of course." I dismiss her idea.

"But forget about it for now. I am just dying to meet the vice president. Shake a leg, there!" She's tilting her head toward the door.

"Okay. Keep your pants on!" I find my lip gloss, my license, ID, the two tickets, and my car keys. Grabbing off the hanger the ivory mink jacket my first husband, Frank, had given me for our first anniversary, I grin at my mother, who herself looks tantalizing in bright Texas red. "Let's party!"

The Willard Hotel is one of the grand dames of Old Washington City. Built in the 1850s and renewed and refurbished in the 1980s, the huge alabaster hotel and its newer components sit at the corner of Pennsylvania as it turns briefly north at the Treasury Building and westward toward the White House.

Tonight, I step out of the Tahoe, give the keys to the valet, and walk up the red carpet into the marble-tiled foyer and along Peacock Alley toward the ballroom where the dinner dance will be.

Cocktails—a ritual in a town where talk is either worth its weight in gold or a plug nickel—are the order of the hour. Sadie and I enter the ballroom, endure the Secret Service security check because the vice president will be here, and within a minute we are no longer alone. Sadie obviously called one of her friends here in town—and made arrangements to meet him here.

"Not to worry about me," she confides to me as the secretary of agriculture, one of our Texas friends, offers her his arm. We make small talk and then I see her hone in on him, chewing his ear about the drought and immigration issues. Before he leads her away to meet another guest, she tells me, "I think there's a couple over there you need to visit with. By the wall, in the green chiffon."

Lo and behold, in a flowing green chiffon gown that lights up her platinum blond hair and cornflower blue eyes, is Norreen Bunting on the arm of her husband, Henry. Norreen is a mix of anomalies. Once a professor of political science at a small college in Kentucky, she is now in her late forties and retains a lithe, youthful appearance that belies her age and brainy profession.

I make my way over. "Good evening," I greet Henry, and he shocks me to my toes when he pecks me on the cheek. "How are you?"

"Good, thanks to you." He smiles wholeheartedly. "Meet my wife." And as he does the introductions, I understand how Norreen preserves herself. She doesn't waste emotion on people she doesn't know.

"Wonderful to know you, Norreen," I begin, my hand still holding hers from our handshake. Her flesh is chilly. Her regard, arctic. But I've met colder fish than this, so I remain at small-talk level. "Have you had an opportunity to look at the auction items?" Along one wall are instant prizes that will go to the highest bidder for hundreds or thousands of dollars, while even costlier items—like a week in the Bahamas—are priced into six figures.

"Not yet," she tells me. "I tell Henry he must be so careful what he bids on. This may be charity, but you know, we never want to be winning anything that any of our constituents would consider improper."

I smile. If office-holders win something at such an event as this that is against campaign or ethics rules, they usually cut a check and turn over the item to a nonprofit and sidestep any violations.

Henry purses his lips. "Norreen, there's no need to bring up such an issue."

"I want to be certain, Henry," she fires back in such a way that I assume I am listening to a sidebar of a marital squabble.

"Yes, well, we should be checking a lot of things," he responds under his breath, "shouldn't we?"

The awkward silence that stretches before us roots me to the floor and when I get nothing more on this subject, I shift for propriety's sake to a different one that interests me. "Tell me, Norreen, how is Sherry?"

Norreen stiffens, as if this is a sacred subject and I have intruded on her privacy. "She's well."

The silence again leads Henry to fill in. "We have restricted her to her room after the other night's events."

Norreen adds, "She'll be going away to a dude ranch for the summer." Her announcement sounds like an accusation. But why I should be blamed for Sherry's infringements and her exile eludes me.

"In Texas, as a matter of fact," Henry fills in. "Bandera. You know it?"

"I do, very well. Bandera is just north of my district line. But I thought Sherry was going to go to a summer day camp here in the Washington area. Was I mistaken?"

"No," Henry tells me, "you weren't. I decided it would be a good idea to get her outdoors each day, rather than sitting inside at a computer camp in Frederick for six weeks."

Computer camp? In Frederick? Did Jordan tell me Sherry was going to do that this summer? If she did, I couldn't recall. "But it does sound like more fun to learn how to ride a horse and team-rope a heifer than wrestle a computer to the ground!"

Henry laughs. "I sure think so, but Norreen is not convinced."

"Sherry loves computers," Norreen announces in what is, I note, a full-blown snit.

"Too much!" Henry retorts. "We'll get it out of her yet." He bends nearer to me and under his breath says, "I was determined to make her forget all she's been through."

Norreen huffs. "Henry, please. Like you could. She's a young woman."

"Hell she is, Norreen. She's a kid and she made a kid's mistake."

Norreen bristles, her face hard with anger. "I disagree, Henry. I vehemently disagree." And her cornflower blue eyes turn on me and vehemently encourage me to scram.

But I can't until I ask her to confirm the issue that confounds me. "I'm interested, Norreen, in how you recommended this gaming group to Marie Deeds."

"They were referred to us," she tells me.

"Referred?" Henry declares. "You said you knew this Victoria Enrici."

I have to hear her say something definitive on this. "Where did you meet her?" I persist, and she blinks. "How?"

"Oh, innocently enough," Norreen confirms—and her choice of words intrigues me. "Vickie was in two of my classes in undergraduate political science."

At her admission, my insides crawl. "In Kentucky?"

"Yes, yes, of course. She minored in poli-sci—and I always said it should have been her major. She's articulate and should work on the Hill."

Looking at his wife like she's sprouted three heads, Henry hoots in laughter. "The hell she could. Girl's got the personality of a flea."

Truer words were never spoken.

"Did you meet her?" Henry asks me, and his brows knit a fraction, as if he truly seeks my opinion—and I wonder why.

"Briefly. She's very reserved," I answer him. "Did you like her?" *Interview her? Tear her a new one for helping your daughter sell pictures and potions?*

"No, I absolutely did not," he tells me.

Norreen inhales. "You didn't give her a chance, Henry."

He smiles tightly at me. "You can see we have different ways of looking at the girl."

I can see you two have more problems than a difference of opinion on Vickie Enrici, or whatever her real name is.

My mother floats into view and our topic has died an aborted death. Taking what I can from the conversation, I introduce Sadie around and she tugs at my elbow. "Shall we sit down, Carly? Time for dinner."

Wavering between joy or dismay at my mother's appearance, I excuse us both from the Buntings as I question their conflict as well as the contradictory information I have once more confirmed about Vickie Enrici's college education. So I go. I sit. I smile and greet others already at the table.

The Deedses, who were to have sat at this table, are of course not here. Poor Goodwin, from accounts I read in the papers, will be buried Saturday or Monday. Marie has not yet decided when and where the services will be. I feel ill, no appetite for food, let alone laughing or dancing. I slowly sip the table's sharp chardonnay—and pine for a stiff gin and tonic. My mother, bless her heart, carries the conversation. Then our last few arrive at the table: the director of the Metro Hospital Group, Dr. Donald Graves, and the honorary guests for tonight, Vice President Raymond Barr and his wife, Thea.

Gremlins must have arranged this table seating, because I sit sandwiched between the vice president and the director, both of whom have taken a good dose of Chatty Cathy pills. Dr. Graves, judging from his very close attention to my wineglass and my cleavage, is also very interested in wooing me. While I suppose I should be complimented by his attentions, I'm put off at his effusiveness—and encouraging him anyway because of what I need to learn about Trainor—and Marie. True, Marie Deeds had told me Graves wanted to meet me, but reason says my womanly charms hardly extend to men I have not yet met. And if Graves and Marie are somehow in cahoots over the blackmail of Gunther Halstead, I need to be kind here to learn it. That makes me so bewitched, bothered, and bewildered that by the time dessert rolls around, I need to escape to the ladies' room for a few moments of quiet contemplation of what I now know.

I'm pushing my chair back and making my excuses when Dr. Graves informs me he's signed us up for the dance contest. "I wrote us down without asking you. I hope you don't mind."

Not as long as you can talk while you dance. "What did you decide we'd do?"

"The cha-cha." He's pleased as a puppy with a new toy.

"That's wonderful!" I'm sizing him up for his looks, which I'd describe as blond, tall string bean. *Another pale Anglo fitting the description of the person Jordan saw run from the Deedses' house!* "I like the cha-cha," I reply with anxiety growing in me that I can induce him to get honest with me. "Are you good at it?"

"The best." He winks at me—and I smile weakly. On the dance floor, I'm known to suffer no fools. With legs that won me the title of Miss Texas years ago, I can still out-waltz, out-samba, out-tango half the men in all the ballrooms in all the world. I don't grope for form and I don't lack for rhythm: A man's gotta have both with me—or I wind up making him look like a mop. With very few men would I ever be so unkind as to clean the floor, and, in this case, the director—especially if he's guilty of theft, blackmail, and murder—is not one I wish to make look like a fool.

So as the orchestra takes up their instruments and the announcer begins his intro, I decide to pour on the charm—and no better way to entice a man than to ask him to talk about himself. "Tell me about how you came to Metro, Doctor. I understand you hail from Minnesota."

He begins a monologue that I am saved from by the start of the first dance, which is, thank you, god, the cha-cha. As we move to the floor and begin, I figure unless I want to spend the entire evening with him, I better get a move on to discuss Marie, when, lo and behold, he opens the subject himself.

"Have you known her long?" I get to ask when I realize his skill at this dance is of the high school variety where we're going to do a few turns and that's it.

"She was in place when I came on board. Nice lady. Sad what happened there." We do a turn and he asks, "You must've been very upset for your daughter."

I nod. "And for Goodwin." We do another spin. "Did you know him well?"

"No, no. Not really." Graves lets that topic die.

"Marie, is she competent?" I press.

"Enough. Why do you ask?" He's growing miffed at this topic.

I'll lose him entirely if I don't probe now. "There have been a few patients' records missing, I hear." Now, this is a slight variation on the truth, but I don't want to show my whole hand. "Does Marie enforce tight security with records?"

He's losing what little grace he started with as he frowns at me. We turn in unison and spin when he asks, "How do you know this?"

I arch both brows to appear, one hopes, secretive and seductive at the same time. "Sources. We have all kinds of sources."

"Like the FBI?"

"Among others," I wheedle.

"You've heard from others"—his voice deepens in alarm—"that our records have been tampered with? Who said this? The FBI?"

"I can't reveal that, Dr. Graves." The number, praise my stars, is coming to an end.

He has a hand on my elbow and his fingers dig in as we come to a stop. "The D.C. Police? Is that who it is? They're investigating this murder, aren't they?"

"They are."

"Have they said things to you about the Hospital Group?" He doesn't wait for an answer but rolls his eyes over the ballroom. "They have. Oh, Christ. I wanted to get ahead of the police and the press on this. Come over here with me." He leads us toward a bartenders' station. "When did they talk with you about this?" He looks weepy, whipped.

"They didn't. Not really." I have to be honest, don't I, because I don't have anything more to torment him with.

"But I don't understand," Graves says.

"I didn't mean to upset you," I offer, but I'm thrilled I did.

The MC announces the finalists in the last dance and we are not among them.

Wanting to make my getaway, I give Graves a watery smile. "Perhaps we need more practice another time." *Hell, Carly, what are you saying? You want to dance again with him like a rattler wants to go 'round with a jaguar.*

"But first," says a mellow bass voice to my right, "you promised me the next dance."

And I find myself looking up into the electric eyes of the creature standing in front of me, grinning at me like a long-lost cousin. Jones.

"Hi, there, ma'am," he greets me with a drawl as if he were from Texas, not Baltimore, Maryland. Damn if he isn't dressed like he just stepped out of *GQ,* too. Black tux, fat onyx studs, formal shirt, starched to kingdom come, white, and showing up his tan and his pecs. Slacks, fitting those hips and thighs like he'd been melted down and poured into them. And he's spruced himself up in other ways. His thick dark hair is trimmed even more than the other night when I saw him on the Mall. Now it's clipped tight to the sides and slicked back with gel, framing a face that could launch a thousand ships—and charm the gloss off your lipstick. "Saw you across a crowded room." He grins. "You look good, too, ma'am." He is faster on the draw with compliments than I am. "'S'cuze us, will you, sir?"

Graves, concerned as he is for his company, leans forward and says to me, "Later, we'll talk later, yes?"

"Of course," I agree, but don't mean to.

"Do you know this man?" Graves asks, his gaze narrowing on Jones.

"Absolutely." Jones smiles, extends his arm to me. "You surely do remember me, ma'am. Doc Winthrup's the name. We met a while back at—"

"Another big event," I supply, looping my arm through his, grinning all over myself like a coed who's been rescued by the snazzy quarterback. "Yes, indeed, Doc."

"Winthrup . . ." Graves scowls. "I don't recall you on the invitation list."

Jones smiles like he has all day to chew the rag with this guy. "I assure you I had one," Jones declares in a tone that brooks no argument, and leads us away.

"That was helpful," I praise Jones as we're walking out to the dance floor.

"Rescuing damsels from distress is my specialty." He grins, wide as the Texas plains, patting my hand like a sugar daddy.

I am snickering, can't help myself. "Want to tell me how you really got in here?"

"Why, same as you," he says, eyes twinkling like little stars, and enticing as moonshine on Saturday. "I got an invite."

"From whom?" I chuckle.

He turns me to him, wrapping his arm around my waist and taking my hand for the start of a new number. "My client."

Right. That makes me want to stomp on his foot. "He thought you should be here to see what's happening?"

"More than that. He sent me to share information—and protect you."

Can I believe my ears? "Kind of him. Do you charge him extra?"

"No. This is a courtesy call." The orchestra goes into a little medley.

"Don't strain yourself. I'm a big girl—and not much can happen to me here." I offer this with more bravura than confidence, Donald Graves notwithstanding.

"No? From what I just saw, you were going to either make him cry or he was going to make you cry if you had to dance with him again."

"You do speak truth to power," I admit.

He grins and says, "I'm here to speak more truth to you." His eyes circle the room and then he smiles down on me, like . . . I shift in my skin . . . a beau. "There are things we need to share."

Really? "I'm dog-tired of you giving me the runaround. I need to find out who killed Deeds. And I'm angry enough with you to spit. The audio you attached to my hall phone—"

"Was necessary." He grimaces. "I can explain. Meanwhile, look enchanted with me, will you? This number is a waltz. You do waltz?"

"Yes." I bark in laughter at the absurdity of a black ops dude who climbs walls, possesses techie toys, sinks spyware—and waltzes. "Look, Jones—"

"Kermit," he corrects me.

I am pained to hear it. "As in *green* and *frog?*"

"As in Winthrup and Doctor."

"Of *what?*" I ask as he pushes us off in a Viennese waltz.

Jones doesn't look at me, but instead at where we're both going. "Plastic surgery. My expertise is facial reconstruction."

I narrow my gaze, my brain working overtime to weigh this tasty bit of info. "More like because you've had it than done it."

But as he circles us around the floor, the big fact hits me, damn my eyes, that we're as smooth together as molasses and July. And as we pass the sea of guests, I catch a glimpse of our effect on those who are not dancing. Admiration. Even on Sadie's face.

On a turn, I ask him, "Who teaches a security guy from Baltimore to waltz?"

"I could say the CIA."

I snort. "Where did I miss *that* little line item?"

"Off the books, for sure." He's grinning and I'm matching him as he directs us expertly. "No, really, my mother taught me. In the kitchen."

"My daddy was my teacher. Same place." We do a few steps and I have to put two and two together. "Did you just choose to become a plastic surgeon for this evening?"

"Not just for tonight. It's one of my covers we created for me a long time ago." He grins, beguiling as his finesse on the floor. Meanwhile, I note he said *one* of his covers. "I know a lot about plastics, not because I ever needed it . . ."—he whirls me around in perfect step—"on my face."

Well, hell, honey, I doubt there's anything else anyone would ever decide needs fixin' on you. I clear my throat. "What, then?"

"My hands."

We go around and I catch my breath. "Pardon me?"

"I've had my fingerprints done."

Now I really am chortling. "You've had your fingerprints changed?"

He winces. "Pipe down. Sure," he acknowledges, light as bubbles. "Doesn't everyone?"

I nod a few times, listing the ramifications of that. "Then how does your employer really know you are you?"

He leads us in reverse rounds now. "Retina scans."

"Ah." I shrug mentally, because the man is keeping me busy churning up my brain. "I think I'm getting dizzy."

"Take it easy," he croons, and for a few more circles, we are going just fine, others being disqualified and moving off the floor so that only four couples remain.

As we swirl past, I catch sight of a very pissed Graves—and a curious Chad Elliott—and I stiffen up.

"Loosen up. Enjoy this. You can. We're not nuzzling each other. Your reputation is in good hands," he offers as he navigates a good turn and takes me with him in a rhythm that I admit I have rarely enjoyed with a man. "Tomorrow the Post'll sizzle with tales of the Texas gal who can cut a rug."

"Even if she finds dead men wherever she goes?"

"Now, now. Bad luck should not make you cynical."

"It makes me lose sleep, gets me a house full of kids and robots, gains me my mother on my doorstep with her chili pot in hand. Why not cynical?"

"Tut-tut, my dear," he whispers in my ear as we come to a graceful stop—and the audience applauds us, the last couple left dancing. "We're done, we've won—curtsy—good, and I will bow. Come with me as I pull out my checkbook to pay for the privilege of showing you off."

I enjoy the sight of Jones signing a check as Kermit Winthrup, M.D., for five thousand big ones to the Metro Hospital Hospice Fund for the Homeless. As he inserts his checkbook inside his jacket pocket, he takes my arm once more and says, "Time to work. Direct your glass slippers over to your table and introduce me."

"You're coming with me to the table? *Why?*" Stick a fork in me, I'm that astonished.

"I want to meet them," he supplies, as if it were the most natural thing in the world to present yourself to half the known Washington world as a fake physician.

"You want to meet *which one?*"

"All." He puts a hand to my bare back, propelling me forward like a gentleman.

"And by which name might I introduce you?"

"Dr. Kermit G. Winthrup. Johns Hopkins. Geneva Clinic of Rejuvenation. I've got a reputation—now, now, no laughing. I've authored many AMA articles on the psychological benefits of plastic surgery for those over sixty." He grins while the band strikes up another tune, this time a samba. "Introduce me." He tips his head toward our table. "Let's get to it."

The cluster we approach first are the vice president and Henry, who pause as Jones, shock me to my bones, puts out a hand to Vice President Barr. "Hello, sir," he says with warmth, "how are you?"

Raymond Barr grins like he's welcoming a prodigal son. "Terrific. How are *you,* Dr. Winthrup?"

"Good, sir."

I'd be speechless if my curiosity would die. "You two know each other?"

The doc smiles, and the vice president matches him. "Yes, of course," they say in unison.

"Doc Winthrup fixed my profile, didn't you?" the vice president tells us with a slap on the back to the man in question.

So, I'm thinking here: The only way the veep had a little help from my friend is if the number two honcho needed security work. Jones, aka Winthrup, may have skills doing so-called profiles with a knife—but they'd be in the arts of terminating, not tucking.

"I did. I did," Jones says with a blush of humility. "Good to see you again, sir."

"And you know Carly, I see," the vice president declares, and asks, "Well?"

I arch a brow. "We became acquainted a few months ago," I inform him, licking my chops over the possibility—the outlandish possibility—that the vice president hired Jones to protect me. How could that be? *And why? He's the opposition, for god's sake.*

"Well, glad to hear it. He's a good man to know, Carly."

I smile. *Depends.* I watch then as the vice president introduces Jones to Henry. Here I see no hint of any recognition. No suggestion that Jones knows Henry, who admittedly knows Jones's friend Brad Wilson. And after we all exchange polite conversation for a few minutes, Jones and I are alone again.

"Well, that was interesting," I announce. "Anyone else in the room who might know your talents as a surgeon?"

"No. Just the vice president."

"That was enough. So what happened to 'I don't know my clients,' and the other tempting possibility that he may have hired you to help me with Alistair's murder?"

"Shhh. That would be revolutionary, don't you think? What reason has he got to save your hide?"

I scoff at that. "What reason does anyone have?"

"I do."

"And what might that be? Aside from your client is paying you. Again."

Jones is steering me toward the edge of the room, where my steam might not singe anyone. He says between gritted teeth, "I call saving you enlightened self-interest."

"You can call it anything you want, but when it comes to helping me find mur—" I lower my voice. "You get me."

"Yeah. Don't I," he complains. "We can duke this out later. Right now, tell me who that guy is over there."

"Where?" I see a lot of folks I know.

"Careful, don't go looking just yet. The little roly-poly guy standing against the column in the white dinner jacket. He looks like a vanilla drop. He's had his eyes on you all the time we've been talking."

I make a bit of nonsensical small talk, then turn to find the man Jones refers to. "Chad Elliott. Louise Rawlings's campaign director."

"Friend or foe?" he asks as he turns to nod at someone across the room, feigning a light conversation with me.

"Right this minute, he's my nemesis. Wants me to—" I stop, realizing I'm about to share info with Jones that is personal, political, and relates to this murder case, even in a tangential way. Do I trust him to tell him this? I play with my diamond necklace.

Jones gazes down at me, concern in his face and tone. "Wants you to what?"

"Figure out who killed the judge."

"Why?" Jones's eyes narrow on Chad like pinpoint little X-rays.

"Because he's a twerp. No, no." I inhale and try to look social, happy to be here. "Because it's an ultimatum. He thinks he can cut me off from Lou if I don't . . . ah . . ."

"What?"

I smile ironically, tragically. "If I don't change my profile."

Jones grins like there's no tomorrow. Then takes my hand and loops it through his arm. "I'm great at profiling."

I guffaw. "Doc, I wish I could avail myself of your services!"

"Congresswoman Wagner, ma'am. That's why I'm here. So let's go share a few facts, shall we?"

My eyes say no. "Not here. Too open. Others might overhear. Besides, my mother came with me and I can't just leave her here. Best to save it for later."

"No need." He presses something square and cold into my palm. "I got a room."

"Ohhhh, no." I'm not waltzing into a hotel room with a man unless it's . . .

"To talk. Only. I scoped it out. End of the corridor, recessed doorway. Take the service stairs to five. No house cameras can track you or me going in or out. You're safe with me."

I gaze into his electric eyes. There, inside, is the man. Professional. Earnest. Dare I say honorable?

Who do you trust, Carly?

Every day in every way, it is I who trust myself. That's how I got here. How I stay here. How I look myself in the mirror each morning.

I finger the key. "What's the room number?"

fourteen

The room is posh. The man . . . just as. The smooth talk should be even better.

"Wine?" he lets himself in, a bottle cradled in his arm as he closes and double-locks the door.

"I'm not here to drink." *Do I give in to suspicion, since he's brought alcohol?*

"You weren't doing it downstairs, either," he jokes. "You hate chard—" He offers one of those little factoids he knows about me that I can never seem to trace to anything that's written down anywhere. "And I don't blame you. That swill they served downstairs was shameful, for what they charged per ticket for this soiree." He goes to the bar, corkscrew in hand, working down, down, down on a bottle of . . .

"Bordeaux," he informs me as he pours. "Château Gruaud-Larose, 1978. From the bar." He turns and walks forward to place one glass in my outstretched hand. "It's the best I found on their list. Shocked I know wine? Don't be. I know a lot of things you can't imagine."

I accept the glass. "Amen to that."

"Try it. It's one of the few you can drink without food—and not fall over. I figured you wouldn't let me feed you—although I must say, you need some sustenance. You look—"

"Like hell."

"Starved," he corrects me.

"For answers. For answers, Jones." I sip and close my eyes, savoring the silken red going down my throat. I open my eyes to find him watching me, a fondness in his face I'd say was somewhere between concern and admiration. I turn away. Find a chair.

"You start," I instruct him when I've had another sip and gotten a slower pulse. "After all, you owe me an apology, followed closely by the reason for bugging me."

He smiles sadly, comes forward to stand in front of me. "I wasn't just doing you a favor Friday night bringing Jordan home. I billed it that way, but I was also motivated by fear for both of you. I had no idea what Jordan knew about this case—and to learn, I planted the bug. I knew I could use our friendship—" At his word my brows fly high. "Okay, our relationship—"

"Hardly more definitive—"

"The hell it isn't," he bites off, and I bristle. "Call it whatever you want, you know we can work together or you wouldn't have asked me to help you last Saturday night. And last Sunday. And Tuesday night."

I put up a hand. "Agreed. Get to it, Jones."

"For over a month I've been on a team investigating leaks of personal data from different locales around the country. The crimes were so diffused, we didn't at first think they were connected. We couldn't find the source. We couldn't find a pattern. We had reports that many types of private data were missing, misused, or appropriated. Some data was the property of federal government agencies. Some came from private corporations, banks, investment houses. But once my team and I were hired—"

"Brad Wilson?"

Jones takes a drink, rolls it around his tongue a second to sample it, and shakes his head. "No. Brad's not with me on this."

"Is that right? Well, I've learned that Wilson works for Howard and Roth."

Jones purses his lips. "No wonder you haven't had any sleep."

I ignore him and murmur, "Do you work for Howard and Roth?"

"No. Wilson and I are with different companies. But on this job, I gather, we've got different clients, all with mutual interests," Jones confirms.

That makes sense to me, since I have information that seems scattered and unrelated. "Have you found anything that does make sense?"

"Only the MO is the same. A missing piece of hardware. Laptops. Along with that, a missing computer tech from an Army base, a bank, or whatever. The computer tech would just disappear, too. We now think they change identities after they take off with the data. They change them often so that they can't be tracked easily by credit card purchases or driver's licenses."

"And what do they use this data for? To buy things? To use other people's credit and then vanish?"

"At first we suspected that. It's the usual reason for identity theft. Then, later, because most data was all military personnel info, we thought it might be a slow leak meant to drain sensitive defense data, arms, troop allotments, deployment schedules, and the like. But we don't see that kind of intel popping up in foreign hands."

"What *do* you think it is?"

He rolls his shoulders, takes another drink, and sits on the arm of the chair opposite me. "Still not sure."

That makes me wonder about the Halstead issue, but before I go there, give away a politically sensitive issue, I need groundwork— and I ask a more pertinent question for me. "Why did you go to the gaming party Friday night?"

"We saw some stolen data coming out of this gaming group and we weren't certain precisely who it was coming from. We had ideas, but no proof." He stares at me, and I know I won't like this next. "We had to determine who our primaries were."

"And who were they?"

"Quite a few in that gaming group. Five living in Frederick."

Five in Frederick. What had Jordan said? There were gamesters from Frederick who disrupted other youths' games by adding spam and cheating. *How does that relate to a missing Army laptop that turns up, days later, in Frederick—and Halstead's rehab in Frederick?* Coincidences or not? I hold my breath—and wonder why Jones, who was focused on five in Frederick, would turn to hone in on Jordan. I go back to his train of thought and his so-called primaries. "Who were the others you suspected?"

He frowns into his glass, then locks eyes with me. "Sherry Bunting and the Deeds twins."

Not Jordan?

He takes a hearty swallow. "When I saw Jordan at this party Friday night, I got alarmed. But then I saw who she was with."

Oh, that I did not want to hear. "And that's when you decided to bring her home to me—and plant the bug."

"To protect you both."

He's so adamant—again—that I am convinced of his devotion to Jordan's and my welfare. "So here the ends justify the means?"

"In this case, yes."

I dismiss it with a hand, daring not debate a subject that I myself must resolve for my own good conscience. "Did your friends do the same in the Deedses' home and the Buntings'?"

"Wilson sank one, yes. But our colleague who took the Deeds twins home never got the opportunity. He was ushered in, kept in the front hall, and never near furniture. The only info we could capture was from tangential phone taps like the judge's clerk. And those gave us zip."

"Sad, too," I add, "because if you'd been successful, you might have heard what occurred in the house the night Goodwin died. Or at least who came in the door."

"And who came in the kitchen door, too. The audio is very sensitive. Picks up any vibration of sound within a forty-foot radius. We can translate the drop of a pin. Whispering." He smiles. "Even kissing."

Am I blushing? "Must be very entertaining."

His electric eyes go neon. "Helps on the slow days."

I take another drink of his wine and put it aside. "What did you learn from the bug that Wilson planted in the Buntings' home?"

"A lot of arguing. The Buntings are headed for divorce, if you ask me."

I look him square in the eye. "Why?"

"Evidently Henry thinks she lies. Often. To him. Bad joss."

I agree. "Nothing more?"

"Lots of accusations about not being a good mother to Sherry. Why?"

"Did you or Wilson do a background check on Norreen?" When he says no, I tell him he should. And when he asks why, I say, "Because she knows Enrici, one of the gaming organizers. And I am not clear how she knows her. Not yet."

"Not *yet?*" Jones gets his dander up. "Ma'am—"

"I'm pursuing what leads I can."

He exhales. "You can be very trying."

"Makes two of us, then," I tell him, and go to the subject I want more on. "So you have numerous breaches of security at multiple military facilities nationwide?"

He nods. "And banks, universities, a long list."

"Okay." I go on. "You have a group of people who change identities and use new ID cover to steal more identities. You have some trail that leads you to Frederick, Maryland, and a group of gamesters who can do what?"

"Hack information from those children who play the games. But they don't do it online. Or so far we can't find evidence of how they trail in."

"Meaning what?"

"They don't access the children's computers from the Internet.

They don't use worms or bugs to mess with the childrens' computers."

I raise a finger. "Worms or bugs?"

"Worms that lock up a hard drive or bugs that eat computer bytes like—"

"A shark." *Or how about an eagle?*

"Exactly," he says, falling silent and swiftly attuned to my alarm. *"What?"*

I'm anxious to have this over and done. *It's time, Carly, for all good girls to bring what they can to this party.* I rise. Walk around the room.

Jones suddenly stands before me, offering me a cigarette he's lit.

I take it, inhale like a junkie, and turn to pace. "I know a lot that might be useful to you. Then again, it might not. I'll tell you everything. See if it makes sense." I take a drag, enjoying the rush from the nicotine . . . and not enjoying the dizzy wave that rolls over me. I steady myself and go on.

"When you brought the four of them home Friday night, I felt there was something you were tracking and I knew it was nothing small or insignificant. I couldn't get Jordan to open up. But I knew she was hiding something. Then, after she found Goodwin dead Saturday night, she panicked and told me and Sam that Sherry was a wiccan and she was selling pictures of herself and potions. Jordan said it was all harmless, but I knew that if someone wanted to make political capital out of it, they could embarrass Henry Bunting with his daughter's activities."

"But there were other things Jordan was keeping secret," Jones points out.

"Yes, things I didn't know. Such as . . . the fact that she saw someone leave the Deedses' house Saturday night just before she went over and then discovered Goodwin dead. She was afraid to say who it was, for fear—"

"For fear it was someone she knew," he provides. "I heard her tell McGinty and Sullivan that yesterday." He lifts his brows. "The transmission was all good."

"I guess so. Anyway, you heard her. She thought it might have been Nicholas. Only because the person she saw leave was tall, thin, and blond. And let me tell you"—I run a hand through my hair and exhale—"everyone I meet these days fits that description."

"What else?"

"The Deedses were having marital problems."

"Got that. And?"

"Marie wanted a divorce."

He crosses his arms. "I know that, too."

"She works for Dr. Graves, downstairs." I tip my head toward the door. "An okay guy, except when you talk to him about his patient data security."

Jones straightens, uncrosses his arms. *And is he alarmed?* "Why would you?"

"I've learned about a certain psychiatrist who folded his practice in Metro's group health service a few years ago and one of that doctor's patients is now a very high-profile government official." I watch Jones carefully. "This official is soon to have—if all goes well and he survives a blackmail attempt—a much higher government position."

Jones stares ahead, thinking so hard I can see smoke coming from his ears.

Why? I take a step toward him. "Does this ring a bell?" *Is the Halstead leak your case? Is Chad Elliott—or my party—your client?*

"Go on."

I sigh at his intransigence. "I asked Graves about it while we were dancing and he got all hot under the collar. That's when you stepped up and whisked me away."

Jones is cooking a new idea, his eyes X-rays into space. "So that means," he says, still ignoring my question, "Graves is either damn sensitive about his data's security or he's got something to hide." He falls silent. "What about Marie? Marie would know if

Graves were doing something shady. She's in charge of the records." He shakes his head. "I think she's smart, but not creative enough to work this theft."

Oh, I do agree. "But how is Graves connected to this Frederick group? That seems far-fetched to me."

His features fall to gloom and doom. "How far-fetched would it be if I told you he was the second person in the front door to see Deeds Saturday night?"

Now, that is news. I stub out my cigarette in a nearby ashtray and rub my arms at the creepy thought. "And I danced with this guy."

"The first one who visited was Turner—who, from a reliable source, went right home. But Graves's face—I couldn't place him. None of my team could. I recognized him here when I saw him dancing with you."

I ponder a minute. "So you think Graves would have known Deeds was alone in the house so he took the opportunity to go back and kill him?"

"Maybe. But why go around back?"

"He wouldn't know if the back door was open." *Who would?* I ask myself. *Only someone who had gone in and out of it before . . . regularly. The twins or Jordan or Marie . . . or Norreen.*

Jones adds, "Why not just stay and finish the job?"

"Right," I say, foiled. "Plus, Graves wouldn't have known you were taping the front door."

"Try the whole block."

"You mean—*us, too*?"

Jones exhales. "I told you I was trying to protect you both."

Not happy with that revelation despite the motivation, I'm more disturbed by Jones's logic. I walk forward. "So be it. If Graves killed Deeds, what's his motive? He doesn't kill Goodwin because he figures Marie has been siphoning info and selling it. That's misdirected."

"He kills him because . . . ?"

We stare at each other, stumped.

I put a hand to my mouth. Go back to basics. "Look at how he was killed. The room was a mess. The PCs—all four of them—trashed. Not the gaming consoles. The killer doesn't care about those because he's looking for something."

"Data on the PCs," Jones whispers.

"That's why he slashed Goodwin's hand to get the computer access out. Goodwin's cleaning his hard drives—and pops a disk in his mouth when he can't finish deleting files. Goodwin wouldn't give him what he wanted, so the killer attacks him. He's angry. Needs access himself. *Why?*"

"Because he wants to access data," Jones supplies.

"Or cover his tracks," I add.

"Or remove something himself?" Jones asks.

"And meanwhile Goodwin has stayed home while the rest of his family has gone to the beach. He's cleaning the hard drives—and this disk. That could only mean Goodwin was hiding something. . . ."

Jones is pacing, too, now. "Something he saw—something he feared would . . . incriminate someone."

"So who knows he's home alone?" I ask my partner in crime detection.

"Marie and the kids."

"Did you check their cell phone records?" I ask him.

"No. Never saw the need." He shakes his head. "I will now."

I put my head in my hands. Rub my temples. "That gives us rationale for the scene, but no solid suspect."

"I'd say my job is to find if any link exists from Marie to the Frederick five—and the missing data about Halstead."

At the name, I beam. "So you do know about him?"

Jones grins. "Why, ma'am, I always know what the mission is, even if—"

I chuckle. "Even if you never know your client." But my thoughts turn dark. "How are you going to look for this connection among them?"

"I'll start by going to the next gaming event."

"Tomorrow night?" I ask, and when he nods, I tell him, "I'm going with you."

He gets his stern-daddy look to him. "No. You cannot come."

"But they know you!"

"With more hair and wire glasses."

"Right, so if you arrived dressed like a hood and with your old lady in tow, they wouldn't remember you as part of a couple." I sidle up to him and bat my lashes. "I'm very good at snooping. You know I am."

"I'll think about it." He stands aside. "Right now you better get out of here before someone suspects you've been gone too long to just powder your nose."

"And you?" I turn at the door.

"I have work to do."

I frown. "I can't call you."

He's pained. "Yeah. I'll get you a new phone—"

"With an on-off switch."

"Check. Just promise me not to throw it away, okay? They're expensive."

I look nonplussed. "Don't you just put it on the client's tab?"

He puts a hand over his heart. "But I feel bad. And I have to explain, too, you know."

"Even 1978 bottles of Bordeaux?"

"Some things you do for yourself. I'll call you with details about tomorrow night. Now get out of here." When I balk at his tone, he adds, "Please. Ma'am."

I turn the knob, careful to make no sound, and peek out the doorway, then slither around the frame and push wide the door to the service stairs. Picking up my skirts, I rush down to the first floor and push open the double doors to head toward the ladies' room.

I get inside and take a gander at my reflection. Wonderful to look flushed with red wine, good conversation, and a degree of success with Mr. Tight Lips himself. I do my ablutions, then come to stand before the mirror and apply a new coat of lipstick.

Taking a comb from my purse, I begin a repair job on my hair when Norreen Bunting sails through the door. Seeing me, she halts in front of me a moment and heads for a stall. Suddenly she's back, smiling at me as if she were gravy on biscuits. "I've not been very appreciative to you, Carly." She drops her voice, but no one else is in the room except us chickens, so she's safe. "I am grateful for what you told Henry."

"I would hope for the same kind of help, had that been Jordan."

She puts her purse on the counter and washes her hands. And as she does, my eyes drift down to her hand, her wrist—where, peeking out just beneath her diamond cuff bracelet, is a scar. A botched attempt at removing a tattoo. Small. But still distinguishable. An eagle. In full cry.

I try not to stare. I smile and try to think. But all I get is one question: *What the hell is Norreen Bunting doing with a tattoo that is a miniature duplicate of Jim Wyatt's? And the business card of the Eagle Eyes guys who invaded my home?*

Where is Jones—or his phone—when I need him?

What can I do here anyway? Bluntly ask her what the tattoo is? Oh, right, and invite her to slug me? Hell, I'm not combat-ready. Mentally or physically. And I have no backup. So I smile as best I can.

"I should have said thank you in the beginning," Norreen explains. "And I am also grateful to you for keeping this matter of Sherry's private."

"You're welcome, Norreen." *Although when I tell my partner in crime about your tattoo and my suspicions, you may eat your words.* "Good night," I tell her, knowing for me it certainly has been.

fifteen

At our agreed rendezvous point——the parking lot surrounding the Rockville Metro stop——I wait only a few minutes on the sidewalk until I see a red Ford 4×4 pickup pull up and the profile of Jones in the cab. He rolls down the window and motions to me to hop in.

I'm grinning like a fool as I get in. "Thought you'd look like a Texan, huh?"

"Your idea of different attire was a good one, and I wanted to make the image complete." His own is what I'd call grunge with holey jeans and Marilyn Manson T-shirt, wraparound shades, and gelled spiked hair. He pulls out of the lot and we head toward the main drag, the Rockville Pike north. "You have the address of the gaming party?"

"The new convention center in Gaithersburg, east off the pike."

He glances over to check out my faded jeans and black polo. "You came dressed for this party, too."

"Sure. Even brought these along." I don a pair of horn-rims and vogue for him.

"Whoa. Ugly."

"Gee, thanks," I respond, proud of myself.

"How are you tonight?" he asks, eyes on the traffic. "Dizzy still?"

"Wow. They train you to notice everything," I complain. "I missed my appointment at the dentist last month, so tell me, how are my teeth?" I bare them for him.

He gives me a woeful glance. "No more butts for you."

He's right. They drive up my blood pressure. "I'll be fine with some sleep. And now that everyone in the house is gone to Texas, I feel better. After those computer geeks charmed their way into my house the other day, I'm nervous as a cat about anyone hurting my own."

"After this is over, I'll fix your house alarm system."

Do I want another favor from Jones? There's a topic to keep me busy in my off-hours. "I doubt anything'll help. The house is so old."

He turns to capture my eyes. "Trust me, I'll do the wiring myself."

I smile and change the subject. "Have a present for me now?"

He jerks his head toward the backseat. "Newest version. Put it in your purse."

I reach for it. This one does look a tad larger—and has a button, which I would assume is for on and off. I might want to contact Jones, but I certainly do not want him living my life along with me. "Thank you."

He shifts his gaze toward me again . . . and the two of us exchange silent questions about trust without any answers that seal the deal.

I break into the quiet, sharing with him details about Norreen, her apology, her tattoo, how it matched—were it still very visible—Wyatt's and the computer intruders'.

He listens, inscrutable until we pull into the parking lot of the center. More than four hundred people, mostly teenagers of all ages and younger ones more Jordan's age, are streaming in, smiling and eager to play. "You keep your purse and your phone on you at all times. What do you know about how to play games and bangs?"

"Pardon me?" I startle at the last word.

"Bangs is the term for group games. Comes from Korea, where they are huge. What's your IQ on games?"

"I've watched Jordan a bit. Aside from that, I'm a rube."

"Okay, stick with me, then. You're my fanster. Mine. Act like you support me. Clear? I'll do the talking—and the playing. You run for drinks and chips."

"Like a good wife. Will do."

"Okay." Jones pulls the keys from the ignition. "Let's rock."

We go inside, pay our fee, and hang out in the lobby. Marveling at how Jones's gait and demeanor have now become more Hells Angels than Special Ops, I notice that about two hundred teenagers register and pay their fees, then make their way to their assigned computers.

Jones and I do, too. And we sort of stick out because not more than ten of the players are adults. Our disguises are super—but they can't change our ages. Jones is assigned a personal computer about midway in front of the podium and massive plasma screen.

We settle in. The program opens with a rah-rah event that reminds me of my years on my high school cheerleading squad. And the hype, the yelling, is wild. These folks are itchin' to get started. And as they sit and many begin to do finger exercises to get their dexterity flowing, one organizer bounds to the stage. James Wyatt. Tonight, just like the other day, he's emoting like he's running for Mr. Personality. Onstage, his tall, blond good looks appear even more middle American. Lest he see me and know me, I sink in my seat behind Jones as I murmur to him that this is the guy I met the other day with Vickie.

Meanwhile, Wyatt does a little sis-boom-bah and says, "And just to show you how pleased we are you're here tonight, we've got a few presents for you. Let's do one round and I'll be back to tell you about it!"

A wild cheer goes up from the audience—and the games begin.

Jones starts and he's surprisingly good. Fast, dexterous—and

I'm wondering when the hell he has time to play games while he's working as a jack of all spooks. No, he doesn't win anything, but I'm absorbed in his abilities and how he stays in the game. About an hour into this, I am bored silly with playing step-and-fetch-it for Jones. I need a new diversion.

Heading for the ladies' room, I pass along the row and listen to the silence of utter concentration on the game by these children. I suspect their history teachers cannot rely on as much devotion to their subject. That's when I turn and see a tall, blond, willowy figure that I know well.

Near the far wall in crisp white polo and neatly pressed khakis with golf visor, hair up in a ponytail and wearing huge Jackie O sunglasses, is Norreen Bunting. She's pushing past the crowd of fansters at the back and moving toward . . . Enrici. When she gets next to her, she tells her something that looks like *Come with me.*

And Enrici refuses, hand out, indicating she has to stay here, do something, whatever.

But Norreen's insisting and the two of them head for the side door and the promenade to the parking lot.

I am pushing my way through to follow them, but I've got a quarter of the room to cover. I duck out the first side door I come to and run down the empty hall toward the glass-encased promenade to the outside. I stand at the end of the promenade, surveying the sidewalk and the cars. There, near a huge truck, I see them standing and talking. But really, they're arguing.

I head for the door and, careful to open it quietly and close it just as carefully, I jog around to the side of the parking lot to head toward the truck. And I'm praying they're still at it when I get there.

And as I slow to a cat's walk and sidle up to the opposite side of the truck, I give thanks I wore my tennis shoes. I stifle my heavy breathing and cuddle up to the cab.

"I'm telling you, this must stop," Norreen declares. "You're in way over your head."

"You know I can't, Nory. It's what I promised to do. The oath I took. I can't back out now. Not after all the mission has done for me."

"Gotten you out of Louisville with a new name and new future. But what's it worth, Karen, if you continue to steal? If you wind up in prison?"

"Don't be silly. I'm fine. We're fine. It's you, Nory, you who has the problem now. You doubt. And you know doubt kills."

"Yes, I doubt the mission. You should, too, with what it's become. And as for me, I love my daughter, Karen. And my husband. I want to stay here and I can't do it if you keep hounding me."

"Well, you know, we all pay prices. You, too, Nor. You knew that when you took the oath. How long ago was that?"

"When I was too young to know better," Norreen spits back, "just like you. Christ, Karen, I was sixteen. Living in poverty in a town no bigger than a pig's eye, with a father who thought women were for scrubbing and screwing—and a mother who let him believe it. I thought the Eagles had a fine vision, but in their success, they've changed, becoming a bigger monster than the one they want to replace. What kind of revolution is it to steal everything from people? Their names, their savings. Goddamn, even stealing their medical records for fun! Marie Deeds wanted money for those hospital records—not murder!"

"Now, now. You're just getting carried away, here, Nor. Pipe down. This thing with Deeds will blow over."

"The police will find out about this, Karen. I know they will. Once they figure out why Goodwin was sitting at his PC."

"Look, Nory. Go home and take a pill, will ya? I am certain things are just fine."

"No, they never will be until all of you hear me: You've had what you wanted from me and there is no more."

"Nory—"

"Do not come near me or mine again." And she walked away—thankfully, in the opposite direction from where I stood, frozen like a stone statue to the pavement.

I wait until Vickie, or Karen, walks away before I move a muscle. Then I run like hell back toward the promenade door and let myself in. Within minutes, I find Jones in his chair, exactly where I left him. I nudge his arm. "Come on, we have to go."

He raises a hand. "No, no, hush, sit down. Wyatt's coming on again. Where the hell've you been?" He glances at me. "And what've you been doing?"

"Helllooo, gamers!" Wyatt's yelling from the stands. "I promised you a surprise if you stuck with us tonight! Having fun? Good! Good! Well, here it is—our newest games for your PCs at home! Star-Raider and Double-Spy! Pick 'em up at the back desk. Take 'em home and bring them back with you at your next visit with us and you get a free entry—and when we read your disks, we not only give you the upgrade free, but bring 'em five times and you get ten free entries!"

"Oh, my Christ," Jones murmurs. "Boy, do I need those disks!"

"Listen to me, you need a disk like a hole in the head," I insist. "Let's get out of here. Now. I have to talk to you."

He examines me now and says, "You are a little harried-looking. Where'd you go?" I roll my eyes at him. "Okay, okay, give me a minute. Go to the truck."

Twenty minutes later, he climbs into the cab of the truck, throws the copies of the gaming disks into my lap, and off we go down Rockville Pike. "I think I know what they do. I want to analyze those." He nods at the software.

"For worms and bugs?"

"Mmm. Maybe," he says as he heads south toward Rockville and my Tahoe parked at the Metro lot. "But if I'm right, they work in a way we never imagined. They give those disks away, offering incentive to anyone who takes them home and uploads them to their PCs. Then, when the kids play and bring them back . . ." He smacks his lips. "Whatever was on the PC at home is now on the disk and automatically uploads to their computers that they use in the parties."

"So all they have to do"—I see the simplicity of it—"is download whatever data they've gotten from the party computers—and they have a treasure trove of data."

"Yeah. To use however they wish. To take identities, info about bank accounts, and IRA investments—"

"Army installations and hospital medications and health care records.

"And I know why." I tell him about Norreen's tête-à-tête with Vickie-Karen, the Eagles as a club for thieves and scam artists, probably a fringe political group gone awry.

With the enormity of that sinking in, we're both silent as the dead for a few more miles.

As he pulls into the Rockville Metro stop again, I tell him where I've parked my car so that he can drop me there. "Even if this is true," I say as he comes to a stop, "it still doesn't tell us who killed Goodwin."

"Right," he murmurs. "Only that he probably discovered something on his home PCs that for sure, as a techie, he would have definitely not liked. Whether it was Metro Hospital medical records that Marie was selling to the Eagles or whether it was Sherry Bunting's wiccan ways, he got taken down because of it, I bet you."

I sigh. "Call me when you learn more about the disks."

"I will. Go home and lock up."

"Hey, I've got my gun to keep me warm."

"Yeah. And a phone you should *use!*"

"I hear you," I tell him, then get in my Tahoe and he follows me out of there. At one of the roads leading west to Potomac and down to Georgetown, I peel off and he flashes his lights good-bye. Within minutes, I'm pulling into my garage, the street silent, reporters gone, my home dark. I lower my garage door, let myself into the kitchen, and plunk my purse onto the kitchen island.

"Hey, Abe, how you doing, buddy?" I walk over to his cage

under the desk of the kitchen counter and unhook his door
latch. "Want to go out?" Poor guy has been locked up most of
today, what with me at the office and then out tonight. He needs
exercise.

He comes out and yammers at me awhile. I figure he wants to
go out in the garden and take care of business. So I go to the
control panel for the house security system and plug in the code.
Why I continue to do this when I have evidence this makes me
no more secure beats me. I open the French doors. He zooms
out and I walk out behind him.

The night is lovely, soft and warm. The sound of my neighbor's fountain makes me close my eyes, admire the peace—and
yearn for more, and soon.

"Come on, Abe," I call to him, because he must be behind
one of the forsythias. God, I need to go to bed and sleep for a
year. Tonight I'll leave him out of his cage. He can do his watch-
dog job.

And as I turn, a dark figure looms before me. "I thought you
went . . ."   the man comes into view—"home."

But this is no Jones. No friend. No ally. No, no. This is . . .

"Wyatt. What are you doing here?"

"I wondered why you were at my gaming party." He saunters
forward. "Who was the guy you were with?"

Great, he makes me, but not Jones. So much for my abilities to
dress up and play detective. "Why does it matter to you?" *Aw,
Carly, cocky is not what we want to make this guy disappear.*

"Sure it matters. You didn't come to play games. You came to
watch what we do. What did you learn?"

"Not much. I'm not that proficient at—"

"Cut the crap." He's crowding me and I'm backing toward
the house, my phone, any phone, my gun. . . . "You wouldn't
come back unless you knew things you shouldn't."

Okay. Now we're gonna compete for the biggest buckle
at the rodeo. "Like how you plant software into children's

computers so that you can lift their parents' files for your own profit."

"Shit. That's the Mickey Mouse stuff." He takes a few steps more and I dance backward in time with him.

"Yeah? What's the bigger stuff?" *Go on, Carly, girl, let him have it. Hey, no guts, no glory—and no answers.* "Theft? Fraud? Blackmail? Turning a political election?"

He grins and in his eyes there is a lunacy I've seen before in the eyes of those for whom compromise is not a commodity they prize—and in a democracy, not one they care to honor. "Masterful, if you ask me." He whips from his pocket a cord—and I note plastic gloves on his hands.

"You can't kill me like you did Goodwin."

His expression narrows to the abandon of his purpose. "Watch me."

And in that second, Abe lets out a yell that in the jungle must signal war of the worlds. I step aside as I realize that ol' James Wyatt is going facedown. And to the beat of sixty pounds of mad monkey on his back.

I dash for the kitchen. Grab for the phone. Wyatt has been able to beat Abe back and escape for the few steps needed to lunge into the kitchen and grab my ankle and twist. I kick him in the face. He growls and clamps a hand over his eyes—and that's when Abe is on him again, jumping up and down and screeching at octaves all of Georgetown must hear.

I get to the phone and push 911—and the operator comes on and I yell for help and my address. I figure she better trace the cursed number, because I'm headed for my car. I get the kitchen door open and damn me if Wyatt isn't hauling me back, but this time I put my foot squarely in his family jewels. And he yowls, almost matching Abe, who now is pummeling Wyatt like a punching bag. I run to my car, yank open the door, lunge across the seat. I reach for the glove compartment—flip it open, grab my SIG-Sauer, whirl, and double-hand it to aim at my target.

"Wyatt. Unless you'd like me to crochet you a new belt with a few bullets, lie still and stop hitting Abe."

Suddenly we have peace. And we wait for the police, me with my gun drawn and Abe sitting on his captive as if he were the monkey king and Wyatt the creature who became his slave.

sixteen

Chicago is my kind of town. A cool breeze, even in late August, a view of the lake, savory deep-dish pizza—and a change of scenery.

My staff is checking us all into the Drake for the week of the presidential convention—and I'm joining Louise, Chad, William Scott Preston, and Gunther Halstead up in the Tea Room on the upper level overlooking the lobby as others below await assignments of rooms. One of them is Sam Lyman, who is still missing in action in our relationship since the night Goodwin died. I haven't had the time or inclination to miss his company. I don't acknowledge him now as two Chicago media types ascend the stairs and spot us five, then come over to have Chad introduce them to all of us.

And I once more try to demur and not allow the capture of James Wyatt and his political fringe group, the Eagles, to seize the spotlight from Louise and Gunther in what should be for them the finest moments of their political lives.

Yes, I get to bask in the limelight of having captured the man who murdered the Good Judge. Yes, reporters still allude to it, more than two months after that night when Abe beat the stuffing out of James Wyatt—and took down the man who would have destroyed one man's life and corrupted many Americans' political way of life. But I am also quick to correct reporters that it was my chimpanzee who really felled the guy—and that I was lucky enough to have a gun in my glove compartment to ward off Wyatt from further destruction.

We had a lot of hoopla that night. McGinty arrived minutes after the patrolman who responded to the emergency call. Sullivan was close behind. Both told me afterward that they were hot on the trail of Norreen's ties to Vickie Enrici, alias Karen somebody from a small town in southern Kentucky. Other than that, they had few clues, evidence, or suspects.

When Wyatt confessed, he told them that he had been watching the Deedses' house Saturday night, thinking they'd all gone to the beach, only to discover Goodwin still there, or so he claimed. Not realizing Goodwin was deleting everything from his home PC hard drives because he was wild that his wife Marie had all kinds of Metro Hospital patient record data on the home hard drives, Wyatt goes in and stumbles on Goodwin, and they argue. Wyatt kills Goodwin in frustration over his failure to access the hard drive. Even carrying the access chip from Goodwin's hand, Wyatt can't get into the PCs and runs away.

Marie herself confessed the next day to selling the Metro Hospital data to the Eagles. If she couldn't fund her way in divorce with Goodwin's money, she had decided to get it any way she could. Selling it to the Eagles seemed like an efficient way to screw the entire status quo.

Now, without even a stepmother, the Deeds twins were to go live with an older cousin of theirs in Leesburg. With Norreen Bunting under investigation for conspiracy to commit identity theft, she and Henry were probably headed for that divorce. Sherry, meanwhile, was enjoying her stay in Bandera—and had visited the Rocking O earlier this month. Jordan claimed Sherry even wore pink these days. A sure sign we had some hope of good things to come.

Chad interrupts my reverie and leans across the table to pour tea for me into a delicate china cup. "What I marvel at is how Marie set up Wyatt so that he'd have to confront her husband."

I accept one of the tiny scones, pass the tier to him, and tell him what I now know, courtesy of McGinty—and Jones. "That Saturday night, as Marie and the twins left for the beach, Marie called Wyatt. She knew Goodwin had discovered the gaming thefts. But she told Wyatt about Goodwin's hand chip, and that he was copying files to give to the police. Crafty soul that she was, she purposely incited Wyatt to go to the house, confront him, and kill him. Marie couldn't get a divorce, so she took advantage of an opportunity to make herself a free woman in another way. Now she gets to sit in prison for the plot."

"Goodwin died," Louise says, "because of the combined venal behavior of so many people, all of whom came together for the wrong purposes and, sadly for Goodwin, at the wrong time. Tragic."

Chad nods, patting his lips with his napkin. "He deleted evidence that his wife could use to gain ill-gotten monies—and withheld other evidence to protect children who would otherwise have been harmed."

Chad and I gaze at each other. "Goodwin died a noble death to save children." His reference to Sherry Bunting also has another reference to the saved reputation of her father, Henry—even if Norreen Bunting's admission of her abandoned membership in the Eagles fringe group left their marriage in shambles and her future in doubt. "Goodwin personified the name so many had given him. He was indeed the Good Judge."

Gunther leans forward, raising his teacup to each of us in turn. "Thanks to all of you, too, for helping me."

Louise grins. "I'm proud of you, Gunther, that you didn't cave. Pleased to see if we can put us both into new housing come January."

"I stuck it out only because you encouraged me, Lou." He grins, relaxed and looking better rested than any of us.

I see Aaron below give me the high sign and hoist a few square room keys. I finish my scone, lift my napkin to my lips, and offer up my excuses. "I am still bone-tired from those wild days of learning who killed Deeds. So if you'll pardon me, I'm going upstairs to take a long night's rest before we begin tomorrow."

The gentlemen push back their chairs and I wave them down. "Don't. Not necessary." I grin. "Thanks to all of you for offering me the speech Monday night—and keeping me there." I don't turn to Chad, but hey, what thanks does he deserve for his opposition?

Minutes later, Aaron, my press secretary, Dana, and I are all going up in the elevator to the floor where all our rooms are, when the fatigue floors me. It's five, but I'm ready for the sack. Within minutes, I'm inside my suite, which opens into a huge bedroom with king-sized bed and a wide-screen plasma TV. As I kick off my shoes, a thought hits me that what I really need is solitude, a movie, and a big burger and fries. I reach for the phone.

"Aaron"—I've dialed up his room down the hall—"I'm going to pass on dinner tonight. You, Dana, and Tony go. Have fun. I'm ordering room service." We hang up quickly because Aaron knows enough not to argue with me—and within half an hour I'm into yoga clothes and a good down-dog to relax my shoulders, when there's a knock at the door.

And as I open it, there stands the waiter, his rolling cart with my dinner—and behind him, back to me, is a tall, dark, very familiar man inserting his room key into the door.

No, I tell myself. Why would it be?

"Come in," I tell the waiter, and stand aside for him to go past me. And at that moment, the man I know so well, the man I know too well, the man I wish I did not know so repeatedly in such sad ways as murder, turns on his heel and stares at me.

I have not seen him since two months ago, when he came to install wiring in my house for a security system, took three days to do it—and brought a bottle of very fine wine each night for us both to drink after his day's work.

Tonight, he's here. He's tall, he's dark, he's goddamned handsome. He's got no glasses, no mustache, but he has a deep golden tan garnered from some Caribbean vacation, I'm betting and whetting my appetite for. His eyes—oh, boy—are stunning silver coins of contrast. His hair is long. I mean, so long that he's caught it at his nape with a nifty leather tie, the wealth of it hanging down his back like a native American Indian's. He's dressed in a snuggly fitting hand-tailored suit, just like he belongs at the Drake. And I'm wondering why.

And scared to ask.

I can't afford to. Not now. Not here. Not again. Not so freaking *soon*.

Our eyes meet. He smiles with hot intent.

The waiter comes to stand beside me, wanting me to sign his receipt. I scribble something. Look at Jones. "Might we have met before?" I ask him, because the waiter lollygags, curious at our silent musings.

"No, never," Jones says, but takes the two steps and puts his hand out. "Chief John Light Horse. Delegate from Arizona."

"Apache?" I venture.

The waiter scurries away.

Jones's gaze goes molten as he grins. "Yes, ma'am," he lies through his perfectly white teeth. "I'm working this convention. Just like you."

Not what I wanted to hear. I take a few steps backward and shut the door, as if I could put a barrier between us. Yes, I brought his nifty little phone with me. No, I don't leave home without it anymore. Today it's in my luggage, convenient. All I have to do is turn it on. And then, do I call him and ask for details on his newest job?

No. I absolutely will not. I'll play this like speak no evil, hear no evil, see no evil.

I sink to a chair.

Who's whistling Dixie here?

I am.

Because for certain, wherever Jones goes, not far behind is murder.